"I know you did not wish to wed me," Isabel began, not really knowing what to say.

The awkward silence stretched further when Patrick picked up the oars and began rowing toward the shoreline.

"It is a great sacrifice," she said dryly, "having to spend time with me."

"More than you know," he muttered.

Isabel dipped her hand in the sea and flicked a palmful of water at his face.

Patrick's face darkened. Droplets of salt water slid down his bristled cheeks. Before she could move, he trapped her hands in his and pulled her arms around his neck. She clung to him for balance, her heartbeat pounding against her chest.

He wasn't going to kiss her. She could see it in his eyes. He was fighting against it.

But he didn't let go of her. His hands caressed her back, holding her, and a secret part of her ached to welcome him. She needed more than this, and yet he held himself back. Embraced in his arms, she pressed her breasts close to him, her body trembling. Her mouth parted, wishing for what he would not give.

Then she lifted her face and kissed him.

* * *

Her Warrior King
Harlequin® Historical #882—January 2008

Author Note

I have always loved stories of royalty, and, during my research, I found fascinating tales about the many kings of medieval Ireland. The High King was chosen to lead the country, but there were provincial kings and petty kings as well who would reign over their territories. Kings were not born, but instead were selected by the people. They could also be deposed if the people were not satisfied with their leader. Approximately 80–100 kings reigned over the tribes of Ireland for hundreds of years.

Her Warrior King is the story of a man struggling with the burden of kingship and a forbidden love of the enemy. I hope you enjoy Patrick MacEgan's tale. As always, I love to hear from readers. Visit my Web site at www.michellewillingham.com for extra features in **The MacEgan Brothers** series!

Available from Harlequin® Historical and
MICHELLE WILLINGHAM

Her Irish Warrior #850
The Warrior's Touch #866
Her Warrior King #882

HER
WARRIOR
KING

MICHELLE WILLINGHAM

TORONTO • NEW YORK • LONDON
AMSTERDAM • PARIS • SYDNEY • HAMBURG
STOCKHOLM • ATHENS • TOKYO • MILAN • MADRID
PRAGUE • WARSAW • BUDAPEST • AUCKLAND

ISBN-13: 978-0-373-29482-4
ISBN-10: 0-373-29482-4

HER WARRIOR KING

Copyright © 2008 by Michelle Willingham

www.eHarlequin.com

Printed in U.S.A.

To my husband Chuck, who has always
supported my dream.
You're my own Irish hero.

Chapter One

England, 1170

Every woman considered stealing a horse and running away on her wedding day, didn't she?

Isabel de Godred fought the restlessness building within her. It was her duty to obey her father. She understood it, even as she clenched the crimson silk of her kirtle and eyed the stables.

In her heart, she knew an escape was futile. Even if she did manage to leave the grounds, her father would send an army after her. Edwin de Godred was not known for his tolerance. Everything was done according to his orders, and woe to anyone who disobeyed.

The marriage might not be so bad, part of her reasoned. Her betrothed could be an amiable, attractive man who would allow her the freedom to run his estates.

She closed her eyes. No, highly unlikely. Otherwise her father would have paraded the suitor before her, boasting about the match. She knew little about him, save his Irish heritage and rank.

'Are you ready, my lady?' her maidservant Clair asked. With a conspiratorial smile, she added, 'Do you suppose he's handsome?'

'No. He won't be.' Toothless and ageing. That's how the man would look. Panic boiled inside her stomach, and Isabel's steps felt leaden. Her rash escape plan was looking more and more appealing.

'But surely—'

Isabel shook her head. 'Clair, Father wouldn't even let me meet the man at our betrothal. He's probably half-demon.'

Her maid crossed herself and frowned. 'I heard he's one of the Irish kings. He must be wealthy beyond our imaginings.'

'He isn't the High King.' And thank the saints for that. Though she might rule over the tribe, at least she did not have the burden of ruling a country. As they walked down the wooden staircase outside the castle donjon, she wondered how her father had arranged a betrothal in such a short time. He'd gone to aid the Earl of Pembroke's campaign only last summer.

'If I could, I'd take your place,' Clair mused with a dreamy smile.

'And if I could, I'd give him to you.' Unfortunately, that wasn't possible.

Isabel's imagination conjured up a monster. The man must be unbearable to require such secrecy. Though she knew it was unfair to pass a judgement before she'd met her intended, she couldn't help but imagine the worst.

'You'll be mistress of your own kingdom.' Clair sighed. 'Imagine it. You're to become a queen.'

'I suppose.' And that added even more fear to the forthcoming marriage. What did she know about being a queen? She knew how to run an estate and make it profitable, but that was all.

Her father Edwin de Godred, Baron of Thornwyck,

awaited her outside the chapel among a small crowd of guests and servants. Tall and thin, his greying beard and moustache were neatly groomed. He examined her with a glance, and Isabel felt like a mare about to be traded. She resisted the urge to show her teeth for inspection.

No, it did not bother her to leave this place. But what should she expect from the Irish king? Was he kind? Cruel? Her nerves wound tighter.

'Is he here?' she asked her father, staring at the men waiting near the church.

Edwin gripped her cold fingers, keeping them in a tight grasp as he escorted her to the church. 'You will meet him soon enough. My men sighted his travelling party a few hours ago.'

'I would rather have met him at our betrothal,' she muttered. Her father only grunted a response.

Isabel shivered. Until she saw this man with her own eyes, she'd not surrender her escape plans. With each step, she felt more alone. Her sisters were not here to lend their support. Edwin had not permitted it, and it had hurt more than she'd thought it would.

When they arrived in the courtyard, a well-dressed man was speaking to the priest. He had little hair, save a snowy fringe around his pate.

'Is that him?' she asked. Her father didn't answer. He seemed preoccupied, his gaze focused into the distance.

The older man swallowed hard and wiped his palms upon the hem of his tunic. He glanced around as if searching for someone.

Isabel sent up a silent prayer, her cheeks flaming. *God, please save me from this marriage*, she thought, even as her father's hand closed over her wrist.

A moment later, she heard the sound of a horse approaching. Startled, she glanced up at the heavens. 'That was quick.'

'What is it?' Edwin demanded.

'Nothing.' Isabel forced a neutral expression onto her face, but the rumbling sound intensified. Her father offered a strange smile, and he motioned for the priest to wait. Moments later, the elderly man stepped among the other guests. So he was not her bridegroom.

The noise grew louder, and her father's hand moved to his sword hilt. A few guests looked to Edwin, the women glancing around with uncertainty. The priest turned to Isabel, a questioning look on his face.

Isabel froze. There, riding towards the guests, a man emerged. His clothes were little better than rags, dried mud coating the hem of his cloak. And yet he rode a sleek black horse, a stallion worthy of a knight.

His sword was drawn, as if to cut down any man who dared oppose him. Guests scrambled to get away from the horse, several women shrieking.

Isabel's heart leaped into her throat, but she held herself straight, refusing to scream. Instead she darted behind one of her father's men, a soldier armed with a bow and arrows.

What was wrong with them? The men hadn't moved, nor released any arrows. As a single rider, the intruder was an easy target. Would no one stop him?

'Do something!' she shouted, but the soldiers ignored her.

The man drew his horse to a halt, sheathing his sword. Isabel's breath caught in her lungs, a strange sense of foreboding sliding over her. No. This could not be him.

Black hair flowed down his shoulders, his granite eyes burning into hers. He reminded her of a savage barbarian, bold and fearless. He wore a strange garment, a long tunic of blue that draped to his knees, and dun-coloured leggings. A crimson, ragged cloak hung across his shoulders, pinned with a narrow iron brooch the length of her forearm. Gold bands encircled his upper arms, denoting a noble rank.

Her father's calm acceptance of the interruption could mean only one thing. The barbarian was her betrothed husband. Isabel bit her lip, fighting back the fear and the desire to flee.

Edwin confirmed it with his words. 'Isabel, this is Patrick MacEgan, king of Laochre.'

She didn't want to believe him. While the barbarian's horse and sword suggested a high rank, the man looked as though he'd come from a battlefield rather than a throne. And where were his escorts, his servants? Kings did not travel alone. Her suspicions darkened.

The king dismounted, and Isabel kept a clear eye on his horse. Now, more than ever, she longed to escape. Perhaps she could seek sanctuary in the abbey. There was a slim chance she might make it.

'You are Lady Isabel de Godred?' he asked. The lilting accent in his voice sounded foreign in the Norman tongue.

'I am.' She stared at the man. 'Is this the way you usually arrive at a wedding? By trying to kill the guests?'

'Isabel,' her father warned. She stilled her voice, fighting back the fear that pounded inside her. His steel eyes studied her dispassionately, and her gaze shifted to his hands. He could tear her apart with them, no doubt.

The barbarian king blinked a second. The fierce expression returned to his face. 'Let us get the deed done.'

Not if she could help it. He wasn't at all half-demon. Full-blooded demon, more like. If she ever intended to make an escape, now was her only opportunity.

Isabel dashed towards MacEgan's horse. She gripped the saddle, trying to haul herself atop the creature before strong arms surrounded her like a shield. Sinewy muscles possessed her in a prison of strength.

Though she fought him, the king lifted her down as though she weighed no more than a fly. He kept her pinioned against his chest. His body heat warmed her cool skin, and the top of her head reached just below his shoulders. In his stance, she could feel the caged fury.

'I cannot wed you,' she insisted. This was not the sort of amiable husband who would sit upon a throne and let her handle the household. He was the sort of man who would lock her in chains and feed her body to the crows.

No one listened to her protests. Father Thomas began murmuring the words to the marriage rite. The king took her hand in his, and blood roared in Isabel's ears.

This could not be happening. This man would steal her away from her homeland, to the island of Erin where she had no family. She'd never see her sisters again. Pain twisted within her skin, and she held back tears.

His hand squeezed hers tighter, and she caught the warning look. Anger rose up within her, permeating and harsh. What had she done to be punished with a husband such as this?

The priest was waiting for her vow. Isabel shook her head and her throat closed up. 'I will not wed you.'

'You've no more choice than I, *a chara*.'

Isabel tried to break free of him, but the Irish king overpowered her. 'You wish to have your freedom, do you not?'

She made no reply. What did he mean?

'Agree to this marriage, and it shall be yours.'

She did not believe him. Every inch of this man was uncivilised. Her father sent her an icy glare. 'Look around you,

Isabel. If you do not wed the king of Laochre, there is none other who will have you. What man desires a disobedient wife? You bring shame upon yourself.'

Hot tears gathered in her eyes, but Isabel held her ground. The wedding guests appeared uncomfortable.

The king softened his grip upon her wrist. Lowering his voice, he brought his mouth to her ear. His breath made her shiver.

'Your father holds the lives of my people under his control: men, women and children. The only way to save them is if I wed you. And wed you I shall, *a chara*, be assured of it.'

A single tear slid free, staining her cheek. The truth broke through, unwanted. Her father's conquest in Erin had made her into a bargaining pawn, her own wishes meaningless. This was a political alliance, and the king's rigid expression made it clear he would not accept a refusal.

Was he telling the truth? Would children and women die if she refused? She turned and studied her father. In his eyes she saw no mercy.

She looked closer at Patrick MacEgan. Past the anger she saw exhaustion. And a hint of sadness. If he was right, if innocents would die without her acceptance… She closed her eyes, knowing she could not escape her fate. In that moment the chains of obligation tightened around her.

When the priest asked for her vow again, she forced herself to nod aye. Within moments, the rite had ended. Her husband brushed a kiss of peace upon her cheek, and Isabel clenched her teeth to keep from screaming.

Throughout the Mass, Patrick kept her hand imprisoned in his. She barely heard the priest's words, her head spinning with disbelief. So fast. Wedded to a man she didn't know, a king who lived a world apart from her homeland.

Afterwards, they walked into the inner bailey. Isabel's stomach roiled at the scent of the wedding feast prepared. Peacocks, a roasted pig, and all manner of exotic fare awaited them. She couldn't imagine touching a bite of it. Celebrating was the furthest thing from her mind.

Patrick stopped in front of his horse. 'We leave now. Say farewell to your father, for you will not see him for a long time.'

His command caught her unawares. 'But my belongings and dowry,' she protested. 'The wagons—'

'We'll send for them later.'

Isabel cast a glance towards Edwin de Godred. No longer did she see the face of her father, a man she had tried desperately to please. Now she saw a man willing to sell her into marriage with the devil, should it further his own ambitions.

Her father moved forward. 'You cannot depart until the marriage is consummated.'

'I have met our agreement.' Patrick's expression hardened, and his palm moved down to the hollow of her spine. Isabel stiffened at the mark of possession. 'You need not doubt the rest. But it will be on my terms, not yours.'

Lord Thornwyck deliberated before at last handing over a scroll of sealed parchment. 'If she is not carrying an heir by the time I return to Laochre, I will require evidence that she is no longer a virgin.'

Isabel's face burned with mortification. Now it seemed they viewed her as a brood mare. Terror lanced her at the idea of submitting to the Irish king. Though he'd granted her a reprieve from the ceremonial bedding, she had no doubt he would want to share her bed later this night. Her skin prickled beneath the touch of his hand upon her body. The awareness of him only heightened her fears.

'At Lughnasa, we'll expect you,' Patrick replied. He did not await a response, but lifted her on to his horse. He swung up behind her, spurring the stallion into a gallop.

The horse raced onwards while strong arms confined her in an iron grip. Neither her father, nor his men, made any move to stop him. Isabel's last thought was, *God, this was not what I meant when I begged you to save me from this marriage.*

Patrick kept the woman in a firm grip as they rode through the fields. He needed to put distance between them and Thornwyck's fortress. Though the Baron had let him leave freely, he didn't trust the Normans to keep their word.

Isabel de Godred had startled him. He didn't know what he had expected, but it certainly wasn't a wife who'd accused him of trying to murder the guests. He'd hoped for a plain-faced, biddable maiden who would follow his orders. Instead, fate had granted him a beautiful woman who looked as though she'd never obeyed a command in her life. Even now her body tensed against his, as though she were contemplating escape.

In silent response, he tightened his hold. Without Isabel's presence, he could not free his people. The orders signed by Thornwyck were not enough. The Norman captain had to see her for himself.

Patrick stared at the horizon, wondering if he would glimpse his brothers. Though he'd ordered them to remain beyond the Welsh border, he suspected they hadn't. During the wedding Mass, he'd caught a slight motion to his left. But when he'd turned, there was nothing.

Then again, his brothers were well trained. Like shadows, if they didn't want to be seen, no one would find them. The fear of anything happening to his family added yet another rope of tension to this tangled web.

Brutal memories slashed at his heart, of the children who had died in the fires. His brother's wife, stolen and killed by the Norman invaders. So much loss. And all because of Thornwyck and the Earl of Pembroke's forces. He could hardly think about the woman he held in his arms, for she was one of them.

After several hours, he drew his horse Bel to a stop. He chose a spot near a stream, out in the open where Isabel could not run. He lifted her down. 'Rest for a moment and slake your thirst. Fill this in the stream, and then we'll go further.'

She accepted the water bag. 'Why did you wed me?' Eyes the colour of polished walnut gazed at him steadily. 'You said the lives of your people depended on this marriage.'

Not a tear fell from her eyes, nor did she scream. Quiet and pensive, she met his attention openly.

'You were part of the surrender terms when your father conquered our fortress. If I didn't wed you, he swore to kill all of the survivors.'

She blanched. 'I don't believe he would really have done that.'

He didn't know what kind of sheltered walls had veiled her eyes, but he refused to equivocate Edwin de Godred's actions. 'Believe it.'

She took a few steps towards the stream, her steps faltering. He doubted if she was accustomed to riding for long distances. If she were any other woman, he'd likely stop for the night.

But she wasn't. She was one of them and not to be trusted. As long as he remained upon English soil, he had no way of knowing whether Thornwyck would keep their agreement. Even now, his people might be suffering. Two score of Norman soldiers held them prisoner.

He wasn't about to waste time with wedding feasts, or with bedding the woman. The sooner they reached Eíreann, the better.

Patrick knelt beside the stream and lifted the cold water to his lips. Isabel sat nearby, her hands folded in her lap.

The wind skimmed against her veil, lifting it to reveal a length of golden hair. With full lips and high cheekbones, her brown eyes illuminated her face. For a moment, he almost pitied her. No woman should have to endure a marriage like this one.

She handed him the water bag. 'What am I to call you? Your Majesty? My sovereign lord?'

'Patrick will do.' Though he had earned the rank of petty king, reigning over his tribe, it had been hardly a year. He had not yet grown accustomed to being their leader. He didn't know how his father and eldest brother had shouldered the responsibility so easily. Every decision he made, he questioned. Especially the agreement with the Baron of Thornwyck.

'You promised me my freedom. Do you intend to give it to me now?'

He shook his head. 'When we reach Eíreann. I give you my word.'

'And is your vow worth anything?'

He folded his arms. It was becoming apparent why Thornwyck had offered his daughter as part of the arrangement. 'Are you always this difficult?'

'Always.'

Her bluntness almost made him smile. 'Good. I've no need for a spineless woman.' He lifted her atop the stallion once more. A flash of irritation crossed her face, but she made no complaint.

She had courage; he'd grant her that. Even still, he could never forget what her people had done to his. Worse, the marriage was only part of the surrender terms. The rest of the treaty made slavery seem inviting. The price he'd paid for the lives of his people was far too high.

As he urged his horse onwards, he could only pray that his tribe could endure what lay ahead.

Isabel clung to the hope that somehow the improper marriage was not binding. She knew better than to try an escape. Without a horse of her own and supplies, she wouldn't survive. Not unless she could find someone to help her.

But who? Edwin de Godred had made it clear that he wanted this alliance. He didn't seem to care that his youngest daughter was now bound to a foreigner, and an uncivilised one at that.

Why had she ever agreed to this? She should have listened to her instincts instead of believing Patrick's tale about captive women and children.

They rode through a forest, the road curving in the midst of fallen leaves. Stately oaks and rowans crowned the path, their branches weaving a canopy high above them. The landscape of her homeland faded into a sea of green and rich earth.

Near the Welsh border, slate-grey mountains wore a halo of afternoon sunlight. They rose above the landscape, beautiful and stark. Flocks of sheep dotted the hills, flecks of white against the sea of green. The spring air cooled her skin, a reminder of the coming night.

Perhaps it would be the last time she saw England. She tried to quell the panic. *You must not be afraid*, she told herself. *Keep your wits about you. Erin cannot be so bad.*

But her stray thoughts kept returning to the wedding night. She glanced down at MacEgan's hands, roughened with labour. They were not at all smooth like a nobleman's. His forearms controlled the horse's reins, revealing a subdued strength.

'Night approaches,' she ventured. 'Do you plan to ride in the darkness?'

There was no reply. She tried again, raising her voice.

'Perhaps when it has grown too dark to see our path, a tree will knock you senseless. Then I could run away.'

Again, silence. The man might as well have been a statue from his stoic demeanour.

'Or if I am fortunate, wolves might devour us.' She pondered the thought, imagining other ideas that could make this day any worse.

'You talk overmuch, *a chara*. In a few hours, we camp for the night.'

Isabel clamped her mouth shut. The thought of stopping for the night, alone with this man, unsettled her. Even now, riding against the heat of his body, kindled her nervousness. He sheltered her, confining her in arms chiselled with a warrior's strength.

Would it be that unbearable to feel his body joining with hers? Her maidservant had sighed over the pleasure of lying in a man's arms, but Isabel remained unconvinced. Her warrior husband had not a trace of gentleness. She dreaded the thought of sharing a bed with him.

After a time, Patrick drew the horse to a stop. The lavender sky swelled with shadowy clouds. She could feel moisture gathering in the air. Ahead, she saw no inn, only more trees.

Her husband moved with a fluid grace, pulling her down from the horse. 'Do not try to run.'

She almost laughed. 'And where would I go?'

'Wherever you planned to travel when you tried to steal my horse.' He took her hands and led her into the woods. From his pack of supplies, he brought out a pile of heavy cloth, which unfolded into a small tent. It was hardly large enough for a single person, let alone both of them. He finished setting up the tent and gestured towards it. 'Wait here. I'll hunt for food.'

Isabel glanced at the swelling clouds, hoping he meant for her to sleep within the tent alone. She started towards the shelter when Patrick stopped her. His gaze held hers, a predatory man who would show no mercy. 'You should rest until I return. We've more riding to do before we stop for the night.'

Isabel gathered her composure. 'Don't you have any supplies here? There's no need to hunt.' She glanced up at the twilight horizon, more than a little fearful. What if he abandoned her in this place?

Patrick's face was close enough to feel his warm breath upon her cheek. 'I'll come back for you soon.'

Her body betrayed her with the warmth that flooded through her. She forced herself to look away.

He deposited her inside the tent and tossed a length of wool at her. 'Cover yourself with the *brat* to stay warm.'

As he started towards the horse, her fear doubled. What if a thief or a murderer came after her? She would be alone, defenceless. 'I would like a weapon,' she added hastily. 'Please.'

He turned and shot her a look of disbelief. 'For what purpose?'

'In case someone attacks. Or an animal.' Isabel crawled outside the tent and pointed to his quiver. 'I know how to use a bow and arrows.'

'No weapons. I do not intend to go far, and I'd rather you didn't shoot me when I return.' He drew up his hood and mounted the stallion, disappearing into the woods.

At that, the rain began. It was a hard, pounding rain that soaked through the silk of her kirtle. A thickness rose in the back of her throat as Isabel huddled inside the tent. Rivulets of cold rain spattered against the heavy cloth, and she cursed

Patrick for bringing her here. She cursed her father for arranging this marriage. She cursed herself for not throwing herself off the horse when Patrick had stolen her.

Mud caked her lower limbs as the rain pounded harder. Her veil clung to her neck in an icy grasp. In the distance, she heard an eerie howling noise. Hastily she sent up another silent prayer.

The last thing she needed was for her new husband to truly be eaten by wolves.

Chapter Two

Patrick's stallion raced across the Welsh plains, the rain soaking through him. The brittle weather helped clear his mind of the resentment.

When he'd accepted the kingship, it had meant making sacrifices. His personal feelings were nothing when it came to the needs of the tribe. He'd married the Norman woman, and now he had the means to free his people.

Shadowed against the horizon, he saw his brothers' camp, the firelight flickering against the orange-and-crimson sunset. When he reached the men, he dismounted.

'Lovely weather,' his brother Trahern remarked. He stood beside the fire, which they had shielded from the rain with a hide stretched before it. Trahern's brown hair dripped with water, along with his curling beard. He towered over both his brothers, his height rivalling that of a legendary giant.

'It seems appropriate for my wedding day.' Patrick tethered Bel, patting the stallion.

Their other brother Bevan stood, pacing. 'I was wondering how long it would take you to arrive. I wouldn't put it past your Norman bride to stab you in your sleep.'

Patrick shrugged. 'She's harmless.'

'We were there behind the church wall,' Trahern admitted. 'She didn't exactly throw herself into your arms.'

'You shouldn't have risked it. I didn't want you to come.'

'And miss our eldest brother's wedding? I think not.' Trahern grinned. He lifted his face skyward and let the rain fall directly on his face. 'The Norman guards never saw us. It was easy enough to remain hidden, so long as we stayed away from the guests.'

'I don't trust Thornwyck.' Bevan sat before the fire, the light illuminating a scar across one cheek. Unlike his brother, he raised a hood to block the rain. 'And we'd never let you go alone. The Normans might have taken you prisoner.'

Patrick neared the sputtering fire and held out his hands to warm them. 'Did Thornwyck's men follow us?'

'No.' Bevan answered. 'But I doubt he'll wait until Lughnasa. He'll bring more forces and try to take Laochre.'

Patrick accepted a horn of mead and swallowed. Grim resignation cast its shadow upon him. 'I won't let our men become slaves to the Normans.'

'And how will you stop him?'

'I have plans,' he lied. But he didn't have any notion of what to do. The orders he carried would free his people. Yet, the rest of the surrender agreement required the Normans to be housed among them. The thought of blending the two sides together made his head ache.

'And what about your bride?' Bevan demanded. 'You cannot allow her to rule as your queen.'

'I know.'

It seemed almost like a faded dream that he'd wed her. He didn't feel married, much less to a Norman. Never would his tribe accept her. He needed to isolate her for her own protection. 'I'm going to take her to Ennisleigh. She'll stay out of harm's way.'

Bevan relaxed, resting his hands upon his knees. 'Good. We've enough problems without her.' He pointed off in the distance. 'I assume you tied her to a tree? Otherwise, you'll have to track her down again.'

'I thought about it.' Patrick recalled his bride's attempt to escape before the wedding. 'But, no, I left her in the tent.'

'Why didn't you bring her here?'

'Because he wants privacy, dolt.' Trahern elbowed Bevan. 'A man should enjoy his wedding night.'

Patrick said nothing, but let his brothers think what they would. He forced back the anger rising inside him. He had no intention of touching his bride, nor making her his wife. He couldn't imagine siring a child with her.

The marriage would not be permanent. After Lughnasa, as soon his tribe drove out the Normans, Isabel and he could go their separate ways. He intended to petition the Archbishop to end the union. A pity he couldn't have wed her in Eíreann. The laws of his own land made it far easier to dissolve an unwanted marriage.

'I should go back,' he said quietly. 'I have to hunt a meal for this night.'

Trahern uncovered a brace of hares. 'Take these to feed your bride a memorable wedding supper.'

'I was going to eat those,' Bevan muttered. But he shrugged and added, 'Safe journey to you.'

'We'll meet you at the coast in another day.' Patrick embraced his brothers and bid them farewell. '*Slán*.'

He slung the hares across his mount and set forth to return to Isabel. He allowed Bel to take the lead, since the last traces of sunlight were slipping behind the mountains.

As he galloped across the fields, he vowed that Isabel de Godred's presence would not interrupt his life, nor would she threaten the MacEgan tribe in any way.

When he arrived back at the tent, Isabel's shoulders were bent forward, her wet hair plastered against her dress. Deep brown eyes blazed with indignity.

'I've brought food,' Patrick said, holding up the two hares. 'And if you can endure the journey, there's an abandoned cottage not far from here.'

She nodded, shivering inside the tent. 'Anything with a fire.'

He helped her pack up the temporary shelter and eased her back on to the horse. She winced, but said nothing about the pain. When he swung up behind her, her body trembled violently.

Coldness iced his heart. She deserved none of his pity. A means to an end, she was. Nothing more. Despite his resolve, guilty thoughts pricked at him for treating a woman like this.

She is a Norman, his brain reminded him. He could not lose sight of that.

Leaning forward, he increased the speed of his mount. Her posture remained rigid, not accepting any of his body's warmth. He should be thankful that she didn't weep or cling to him. And yet it was a first for him, to have a woman shrink away.

As each mile passed, the silence continued. Finally, he reached the outskirts of a forest. Near the edge stood the abandoned hut he'd seen on his journey earlier. The last of the sunlight rimmed the landscape, unfurling the night. He slowed Bel and eased up on the reins, letting the stallion walk towards the shelter.

When they arrived, he dismounted and helped her down. Isabel stared at the thatched wattle-and-daub hut, frowning. 'I can see why it was abandoned.'

The roof needed fresh thatching and one section of the wall sagged, as though the hut might collapse. Patrick let Bel wander over to a small ditch filled with water. Then he opened the door for Isabel.

'Go inside while I tend to my horse,' he ordered. He removed the saddle and rubbed down the stallion. When he'd finished, he entered the hut and was thankful to find a small pile of dry firewood inside. He used some of the fallen thatch to make a pile of tinder. With flint and steel, he sparked a flame. Isabel hung back, watching him.

'I thought you had left me,' she murmured.

'Is that not what you wanted?'

'I had no wish to be deserted in the middle of nowhere,' she said. She shivered again, nearing the small blaze he'd kindled in the hearth. 'I was frightened,' she admitted.

'Wolves?'

Her lips pursed and she shook her head. 'Thieves. Someone might have come, and I couldn't have defended myself.'

There was a grain of truth in it. She was right. He had been negligent in protecting her, but he made no apology.

'Are you hungry?'

At her nod, he continued, 'I'll start cooking the meat. In the meantime, there's a flask of mead tied to the saddle. Go and fetch it.'

Isabel stepped outside, and Patrick tended the fire until he had a strong flame burning. He didn't worry she would try to escape. They were miles from anywhere, and the darkness would prevent her from fleeing.

With his knife, he finished skinning the hares and spitted them. He set the hares above the fire and Isabel returned with the mead. Suddenly she shrieked and dropped the flask. It struck the earth, but did not shatter. Patrick drew his sword, but no one stood at the door. A large rat raced past her, darting around.

When the rodent charged, Isabel grabbed a heavy branch from the pile of firewood and swung it, battering the floor and screeching when the animal neared her skirts.

The rat skittered away from the fire, and Patrick ducked when her club nearly missed his head.

'What in the name of Lug is going on?' he demanded. 'The animal is on the ground.'

'Get it out of here!' she wailed. Her horrified expression, coupled with the wild swinging of the branch, forced him to act. Patrick opened the door and kicked the rodent outside.

Isabel stood on a wooden bench, still wielding the branch. She held her hand to her heart, her mouth tight with fear. This was more than the disgust he'd seen on the faces of most women. She'd been terrified.

'You've seen rats before,' he remarked.

Though Isabel nodded, her fear didn't diminish. 'I hate them. And mice. And anything that nibbles.'

He couldn't resist the urge to tease her. 'They're probably living in the thatch.'

A whimper sounded from her lips. 'Please, God, no.'

He moved closer and disarmed her, tossing the branch onto the hearth. Standing before her, he saw her shudder. Her veil had come loose from the thin gold circlet, and she clutched the crimson kirtle. Though she raised her eyes to his, the fear in them was so great, he felt badly for his teasing.

He studied her, the warm brown eyes and the pale cheeks. She smelled like a mixture of honeysuckle and rose, every inch a lady. Though she tried to keep her courage, her fear of something else was stronger. It was the fear of a woman who had never lain with a man before.

Soaked as she was, the silk outlined every curve. His imagination conjured up wicked thoughts, of sliding the silk from her shoulder and tasting the warm woman's flesh.

He could not weaken. He'd not touch her, though it had been many moons since he'd known the pleasures of a woman's body.

Instead he changed the subject. 'That bench is going to collapse.' Isabel grimaced, her eyes watching the floor as though she expected an army of rats to invade the cottage.

At her hesitation, he lifted her into his arms and carried her to the opposite side of the hut. Her body was cold against his, and he set her down upon a table. Isabel tucked her knees up, shivering. Patrick returned to the hearth and turned the roasting hares over. 'Why do they bother you so much?'

She covered her face in her knees. 'My sisters. Patrice and Melisande played a trick on me when I was small. They put mice in my hair while I was sleeping.' She shuddered again. 'I've never forgotten the feeling of them climbing on my face, getting tangled in my hair.'

'Are they your younger sisters?' he asked.

'Older.' She raised her gaze to his. 'I'm not a wealthy heiress, in case you thought to claim land.'

'I have no need of land. And your father and I came to a different agreement during the betrothal.'

An agreement where Thornwyck intended his grandsons to be future kings of Eíreann. Patrick tossed another limb on to the fire. There would be no children, his own form of revenge. Though Thornwyck could take his tribe prisoner, capturing Laochre and forcing an alliance, at least this was something the Baron could not control.

His wife had stopped shivering at last. She removed her veil and finger-combed her long golden hair to dry. It glowed in the firelight, a vibrant contrast to her crimson silk kirtle.

She rotated to warm another part of her body. When she caught him watching her, she frowned. Patrick turned away and checked on the hares again. After a time, the tantalising aroma of the roasting meat filled the air. The meat dripped with juices, and he cut off a piece with his knife, offering it to her along with a hard loaf of bread. She tore off a piece of bread and handed it back. Nibbling at the hare, she murmured, 'Thank you.'

'I was not intending to starve you,' he said. 'No thanks is needed.'

'Not just for the food—' her face flushed red '—also for not bedding me after the ceremony.' She moved her gaze away, staring at the roasting meat.

Patrick crossed the room and stood before her. She needed to understand her role in this union. Resting his hands upon the table, he trapped her in place. His hands dug into the wood and he hid none of the frustrated anger, nor the vehemence he felt.

'You needn't worry that I will bed you now. Or at all, for that matter.'

She blanched, but he held his ground. The marriage was part of a surrender agreement, not a true alliance. She would never be a queen, nor would she bear sons of his blood.

It was best she got used to it now.

Isabel groaned, as rays of sunlight speared her eyes. She tried to uncurl her body from where she'd slept upon the table. Her husband had not protested her choice, and she'd covered her hair with her veil. Even so, she'd had trouble falling asleep for fear of rats.

Such a strange wedding night. She didn't know what to think of Patrick MacEgan, nor their future together. Her husband stood at the doorway, his back to her. Isabel stifled her surprise. His tunic hung near the dying fire and he was bare from the waist up. His bronzed skin glowed in the sun while rippled muscles revealed his strength.

She held her breath as he stretched. Toothless and ageing he wasn't. But he'd laid her apprehensions to rest last night. He'd already said he had no intention of bedding her. She should be overwhelmed with relief.

Instead, it made her suspicious. And uneasy about their arrangement. Why would he keep her a virgin? And for how long would he leave her alone? Her father had threatened them both if she was not carrying an heir by the time he arrived in Erin. Edwin de Godred would not hesitate to humiliate her.

Isabel swung down from the table, eyeing the floor for any sign of rodents. Her limbs felt stiff and aching. And, sweet saints, there was more riding this day. Her backside chafed from the journey yesterday.

Patrick turned around. 'Good. You're awake. Break your fast and we'll go.' He picked up his tunic and donned it, heading back outside.

Isabel spied the fallen length of cloth on the floor and wrapped it around her shoulders. A *brat*, he'd called it. At least it kept her warm in the morning chill. She ate the piece of bread he'd left for her, then ventured outside.

The rising sun glimmered through the forest, while the wet grass shone. 'Aren't queens supposed to travel in a litter?' she grumbled.

'You aren't a queen.'

'But I thought—'

'You are a bride, but not a queen. You will not rule over my tribe.'

There was anger in his voice, a dark threat that made her tremble. What did he expect from her? As his wife and lady, she had responsibilities to fulfil. She frowned as he lifted her atop his stallion. 'Then why bother taking me to Erin?'

'Because the Normans need evidence that I've kept my word. Only then will they obey your father's orders to free my people.'

She did not bother to converse during the remainder of the journey. A flare of annoyance sparked. He did not want her to play any part in their lives. What did he expect her to do? Sit in a corner and spin until she rotted?

Her feelings flamed with silent rage. Aye, she was a Norman, but she had done nothing wrong. She had no choice in this marriage, but she refused to be treated like the enemy.

Last night she'd stayed awake for hours, trying to decide what to do. Though she could behave like a child and try to flee, it would do no good. Either Patrick or her father would bring her back again.

No longer could she return to her home or her people. Whether she willed it or not, as a married woman she had no choice but to remain with Patrick MacEgan.

Her husband claimed Edwin would execute his people if she did not come to Ireland. He'd said there were children threatened.

The very thought numbed her heart. Cruel deeds happened in battle. She'd seen it for herself once, and, even now, she shuddered at the memory of a burning village.

Though her escorts had kept her far away from the carnage, she'd never forgotten the screams of the victims. A young boy, hardly more than three years of age, had stood beside a dead woman, sobbing for his mother. No one had come for him.

She wished she had ordered her escorts to stop. She should

have taken the boy with her, even though she had only been fifteen herself. Likely he had died with no one to care for him.

It was possible that Patrick's people had suffered the same fate as the villagers. She didn't want to believe it. But what if it were true? How could she live with herself if she let others die because of her own selfish fears?

No, until she fully understood what had happened to his people, she could not leave. She'd accompany her husband to Erin, and learn the truth.

Isabel expelled a breath, gathering her wits. Surely once Patrick saw her skills at running a household, he would allow her to be useful. Somehow, some way, she would find a way to heal the breach between them and make a place for herself.

Her future depended on it.

The coastline loomed before them, shadowed by the sunset. The last vestiges of daylight disappeared beneath the clouded horizon, and Patrick saw his brothers' horses grazing a short distance away. Relief filled him to know they were safe.

He slowed the stallion's gait. The waves surged against the sand, spraying foam into the salty air. Their ship waited on the strand for the morning tide, a vessel large enough for their horses and the four of them. Without the help of his brothers, he could not sail it.

Patrick reined his horse near the caves and dismounted. Isabel's eyelids drooped, her body struggling to remain upright. He lifted her down, and her knees buckled before she regained her footing.

'I don't think I ever want to ride a horse again,' she murmured. He let her lean against him as they moved towards the caves. After several minutes of walking, he spied the golden cast of firelight against the cavern.

Lug, but he looked forward to a good night's rest. Only amongst his brothers could he relax. Each would give his life for the other.

'Come.' He led her to the mouth of the cave. Isabel stumbled across some of the rocks, and he caught her. Though her body had a delicate softness, her strength of will rivalled his own.

His brother Trahern stooped near the entrance, his head nearly touching the stone ceiling. 'So this fine *cailín* is your new wife?'

Isabel steadied herself. 'I am.'

'I am Trahern MacEgan,' he introduced himself. 'And it's curious I am—why you didn't run away from my brother? If I had to wed him, I would have done anything to escape.'

She tucked a lock of escaping hair behind her veil and offered a sheepish smile. 'How do you know I did not try?'

'More's the pity you didn't succeed.' Trahern released a laugh. 'Come and eat with us, sister. Bevan here is scowling because he lost our wager. He thought you'd run.'

The scar across Bevan's cheek whitened. He offered no kiss of welcome, and Patrick did not press for the courtesy. He'd rather his brother hold his silence.

He led her towards the fire. Isabel huddled close to the flames, shivering to get warm. Her hand moved to her backside, and she closed her eyes as if to suppress the pain.

'There will be no more riding,' Patrick reassured her. In truth, he was glad of it himself, though he did not relish the voyage at dawn. He hated being powerless and at the mercy of the wind.

'I am glad of it.' Isabel let the *brat* slide from her shoulders. A damp tendril of hair curled across her shoulders, down to a slender waist. She met his gaze with a forthright stare of her own.

He tore his gaze away. She might be a beautiful woman, but he had no right to look. The vow he'd made, to leave her untouched, strangled anything his traitorous body wanted.

Trahern coughed. Patrick recognised the silent message
and moved away from Isabel. His brother opened a pouch,
offering a loaf of bread, then passed a horn of ale. Isabel
accepted a portion of bread and quenched her thirst. He
noticed the exhaustion haunting her face. Her brown eyes
were strained, her skin appearing far too pale.

While he satisfied his own hunger, he watched her sur-
reptitiously. She had removed her veil, turning aside from
them. Tangled locks of golden hair rested against her neck,
and she began rebraiding it. He had never seen a woman
perform the task before, since he had no sisters. It seemed
almost intimate, watching her weave the strands with slender
fingers. She sat beside the cavern wall with her knees drawn
up. Almost like a child.

But the silhouette of her woman's body could not be
denied. The rain had moulded the dress to her skin, and
puckered nipples stood out, making him wonder what it would
be like to touch her.

She was forbidden. It was the only explanation of why she
kindled any form of desire. He moved to the entrance of the
cave, breathing deeply. The night air smelled of salt, and the
last of the sun disappeared beneath the waves.

'What will become of me when we reach Erin?' Isabel
asked finally.

'I will grant you your freedom, as I vowed.' If he kept her
exiled upon Ennisleigh, she could move about as she pleased
upon the island, doing harm to none. And he would not have
to see her each day, nor be tempted by her.

'I wish to know my responsibilities.'

'You need not trouble yourself.'

'Because I will never be a queen, isn't that right?' Bleak
weariness settled in her eyes, and Isabel turned away from him.

Never had she felt more alone. She had not been allowed to bring a maid with her, nor any of her belongings. Desolation rose within her, an icy cloak of loneliness.

A piece of wood cracked in the fire, sending sparks into the air. Flickering shadows cast darkness across Patrick's face. His brothers sat against the opposite wall, their heads lowered in muted conversation.

'What about the estate? I do have experience running a castle household. Or shall I handle the accounts? I am not familiar with your lands, but perhaps—' She broke off her rush of babbling when Patrick drew nearer.

With a roughened palm, he lifted her chin until she was forced to look at him. In the erratic fire glow, a subtle intimacy cloaked the cave.

'You are responsible for nothing.' The smooth baritone of his voice and the nearness of him made Isabel tremble. Beneath the thin fabric of her kirtle, her breasts tightened. She couldn't breathe, her mind racing with clouded thoughts of escape.

Grey eyes, the colour of freshly hewn stone, stared at her with intensity. Isabel wanted to look away, but she forced herself to meet his scrutiny. Her warrior husband could do anything to her, and there was naught she could do to stop him. It was her duty to submit. Even so, her fingers dug into the damp earth.

Patrick didn't move. Gossamer shivers erupted across her skin at the dark heat in his gaze.

'Sleep, *a chara*.'

At the invitation to escape, Isabel scrambled away from him. She huddled against the cave wall, shivering, yet her skin blazed as though it were on fire. Suddenly she was afraid of the unexpected yearning he evoked. Blood raced within her veins, her skin sensitive.

By the Blessed Mother, she had wanted him to draw closer. Though his demeanour was rough and savage, a primitive part of her yearned to know him.

What was the matter with her? What had happened to her loyalty? Everything about this man bespoke his barbarian nature. From her childhood, she'd heard tales of the ancient Celts who rode into battle naked, their faces painted blue.

She could almost picture Patrick's face painted a fierce shade of indigo, fighting against the Norman invaders. He had practically stolen her from her own wedding. He hadn't bothered to celebrate with feasting or participate in the ceremonial bedding. He was unpredictable, and she didn't trust him to keep his vow. One moment he seemed to desire her; the next he grew distant.

She wanted him to stay away. She didn't like the unexpected longings that tempted her. He frightened her with his dangerous manner.

Patrick's brothers disappeared outside, leaving them alone. Isabel buried her face in her knees. Though she shivered partly from cold, her mind clenched with uneasiness.

Moments later, a warm cloth fell across her shoulders. Isabel stood, drawing the shawl across her shoulders. Patrick held out a ragged gown. 'Put this on. You need to wear the clothing of a tribeswoman now.'

The coarse woollen dress was unlike any she had seen, a long gown that draped to her ankles with voluminous sleeves. She turned her back to him while she put it on. 'Am I to be a slave, then? It is the colour of horse dung.'

The edges of his mouth tipped. 'I did not have time to barter for the colours you wanted. You may embroider the *léine* when we arrive in Eíreann.'

When she turned back to face him, Patrick adjusted the shawl around her shoulders. She stood only inches from an embrace.

In time, he exerted a gentle pressure upon her shoulders, forcing her to lie upon the cloak he'd spread upon the ground. He tucked the edge around her shoulders and spread the mantle across her. 'Sleep. We've a long journey on the morrow.'

Isabel turned away to feign sleep. Ever since the wedding, she had felt frozen in stone.

Shadowed against the darkness of the cave, her husband stood guard. She sensed a wildness within him, a feral hunter who would show no mercy.

Patrick turned and caught her gaze. Steel eyes disarmed her, while the flesh of her body rose with heat. What was wrong with her? Why could she not shut him out?

'Will we reach your fortress in a day's journey?'

He shook his head. 'But I will take you to your new home.'

Isabel faltered, suddenly understanding more than she wanted to. 'Where is that?' He wasn't going to abandon her in Erin, was he?

'You wanted your freedom,' he said. 'I will grant that to you. You will remain upon the island of Ennisleigh.'

Her heart sank, a coldness surrounding her. 'Alone?'

He inclined his head. 'It is for your own protection. I cannot say what my tribe would do to you, were you to live among them.'

'I've done nothing to harm anyone.'

'Norman blood runs within your veins. It is enough.'

Isabel huddled before the fire, her mind surging with anger. Did he think she would agree to this bargain? 'I won't be a prisoner there. You've no right to treat me as such.'

'My duty is to keep you safe. It's the only way.'

'Your people disobey your commands, then?'

He tensed, as though her words were made of thorns. 'You

know me not, Isabel. Do not presume to judge me. I seek only to make the best of this arrangement.'

'What is best for you.'

'What is best for all of us.'

She clenched her teeth. So the Irish king believed he could exile her without a fight?

Patrick MacEgan had no idea just how difficult she could be.

Chapter Three

White sails rippled in the wind, and in back of the vessel, the horses whinnied their displeasure at being trapped in one place. Patrick could sympathise with them. After a full day of nothing but grey skies and an endless sea, he longed to walk upon solid ground. Though he sailed when necessary, he disliked being at the whim of the seas.

In the distance, the green hills of his homeland emerged, fragments of the shoreline ridged with sandy earth and limestone. Patrick's chest constricted with emotion at the sight of it. As a lad, he'd once run along the strand, playing with boyhood friends. Now, he held a different memory of these shores. The Norman invaders had landed here, spilling the blood of his people. And that of his eldest brother Liam.

His hand moved to his sword hilt, feeling the unfamiliar warmth of ivory and wood. The weapon was one he'd inherited by right, but he had not grown accustomed to it. A ruby, worn smooth by generations of MacEgan kings, rested in the hilt. Once, they had commanded an imposing presence upon the land. But his father's men were used to tribal raids, not organised warfare. Most could wield a sword, but they had no formal training in how to withstand the enemy in large numbers.

He meant to change that now. The only way to protect themselves from the Normans was to learn their weaknesses. He would bring the soldiers among them, watch their training, and force his men to learn. Then he could use the Normans' own strategies against them in battle.

Mists encircled the island of Ennisleigh while storm clouds gathered along the horizon. The craggy rocks protected a small ringfort atop the hill, enclosing seven stone huts. Only a score of ageing survivors remained. Proud and set in their ways, the folk had refused to join the remainder of his tribesmen on the mainland.

His gaze moved towards his wife. Isabel's golden hair tangled in a web about her shoulders, shadows lining her eyes. She studied the land without any emotion in her face.

'That is where you will live,' he told her, pointing towards the island.

Her posture stiffened. She looked as though she was considering throwing herself into the dark waters. He wouldn't put it past her.

'You will have your freedom there,' he said softly. 'And in this way I can grant you my protection.'

She shook her head in disbelief. 'Protection? We both know it is my prison.' She turned her face away from the island, her veil whipping in the breeze.

'There is nowhere else for you to go.' Why could she not accept the truth? Her father's men had murdered his. His tribe would never bid her welcome upon the mainland. But Ennisleigh had emerged virtually unscathed from the battle. It was an island sanctuary amidst the fighting at his own fortress.

The harsh scent of salt permeated the air while gulls screeched around them. A low fog skirted the ghostly island. With his brothers' help, he drew in the sail, eager to get off the ship.

As they neared the dock, his brothers slowed the oars. Bevan held the craft steady while Patrick stepped on to the wooden pier. He reached down and helped Isabel off the ship. She took a few unsteady steps, and then walked across the planks towards the beach.

'Let the horses off for some food and water,' Patrick directed Bevan. 'Then we'll take them back to Laochre.'

'I'll get food for us,' Trahern offered. 'I'm wanting a taste of something fresh.'

Before his brother could leave, Patrick warned, 'Keep the islanders away. Tell them to remain in their huts for this day and not to bother Lady Isabel.' The islanders loved nothing more than gossip, and he knew his Norman bride would provide fodder for many nights' conversation.

'Should we reveal she is your wife?' Trahern asked.

Patrick gave a curt nod. Trahern took the pathway up to the ringfort entrance while Bevan led the horses along the strand. Sunlight illuminated the ruined *rath* of Ennisleigh. Patrick waited a few moments before extending a hand to help Isabel up the steep walkway.

She did not accept his assistance, but set her face with determination. He kept his pace slow while she steadied her footing upon the path.

'Why are you leaving me here?' Before he could answer, she added, 'And if you tell me one more time it's for my own protection, I might seize your dagger and cut out your tongue.'

He didn't believe she'd do it. 'You won't. After all, you're afraid of mice.'

'I'm not afraid of you.'

He stopped and leveled a glare at her. 'Perhaps you should

be, *a chara.*' Before she could dive towards the blade at his side, he trapped her wrists.

She struggled to break free of him, muttering, 'I should have stolen a horse when I had the chance.'

Patrick didn't know what she meant by that reply, but he would not relent. 'As I said, you have your freedom here. Live as you choose.'

'But stay away from you and your tribe.'

He released her. 'Yes.' There would never be a time when she could be one of them. The sooner she understood that, the better for both of them. For a moment, he tore his gaze from her and stared out at the azure sea.

A stubborn glint lit her eyes. He didn't know what she planned, but he didn't like it.

'Does my father know of my exile?' she asked.

The question was a subtle threat. 'You are no longer his concern.'

'I will be when he arrives at Lughnasa,' Isabel warned. 'If this marriage allowed you to save the lives of your people as you claim, then I should at least be allowed to live among the tribe.'

'I never said you would be living with us.' Her assertion did not concern him in the least. By Lughnasa, his forces would be strong enough to drive out all of the Normans.

'Aren't you afraid of what my father might do?'

'No.' Though he'd conceded defeat in battle and wedded Isabel, he refused to be commanded by a Norman. 'Edwin de Godred holds no power here.'

And the Baron would hold no power within the privacy of their marriage, either. If Isabel ever bore a child, it would not be of his blood. After they'd defeated Edwin's men, he intended to sever the union. It would have to wait until after the harvest, but that would give him enough time to gather the funds needed to coerce the Archbishop.

Isabel strode past him, her mood furious. When they reached the crest of the hill, she stopped short. A moment later, her lips parted in surprise.

She saw its beauty, as he did. One side of the island near the channel was fierce and rugged, while glittering sand embraced the side closest to the sea.

Isabel held herself motionless. Her eyes held a muted awe as she surveyed the landscape.

A moment later, her softness disappeared. Rebellion brewed in her eyes, along with something else…like sorrow. 'I don't belong here.'

'No,' he said softly. 'You don't. But it's the only place for you.' He closed himself off to her feelings. His duty was to his tribe. There was no place for guilt. And yet, he found himself fascinated by the soft lips that argued with the ferocity of a warrior.

'I'll find a way to leave.'

His hand captured her nape, her hair tangling in his grasp. With mock seriousness he added, 'Then I'll have to chain you.'

'You wouldn't dare.'

'I'll dare anything.' He met her challenge, even as her hands struggled against him. Fury flashed in her eyes, and he caught himself staring at her mouth. Full, with an intriguing lower lip.

Immediately he released her, angry with himself for even considering touching her. 'I will return to you this night, after I have tended to my own fortress. You'll need supplies.'

'Why bother? I'm sure your tribe would prefer that you starved me to death and mounted my head upon the gate.'

He didn't comment. For some, she wasn't too far off from the truth.

Tall grasses swelled in the breeze, brushing against their knees as they walked. Up ahead, stone beehive-shaped cottages stood against the perimeter of the palisade wall. He inspected them, searching for signs of damage. He was satisfied to see none. Only his family's dwelling had suffered, and it could be rebuilt.

Smoke curled from the outdoor cooking fires, wisping tendrils of burning peat. His stomach growled as the scent of hot pottage mingled in the air. Just in front of the fortress, a large stretch of land bloomed green with seedlings.

He heard the soft sounds of conversation, but none of the islanders emerged from their huts. Good. They had obeyed his brothers' warning. Even still, he was certain that all eyes watched them from behind the hide doors.

He led Isabel towards the ruined fortress built by his grandsire. It stood on the highest point of the island, its proud walls humbled by fire.

This was the place where he'd often run away from home. Patrick laid a hand against a charred beam, remembering the broad laugh of his grandsire Kieran MacEgan. 'This dwelling is mine.'

'How did it burn?' Isabel asked. 'Was it the invaders?'

Patrick shook his head. 'The islanders set it on fire, so the Normans would believe they were already under attack.'

He didn't blame the islanders for burning it. His grandsire would have wanted it that way. Better to burn it than to let it fall into Norman hands. 'And they saved themselves,' he added.

The main building was mostly intact, save the burned walls. It would not be a comfortable place to live, but it provided a dry roof. In most places, Patrick amended, recalling holes in the ceiling.

At that moment Bevan and Trahern returned with two sacks

of supplies. Trahern held a steaming meat pie in one hand, while he bit deeply into another. Patrick caught a sack tossed by Trahern. He hadn't missed the way Isabel's eyes devoured the mutton pie with unrestrained longing.

He offered one to her, and Isabel half-moaned when she bit into it. Her eyes remained closed, her lips tasting the food as if she'd never been more satisfied.

Patrick jerked his attention away. The look on her face might be unintentional, but his body could not help responding to her. This marriage would be far easier to endure if his wife had a nose missing or hideous scars. Instead, she had the face of the goddess Danu.

Patrick nodded for Trahern and Bevan to accompany him outside the dwelling. 'What news have you heard from the islanders?'

'The Ó Phelan clan is gathering its forces,' Bevan told him. A grim edge of finality lined his brother's voice. 'They're planning to attack while we are vulnerable.'

And here he'd thought matters could not get worse. First the Normans, now another clan. The Ó Phelans had easily survived the invasion. He suspected they had turned traitor, bribing the Normans or making other arrangements.

'Prepare the men,' Patrick commanded. 'They need to be ready for an attack.'

Bevan shrugged. 'I could, but it will be for naught.'

'You think me incapable of defending our tribe?' Patrick asked, his voice cold and hard.

'I do,' Bevan replied. 'Especially since you must open your gates to the foreigners. Norman bastards.' He spat upon the ground, hatred brewing in his eyes. Shaking his head in disgust, he added, 'You should never have wed her.'

'I had no choice and well you know it. Stop dwelling on

what cannot be changed. The men must be ready. Thornwyck has orders to destroy Laochre, do we fail to meet the terms of surrender,' he reminded Bevan.

'At least we'd die without bringing traitors among us.'

'Not everyone wishes to die.' Their gazes locked in an unspoken battle of wills. Patrick knew his brother would lay down his life in a moment, especially after the Normans had murdered his wife in the last battle. 'Open the gates to the Norman soldiers. I will speak to them when night falls.'

'How can you betray us like this?' Bevan's fists were clenched, his eyes burning with fury. 'If you let them in, I'll not stay.'

'Then go back to Rionallís,' Trahern urged. 'You haven't been to your own fortress since Fiona died.'

An icy cast of pain flickered across Bevan's countenance. 'I've no further need of Rionallís.'

'Your people need you there,' Patrick reminded him gently. The past year had not been kind to Bevan, with the loss of his wife and child.

'I have pledged my sword to those who fight against the Normans. If my own brother will not join me, then I will go elsewhere.'

Patrick watched Bevan tread towards the shoreline, but he made no move to stop his brother.

'Ruarc is gathering others against you,' Trahern warned. 'We need Bevan at our side, else you could lose your position as king.'

At the mention of his cousin, the tension inside of him wound tighter. 'Ruarc is more interested in power than the needs of this tribe.'

'Then do not lose the people's faith.' Trahern pressed a hand to Patrick's shoulder. 'They prefer you as their king, but

I cannot say what will happen when you bring the Normans among us. Ruarc has not forgotten his defeat at your hands.'

Though his cousin posed a threat, Patrick could not allow one man's dissent to sway him from his duty to the tribe. He steeled himself, his gazed fixed upon the empty horizon. The sun touched the water's edge, spilling gold and crimson across the waves.

'This night, we open the gates to the Norman soldiers,' Patrick commanded. 'Those who attempt harm towards our people will not live to see the dawn.'

The island held a mystical beauty, almost pagan in its contrast of stone and grass. Isabel's throat grew dry, her eyes burning with unshed tears.

She walked the perimeter of the dwelling, studying the blackened walls. At one time, the wooden structure must have stretched skyward, with stairs leading up to the bedchambers. She kicked one of the support posts, noting that it was indeed solid.

A chill in the air brought goose bumps on her arms. Even now, the ground seemed to sway after being on the boat for so long. Her body ached with the need for sleep, but she could not succumb to it. How could she close her eyes, when she was surrounded by strangers in an unfamiliar land? As small as it was, she needed to study the island and become acquainted with the people.

A hollowed feeling invaded her stomach. Would they try to kill her because of her Norman blood? Patrick had said she would never reign as queen here. A part of her was grateful for it. What did she know about ruling anyone? She preferred to remain unseen, running the household without all eyes upon her.

After her sisters had married, she'd taken care of Thornwyck Castle. Nearly two dozen servants had worked under her command, and she'd taken pride in mastering the inner workings of the dwelling.

Not that Edwin de Godred had ever noticed, or uttered a word of praise.

Isabel shivered and walked back to the entrance of the donjon. In the distance, she saw Patrick speaking with his brothers. Trahern and Bevan disappeared down the slope of the hill, moving towards the boat. Her husband strode towards her, with all the fierceness of an invader.

His black hair fell against his shoulders, eyes of steel boring into hers. The folds of his cloak draped across his strong shoulders, while leather bracers encased his forearms. 'I have arranged a hut for us, this night.'

'I am sleeping here in the donjon.' *Where you cannot touch me*, she thought. She didn't trust him for a moment. He might claim he had no intention of bedding her, but eventually he would want sons.

Patrick seemed to read her thoughts. 'Sleep wherever you wish. It matters not to me. But the nights are cold.'

Her skin prickled, but she did not look away. 'You're not staying here on the island, are you?'

He took another step closer until his body almost touched hers. His gaze assessed her, and in his eyes she saw fury. 'As I said before, I won't be sharing your bed.'

'Good.' *Don't look away*, she warned herself. Though every part of her wanted to run from him, she held steady. 'But I want to dwell at your fortress on the mainland.' Once she saw his home and people, she would know whether he'd lied to her about the damage. And then she could decide whether to stay or leave.

'No.'

Isabel continued, 'I've had no choice in what has happened

to me. I've lost my home, my family and now I'm forced to live here. Put yourself in my place.'

'Put yourself in mine,' he countered, his expression hardening. 'I watched my people die at your father's blade. Did you think I wanted a Norman as my wife?'

Isabel did not let him see how he affected her. 'I've done nothing wrong.'

'No.' He pulled away, his visage growing cool. His glance moved across the thatched cottages within the ringfort. 'But to them, you are an enemy.'

And he viewed her in the same light, it seemed.

'What am I to you?' she whispered.

'A means towards peace,' he replied. 'But you have my protection. Call our marriage what you will.'

Isabel closed her mind to the images he evoked. She needed no imagination to see the coarse barbarian before her. His tunic stretched against battle-hewn muscles. Black hair contrasted sharply against his warrior's face and granite eyes. His face never seemed to smile.

'There was no choice for either of us, Isabel.' Like a droplet of water, his baritone slid over her. The very sight of him made her want to flee. At her belt, she palmed the familiar hilt of her eating knife.

A spark of amusement seemed to soften his eyes. 'Do you think to stab me with that?'

'Widowhood looks promising.'

He reached out and captured her wrist, holding her still. 'I'll return to you later with the supplies you'll need.'

'I hope not.'

He ignored her. 'In the meantime, you may explore the island.' He turned to leave and the wind slashed at his threadbare cloak, revealing its holes.

Her mind warned her not to be deceived by appearances. A king Patrick MacEgan might be, but beneath the cloak of his authority lay the demeanour of a warrior. Merciless, unyielding. And fiercely loyal to his people.

After he'd gone, she began traversing the island as he'd suggested. She needed to learn every inch of her prison, for only then could she find a way to reach the mainland.

Chapter Four

Patrick's palm curled across his spear as he waited near the wooden gates. His brothers held steady by his side, all mounted and heavily armed. His skin prickled with coldness, as though he were standing outside himself. At any moment, the Normans might break their word and attack. He gripped the spear so tightly his knuckles grew white. Silently he murmured prayers that they wouldn't be slaughtered where they stood.

The darkening sky turned indigo, storm clouds rising. He smelled earth and peat smoke, along with his people's fear. And now it was time to open the gates to their enemy.

Behind him stood the remainder of his tribe. A motley group of farmers, blacksmiths, and labourers, their fighting skills were few. His best men had surrendered their lives in battle, and only these remained.

Each held his weapon of choice, from the eldest grandsire down to the youngest boy. The women stood further back, but they held their own weapons in readiness. Pale and stoic, they awaited his command.

'You're making a mistake,' a low voice muttered. His

cousin Ruarc had already unsheathed his sword and looked ready to skewer any man who passed through the gates. 'They're going to kill us all.'

Ruarc wore the blue colours of the MacEgan tribe and held a battle-scarred wooden shield. Like the others, his body had grown thinner during the harsh winter. At his temples, war braids hung down, framing his bearded face. 'We should fight them. Drive them out.' He lifted his sword in readiness.

'We made a bargain.'

'We can still fight. There are enough of us.'

'No.' Enough blood had been shed. Their tribe had been conquered, and surrender was the price of their lives. 'I've kept my word, and I believe Thornwyck will keep his.'

'Your beliefs will not matter if we die,' Ruarc replied. The rigid hatred carved upon his cousin's face would not be swayed. Patrick turned his back, refusing to justify himself. He had made his decision, and because of it, his people would live.

He caught sight of a young boy, hiding behind his mother's skirts. The child's innocent face burned into his mind. He studied each member of his tribe. Once, they had numbered over a hundred. Now, there were hardly two score in total. The heaviness of loss numbed everything else.

All around them, the wooden palisade was the only remaining barrier of protection. The dying scent of burning peat encircled the air. Rays of the sunset filtered through the edges of the gate while dusk conquered the day. It was time to face the inevitable.

'Open the gates,' he ordered.

Two men raised the heavy entrance gate. Beyond them stood two mounted captains and the Norman soldiers, wearing chain mail armour. Patrick mounted his steed and urged the animal forward.

Though he tried to maintain a façade of calm, it was difficult to still the energy rising inside him. What if they broke the agreement and attacked? He prayed he had made the right choice.

From a distance, the Norman army held their weapons and shields in readiness. Swords raised, and with arrows nocked to bowstrings, they awaited the command to kill. Eyes cold, they would fight to the death.

Yet, when he drew nearer, he saw the faces of men. Weary, hungry, like himself. They had obeyed their leader, taking the lives of his people.

Was he expected to welcome them? Though he had restrained Ruarc's sword arm, his own desire for vengeance was harder to quell. For these men had killed his eldest brother.

Regret pierced him at the memory of Liam's death. Though he could not know which soldier had struck his brother down, he'd not forget what had happened.

Darkness and anger filled him at the memory. He blamed himself. He should have reached Liam in time, blocking the enemy's sword. And though he longed to release the battle rage within, he could not let his people's lives be the penalty for it. His personal vengeance would have to wait.

Patrick beckoned to one of the captains, and the Norman approached, his hand upon his sword. Patrick palmed his own hilt, watchful of the enemy. 'I am Patrick MacEgan, king of Laochre.'

'I am Sir Anselm Fitzwater,' the Norman replied. 'Lord Thornwyck gave me command of these men.'

Sir Anselm did not remove his helm, nor did he release his grip upon the sword. The Norman's cheeks were clean shaven, his lips marred by a long battle scar that ran to his jaw. His face was impassive, as though he were accustomed to his enemies surrendering.

'The terms of the agreement with the Baron of Thornwyck have been met,' Patrick said, handing him the orders with Thornwyck's seal. 'Your men may enter our *rath*.'

He granted permission, though it was like baring the throats of his people to the enemy sword. He still didn't know whether the Normans would hold the peace.

'Where is the Lady Isabel?' Sir Anselm inquired.

'She dwells upon Ennisleigh. You may accompany me there on the morrow to see for yourself.' He glanced over at the island, and a sense of guilt passed over him. Though he hadn't wanted to bring Isabel amid this battle, he didn't like leaving her alone either. She would be tired and hungry. It was his responsibility to take care of her.

Sir Anselm shook his head. 'I will see her this night to ensure her safety. Have her brought here.'

Patrick would not defer to the man's commanding tone. 'To do so would endanger her. She is safer upon Ennisleigh, away from this strife.' He didn't want her anywhere near the Norman army.

'You dishonour her, if you do not place her as your queen and lady.'

Patrick's hand moved to his sword. His horse shifted uneasily, sensing his anger. 'She is under my protection, and there are those among my people who would sooner see her dead. I see no honour in that.' The raw wound of defeat still bled in his people's hearts.

'It is her rightful place.'

'Until we have brought peace between our people, she stays where I command.' Patrick gestured for Sir Anselm to follow him. 'Your men will join with mine this night in an evening meal. Then you may resume your camp outside the walls.'

'Our orders are to dwell within the fortress,' Anselm said.

'Your men killed ours.' Patrick tightened his grip upon the reins. 'None welcome you here.'

'If your Irishmen raise a weapon against us, they will regret it.'

'As will your men,' Patrick replied, anger threading through his voice. Though the captain might expect them to cower before his men, Patrick did not fear their forces. It was a larger threat that concerned him. Although this army had strength, it was only with the combined forces of Robert Fitzstephen, the Earl of Pembroke's man, that they had defeated his tribe. He had no doubt the Normans would return, along with the Earl.

Patrick gestured towards the large wooden fortress he'd constructed. 'Your men may enter our Great Chamber.' He dismounted, handing his horse over to a young lad. Bevan and Trahern remained mounted.

'Give your horses over to Huon there,' Patrick instructed, gesturing towards the boy. 'He'll see to them.'

He led the Normans inside, standing at the entrance to the fortress as if to guard them. With bitter expressions, most of his kinsmen turned their backs and entered their own huts. They blamed him for this. A few stared, whispering amongst themselves.

Sir Anselm accompanied him inside the main dwelling. From the way his gaze fixed upon the wooden fortress, Patrick wondered if the Norman commander was assessing its worth.

The Great Chamber held no decorations, nothing save weapons mounted upon the walls. Ever since his mother's death years ago, no woman had made her mark upon the gathering space. The sparse furnishings were functional with two high-backed wooden chairs upon a small dais and five smaller chairs for his brothers and him. The small backless X-shaped chairs were carved from walnut, the seats formed of padded wool.

Now, his duty was to take his rightful place at the head of the table, upon the seat filled first by his grandfather, then his father, and then Liam. He had avoided it, but now he had no choice.

Patrick crossed the room and stood before the table. He rested his hands upon the scarred wood, as if seeking guidance from the men who had stood here before. Then he sat down upon the high-backed chair. The chair beside him remained empty, intended for his wife. It seemed strange to think of himself as married. He'd known that one day he would take a wife, but he'd always imagined it to be a maiden from another tribe. He resented having the choice taken from him.

His kinsmen remained standing while the Normans sat at a low table, helping themselves to the food brought by servants. As the soldiers ate brown bread and mutton, resentment deepened upon his people's faces. These were their carefully hoarded supplies, and now they had to surrender them to the enemy. Bowls of cooked pottage, dried sweetened apples and a few freshly caught fish were also offered with the meal.

Patrick ate, hardly speaking to his brothers who sat at the further ends of the table. He forced himself to eat the baked fish and bread while speculating what sort of plotting was going on at the tables. He and his brothers spoke the Norman tongue, but his tribesmen didn't. He didn't trust either side to keep the peace.

Rising from his seat, he walked towards the doorway, greeting his men as he passed. Near a group of bystanders, he overheard his cousin Ruarc's remark. 'If I were king, we would never have allowed the *Gaillabh* entrance. They would lie dead upon the fields, as they deserve.'

Patrick stopped and directed his gaze towards his cousin. 'But you are not the king.'

'Not yet.'

He could not let that remark pass. He'd had enough of criticism and contempt, when he'd done what he could to save their ungrateful lives. His men might doubt his choices, but he could not let them doubt his leadership.

Seizing his cousin by the tunic, he dragged him against the wall. 'Do you wish to challenge me for that right?'

Ruarc's face turned purple as he struggled to free himself. His legs grew limp as Patrick cut off the air to his lungs. When at last he released his kinsman, Ruarc slumped to the ground, coughing. Black rage twisted his features. 'One day, cousin.'

'Get out.'

Ruarc stumbled towards the door, while the Norman soldiers watched with interest. Patrick took a breath, fighting back the urge to pursue. He'd forgotten himself again and his rank. Kings were not supposed to fight amongst their men. The others appeared uncomfortable at his actions.

'That was a mistake.' His brother Bevan came up behind him. Eyeing Ruarc, he added, 'You made him lose face in front of our kinsmen.'

'He should not have challenged me.'

'No. But he'll be wanting revenge upon you now. I'd watch your back, brother. For that one will be ready with a knife. He still blames you for what happened to Sosanna.'

'I know it. And that is why I have not banished him.' Ruarc's sister Sosanna MacEgan, like many of the women, had suffered during the invasion. Afterwards, Ruarc's fury towards the Normans had increased tenfold.

Patrick gestured towards his men. 'Our men should not stand while the Normans sit and eat. We'll build more tables for the Great Chamber.'

'Few have any appetite for food.'

'Except Ewan there.' Patrick leaned against the entrance

wall and pointed to their youngest brother. Nearly three and ten, Ewan had no qualms about dining with the enemy. He sat at the last table, barely visible amid the heavily armed soldiers.

'A good spy, is Ewan.' Bevan shook his head in admiration. 'We will see what he has learned on the morrow. They don't know he can speak their language.'

'The Normans must be taught Irish,' Patrick said. 'Else a misunderstanding could happen.'

Bevan grunted. 'I'd rather we send them back to England instead.'

'It is too late for that.' He turned to his brother. 'You are needed here, Bevan. Will you stay?'

Bevan's visage tensed. 'I will stay a fortnight. For your sake. But promise me you'll drive them out.'

'I'll do what I can.' A headache gnawed at him, and he thought again of Isabel. She had no supplies, for he had forgotten to send them. His mind had been so consumed with the Normans, he had not thought of it. What kind of a provider did that make him? And yet he could not leave his men alone. He felt as if he were holding two ends of a rope while both sides pulled against each other.

He should send someone to her. Darkness had descended, bringing a moonlit sky. Patrick gave orders for a sack filled with food and several jugs of mead.

'What is that for?' his brother Bevan interrupted.

'My winsome bride,' Patrick commented drily. 'She'll want to eat and drink over the next few days, I presume.'

'You're not thinking of going to Ennisleigh.' Bevan gestured towards the food.

'Later, perhaps.' He didn't like the thought of Isabel alone, especially with the islanders who did not understand the reason for her presence.

'Tonight is not the time to leave, brother,' Bevan argued. 'Not with such a fragile situation. The men need your calm.'

He knew his brother was right. This night he needed to prevent both sides from killing each other. 'Would that it were possible. Sir Anselm wishes to see to Lady Isabel's welfare. He will accompany me to the island later this eventide.'

He glanced over at the knight. Sir Anselm ate slowly, his eyes scrutinising every face as if trying to memorise the men. At this pace, the Norman looked nowhere near to finishing his meal.

'I'll return afterwards,' he assured Bevan.

'Ewan!' he called out to his youngest brother. Ewan was caught in the awkward age between child and adolescent. Despite his gangly thin frame, the boy ate as much as a fully grown man.

His brother eyed the roasted mutton before him, as if wondering whether anything could be more important. 'What is it?'

'I need you to go to Ennisleigh. My bride Isabel has no food or supplies for this night. Will you take them to her?'

Ewan's ears turned red. 'If you wish.' He stuffed a small loaf of bread into a fold of his tunic, then tore off another bite of the meat. 'Is she fair of face?'

'What do you mean?'

'I heard Sir Anselm say that many noblemen wanted to wed her. Like a princess from one of Trahern's tales.'

'She is a woman, like any other.' Even as he denied her beauty, the vision of her face taunted his memory. The stubborn set to her mouth had caught his attention more than once. And her deep brown eyes held intelligence.

Patrick walked outside with Ewan, staring at Laochre. The wooden fortress wore its battle scars like the rest of the ringfort. Once, he'd dreamed of building one of the largest *raths* in Eíreann, a dwelling worthy of his tribe. Now he worried about whether they would survive next winter. Though the corn and barley flourished in the fields, he now had to feed even more people with the addition of the Normans.

He led Ewan outside to where his horse was waiting with supplies. 'Go now. If it rains again, she'll need a better shelter. I fear she'll want to dwell inside the fortress.'

Ewan's eyes widened. 'Why?'

'To spite us.'

'Oh.' He shrugged. 'She'll just get wet, then. But I'll go and tell her you sent the food.'

'Do not eat any of it,' he warned.

'I wouldn't.' The lad's voice cracked upon the last word.

Patrick hid his smile. 'Of course you would. I mean it, Ewan. Not a bite.'

He added another loaf of bread to the sack, tying it off. His brother rolled his eyes and set off to the island. Patrick cast a look towards Ennisleigh. He would come to Isabel later. Though she would protest, he had to make her understand that she had no other choice but to make the island her new home.

'Forgive me for intruding, but might I please light a torch from your fire?'

Isabel spoke to one of the doors, a hide-wrapped entrance with a bundle of wool hanging above it. No one had answered her knock, but she knew they had heard her.

She tried again, knocking upon the wooden frame. Silence. She bit her lip, wondering what they would do to her if she dared open the door. In her hand she held a dead branch she'd picked up from the apple orchard. She had wrapped it in dried grass, but what she really needed was oil or pitch to keep it burning long enough to start a fire.

This was the third door she'd knocked upon. Her quest for fire was not going well, and it was getting dark.

The cosy beehive-shaped stone huts had wisps of peat smoke rising from them. An outdoor hearth stood nearby, but no one had made use of it this night. Blackened bricks of peat remained behind.

Very well. If they weren't going to help her, she'd simply wait upon Patrick. She strode back to the fortress, pushing open the charred oak door. Her barbarian husband would return eventually. Surely he would not let her freeze to death. He'd gone to enough trouble to bring her to Erin that her death would be an inconvenience.

A low growl rumbled from her stomach. She hadn't eaten since that small meat pie earlier, and there was nothing inside the broken-down donjon to salvage. At this rate, she'd be reduced to gnawing upon seaweed.

Isabel sat down upon a flat tree stump left behind as a stool and surveyed her dwelling. She had inspected every inch of the fortress, fully aware that the islanders were watching her from inside their huts.

Good. Let them stare. Let them see she was not the enemy they seemed to believe.

Weaponless and alone, her skin prickled with uneasiness. Sometimes the echo of voices carried upon the wind. They spoke in Irish, a language unlike any other she'd heard. She'd tried to learn a few words, but to little avail. The foreign sound had a musical quality to it, and in no way did it resemble the Norman tongue.

She had to learn it. If the king expected her to weep and gnash her teeth at being exiled, he was wrong. She would find a way to survive here.

Night cast its shadowed cloak upon the land, and she

shivered in the evening chill. Perhaps she should have stormed one of the stone huts, demanding a torch. Of course, given their cool reception, she supposed they'd sooner set her on fire than give her aid.

A harsh wind cut through her woollen shawl, and Isabel moved towards a more sheltered part of the fortress. She should have accepted her husband's offer for a hut of her own.

The sound of footsteps made her heart quicken. Isabel reached down and grabbed a small stone.

Of course, if the man had a sword or arrows, the rock would do naught more than give him a headache. Still, it made her feel better. Was it her husband? Or someone coming to harm her? Isabel clutched the rock tighter.

A man's shadow fell across the darkened ruins of the castle. No, not a man's. A boy's.

A young lad with scraggly fair hair stepped across the threshold. He looked as though he'd never made use of a comb. In his hand he held out a sack.

'What is it?' she asked, but he made no reply. Instead, he moved forward and handed her the bundle.

Bread. The warm yeasty smell made her mouth water. She hesitated, wondering if Patrick had sent him. 'Is this for me?'

He gestured towards the supplies, his eyes watching the food. Isabel took the hint and tore off a piece of bread, handing it to him.

'I suppose you do not speak my language.'

The boy devoured the bread, behaving as though he hadn't heard her. She found a jug of mead inside the sack and took a long steady drink. The food and drink improved her temperament, and she began making conversation with the boy.

'I am sorry I do not have a fire to share. On a night like this, it would make my donjon more comfortable.'

She finished the bread and handed the boy the mead to take a sip. He drank deeply and gave it back. 'Of course, your islanders would not help me. I would build one myself, if I had flint and steel.'

Though he said nothing, his sharp eyes studied her. Despite his rumpled appearance, his face reminded her of Patrick's.

'You're his brother, aren't you?' She stood and circled him. The boy appeared uneasy. 'Well, if he sent you to spy upon me, you can tell him that he isn't much of a king. His hospitality is greatly lacking.' With a glance above her, she pointed towards the burned stairs. 'I should like to retire to my chamber, but it seems I must use a rock for my pallet and dirt to keep warm.'

He rubbed his hands and pointed to the empty hearth. Isabel brightened when he gathered up a small stack of peat and tinder. He reached inside a fold of his cloak and withdrew flint and a steel knife. In moments, he sparked a flame to life.

'I could kiss you, you know,' Isabel remarked. 'Clever lad.'

His ears turned crimson, and he didn't look at her. Isabel's expression tightened. 'You understood what I said, didn't you?'

He made no reply, but his colour brightened.

'I might have known.' She tossed another brick of peat into the fire. 'Well, then, what's your name?'

'Ewan MacEgan,' he admitted. He took a long sip of mead, still not daring to look at her.

'Ewan. And why did King Patrick send you in his stead? Did he have other things to do this eventide besides consummating his marriage?'

Mead spewed from his mouth, and the boy choked. 'He—he was trying to stop a war. Busy, he was. He sent me to give you food and to see what you needed.'

'A war?' She shook her head. 'Do not be foolish. The only

war is the one that will happen when your brother comes back here.'

Ewan glanced towards the sack of food. 'Is all the bread gone?'

'No.' She handed him another loaf, which he ate with enthusiasm. Isabel neared the fire and put her hands out to warm herself. 'You're young to be here alone,' she remarked. 'Who looks after you?'

'My brothers.' Ewan's face turned distant. 'Last summer my foster parents were killed in the battle. Patrick allowed me to stay here, but he hasn't made arrangements to send me elsewhere. He's been busy with the Normans.'

'Shall I speak to him for you?'

'No!' Ewan tore off another piece of bread. Colouring, he added, 'I like staying here.'

Isabel supposed the men let the boy do as he pleased. Of course he would be happy. But then, she knew what it was like being separated from her family. If it did the boy no harm, he might as well finish his fostering here.

'Why don't you take me back to your brother's fortress?' she asked, changing the subject. 'I assume there is more food there.'

'Can't.' Ewan took a step backward. 'If that's all you're needing, I'll come back tomorrow morn.'

'Why won't your brother let me live upon the mainland?' she asked. 'What harm could I possibly do?' Unless it meant seeing things she was not supposed to know about.

'It isn't you. It's the others.'

'Others?'

'Your father's soldiers. Patrick has to keep them apart from our men. Otherwise, they'll kill each other.' He stood and walked to the entrance, eyeing the grey sea. Isabel followed him and squinted at the opposite shore. In the distance, she saw several torches lining an embankment.

'I should be going now,' he said.

She was not about to let the boy leave without answers. Patrick had admitted that the marriage was arranged to save the lives of his people. But why were her father's soldiers still in Erin?

'Tell me why the men are here.' She did not trust Edwin de Godred to bring soldiers without a purpose.

'Thornwyck's orders.' Ewan rubbed his arms, stepping closer to the fire. 'But they may be fighting even now, if Patrick cannot stop them. It's the first night he brought them together.'

Isabel took another bite of bread, struggling to think. 'Does he want to unite the people?'

Ewan shook his head. 'Patrick doesn't, no. It can't be done. The Normans killed our folk in battle.'

'But my father wants them to live together.' Isabel understood the deeper implications of her marriage. Edwin intended to conquer the fortress and put her in command. He was counting on her to bring the men together, to become Lady of both sides.

Lady of two sworn enemies. Dear God, she didn't know if she could manage it. Or if she even wanted to venture into this battle.

It was tempting to hide from all of it, here upon Ennisleigh. Her husband wanted her to stay away. She took a breath, steeling herself. Though it frightened her to even think of visiting a fortress under such conditions, she had to know the full truth of what had happened. Only then could she decide whether or not to stay. Was Patrick telling the truth? Or was he simply holding her prisoner?

'Let me help you,' she coaxed the boy. 'I may know some of the men. I can ask them not to attack.'

Ewan shook his head. 'You must stay here.'

While the boy rattled off reasons why his brother had forbidden her to leave, Isabel ignored him. She could not remain here any longer.

She followed Ewan down the rocky incline to the sandy beach where he'd hauled the boat. His skinny arms struggled to push the vessel into the water, and she stepped inside before he could get any further.

'You must go back,' Ewan argued, his hands poised upon the wood.

'I am going with you, and you will take me to your brother's fortress. I'm not staying here.'

Ewan's hands lowered to his sides. He was staring at something out in the water. Isabel turned to follow his gaze and saw the flare of several torches. The flames cast reflections upon the black sea water.

Amid the harsh glow of the torches, she saw a man with black hair. He wore a dark blue cloak, pinned with an iron brooch. His clothing fairly blended into the night and his boat moved forward with a swift grace. The familiar visage made Isabel grip the sides of Ewan's boat even tighter.

'Going somewhere, my wife?'

Chapter Five

Her husband was not alone. A soldier sat behind him in the small water vessel, wearing chain mail armour and a Norman conical helm. One of her father's men, she realised. Why was he here? Had Edwin de Godred come for her? No, if her father had arrived in Erin, he would be here himself.

'I thought you were occupied with preventing a war,' Isabel said, stiffening under Patrick's gaze. She didn't move from her position, behaving as if there was nothing wrong with sitting in a boat trapped upon the beach. 'Shouldn't you be protecting your people from the terrible Normans?'

In one motion, Patrick lifted her from Ewan's boat and carried her further up the shore. She gritted her teeth, annoyed that he still treated her like a sack of grain.

The Norman soldier blinked at the action, but said nothing. Ewan retreated back to his own boat, rowing towards the opposite shore. He looked eager to be away, and Isabel cursed herself for not seizing the opportunity earlier. There was still the second boat, however.

Patrick continued walking uphill, carrying her in his arms. The outside temperature had dropped, the moonlight sliding

out from behind a cloud. For a moment, she contemplated
struggling and fighting against him. She really ought to, but
his warmth cut through her chilled skin, easing her discomfort. The taut muscles and warm male skin against her own
should have terrified her. Instead, deep within, something
stirred. He made her feel protected, somehow.

'Why did you come here?' she asked.

'To ensure your safety.' Effortlessly, he carried her to the
top of the hill, ducking beneath the entrance to the *rath*.
Behind them, the Norman soldier followed. The man
appeared distinctly uncomfortable.

'Put me down, please.'

Patrick lowered her to stand beside him, but did not relinquish his grip upon her hand. The Norman drew near, his expression frowning.

'Who is he?'

'Sir Anselm. He won't be staying long.'

Isabel's suspicions deepened. The knight was one of her
father's men, but why would Patrick bring him here this late?
'Why did he come?'

'Your father sent him to ensure that I have not harmed you.'

She didn't believe him. There was another reason for the
knight's presence. With horror, her imagination conjured up
another idea. 'He's not planning to…witness anything, is
he?' Her face flamed at the thought of another man
watching. 'You said you weren't going to…' Her voice
dropped away.

'No.'

Thank the saints. Isabel hid her relief. Though she didn't
understand why Patrick refused to share her bed, she wasn't
going to question it.

When Sir Anselm reached them, he bowed before her.

Isabel suddenly grew aware that she looked more ragged than the worst sort of wretch. Her hair hung down, matted beneath a rumpled veil. She wore the dung-coloured Irish gown Patrick had given her. But she held herself steady and inclined her head. 'You are Sir Anselm?'

'Aye, my lady.'

She thought she might have seen him before, among her father's men. But since Edwin had never allowed her to speak with the soldiers, she could not be certain. His shield bore her father's standard, and his chain mail armour was the same as the men who had guarded their castle. Though he was not an old man, his eyes appeared weary of battle. And in them, she saw his concern for her.

'I am Isabel de Godred, daughter of Edwin, Baron of Thornwyck.'

Patrick's hand tightened upon hers. 'Your name is Isabel MacEgan. Wife to me.'

His possessive voice curled around her, invading her thoughts. A rapid pulse trembled beneath her skin. She was not accustomed to the new name, and it made her feel as though she'd lost a part of herself.

Turning to Sir Anselm, Patrick said, 'You've seen what you wished to see. Now go.'

The knight did not move. 'Have you been well treated, my lady?' At Patrick's glare, he amended, 'Your father wished me to ensure your contentment.'

Isabel wanted to laugh. She'd been given barely any food, no roof above her head, and the most awful gown she had worn in her entire life. What was she to say?

'She is quite content,' Patrick interrupted, his hand firm upon her wrist. Isabel wanted to jerk away. There was no need to treat her like a child. But when she glared up at him, she saw an unexpected warning to be silent. The dark cast to his face made her hesitate.

Isabel suspected it would be best not to draw her husband's anger upon her. 'I have only arrived this day,' she said. 'I am certain when my husband brings me to the mainland fortress, my accommodations will improve.'

There. Surely MacEgan would have to bring her to his home now. But instead his steel eyes met hers with unyielding force. He would not be swayed by words. 'In time.'

'On the morrow,' she argued.

'When I have deemed it safe,' he growled. Isabel bit back her frustration. He wasn't going to relent, especially not in front of her father's man. Well, then, she wasn't going to give up either. She wasn't about to let him exile her alone upon Ennisleigh.

To Sir Anselm, Patrick commanded, 'Take the boat back to the mainland. At dawn we will discuss enlarging the *rath* to accommodate your men.'

Her heart sank. She'd thought he would go back with Sir Anselm. The idea of spending this night with him rattled her nerves even more. She had expected a night of discomfort in the broken-down fortress. But at least it would have given her a chance to plan her next move.

Sir Anselm studied Isabel, and she held his gaze. He was silently asking about her welfare. She hesitated, then braved, 'Will I see you again soon, Sir Anselm?'

He inclined his head. 'If my lady wishes it so—'

'You will have other duties to concern you.' Patrick cut him off, sending her a warning look.

The Norman knight retreated to the boat, and Isabel expelled a sigh of regret when he was beyond their shores. 'I suppose there isn't any hope of you leaving also?'

'Not yet.'

'A war could break out,' she offered, panic rising inside her. 'You might be needed.'

She wanted him far away from her. Though he claimed he had no intentions of taking her virginity, something about this man unravelled her sanity. There was a wildness to him, a man who would let no woman tame him.

Patrick took her hand in his, gripping her palm as if to prevent an escape. Though his grasp was meant to guide her towards the fortress, goose bumps rose up on her arms.

What did he want from her? Was he trying to keep up appearances, behaving like a husband? She didn't understand him. Then, too, a small part of her wondered if he did not find her appealing. Some of her suitors had accused her of being haughty. And she didn't know what she'd done wrong.

Isabel cast one last look at Sir Anselm's disappearing boat and the torches flickering upon the opposite shore. A chill crept across her at the finality of her fate. 'I am cold.'

Patrick paused a moment and took the ends of her woolen *brat*. He lifted the shawl to her shoulders and wrapped it around her. Though his hands only brushed against her skin, his light touch felt intimate. 'I'll take you some place where you can get warmer.'

Her cheeks flushed, and she closed her eyes, wishing she'd never spoken. 'It isn't necessary for you to stay with me. You could always go back to the mainland.'

'I will, yes. But later.'

Later? What were his intentions in the meantime? She quelled her apprehensions and blurted out, 'Bring me back with you. I promise I won't be in your way.' At least then, he would be more occupied with the people than with her.

He regarded her, his resolve steady. 'I would not bring a woman in the midst of a war. And that is what it is, *a chara*.'

Isabel huddled inside the *brat*, wondering what more she could do. She didn't like remaining behind, but convincing her husband would take time.

They stopped before one of the huts, and he rapped sharply upon the door frame. He spoke words in Irish, and his commanding tone brought immediate results.

A young family, a husband and a wife, answered the door. Behind them, Isabel saw small children sleeping upon pallets. After another command from Patrick, they roused the children and took them outside. Without argument, they opened the door to another hut and ushered the little ones inside. Isabel caught a glimpse of another family inside and worried about such a crowded space.

'You forced them out of their home at this hour?' she said, aghast. 'What of their children?'

'They obeyed their king's command.'

She could not believe what he'd just done. 'It is their home.'

'And they will be well compensated for the use of it. It is only temporary, and they know this.'

'There is a perfectly good donjon over there.' She was lying, of course, for the remains of the dwelling did not have a serviceable roof.

He opened the door and held it for her. 'They knew of my request before you came, Isabel. I gave them several sheep for it.'

She didn't like it, but it relieved her somewhat to know of the payment. After she entered the dwelling, the deep warmth of the interior surrounded them. To her surprise, there was no fire. The heat radiated from large stones set in the centre of the hut. Likely they had been warmed inside the outdoor peat fire earlier. A faint light came from oil lamps set about the small space.

Patrick removed his cloak and set it upon one of the pallets. Isabel turned away, holding her hands out in front of the stones to warm them.

'Did Ewan bring you food, as I asked him to?'

'He did. Thank you for sending him.' Her gaze moved over to the low straw-filled pallet. The thought of lying down tempted her, but Patrick's presence made her nervous. In the dim light, his dark hair shadowed his face. She felt like a captive, awaiting her fate.

He moved to the low table where a skin of mead awaited. He poured the liquid into two wooden goblets. Raising the glass, he handed one to her. '*Sláinte.*'

She drank, the fermented beverage warming her stomach. For long moments he said nothing. He seemed distracted and reluctant to be here with her. When the silence became unbearable, she asked, 'Did you always want to be a king?'

'No.' He sat down beside the table, his hand resting upon his knee. 'It was the last thing I wanted.' The resignation in his voice startled her.

'Most men dream of such an honour,' she ventured.

'I only became king after my brother died. He deserved to rule our tribe.' For a moment, his shield of anger dropped and Isabel caught a glimpse of the man behind the warrior. He grieved for his brother, like anyone would.

'How did he die?' She refilled Patrick's goblet from the skin and he drank.

'He was struck down in the battle against your father's men last summer.'

'I am sorry for it.' She was close to her own sisters, and it hurt to think of anything happening to them.

'So am I.' He set the goblet down, and she handed him a piece of bread from the sack Ewan had brought. Patrick accepted it, grimacing at the hard texture. A problem with the leavening, she guessed. Perhaps bad water or rot. Mentally she reminded herself to look into the matter.

A thought occurred to her. Patrick had said that his brother had died, but was there still a queen?

'What happened to your brother's wife?' she asked.

'Liam was planning to marry Neasa Ó Connor, the daughter of another chieftain. He never had the chance to wed her.'

'Did he love her?'

Patrick shrugged. 'I doubt it. But the alliance was a way to bring the two tribes together.'

'Rather like our marriage,' Isabel mused, but Patrick made no reply. She sat down across from him, pulling her knees to her chest. The hideous brown skirts draped to the floor.

She studied him, trying to see past the steel exterior he cast around himself. Lines of exhaustion rimmed his grey eyes. 'You look tired,' she said. 'Why don't you rest?'

He took a sip from his goblet, pushing it aside. 'I cannot. Your father's men entered Laochre this evening. Tempers are short, and I suspect a fight is brewing.'

From his guarded expression, she could tell that he did not relish the idea of more Normans among them. Isabel kept her stance steady, though he made her nervous. In the dim light of the lamp, his bare arms gleamed. Like a pagan god, she thought. A warrior who would not surrender anything that belonged to him.

'You should leave me your bow, this time,' she said. 'If the islanders try to murder me while I sleep, I'll need a way to defend myself since you won't be here to stop them.' She didn't like remaining behind, helpless.

'They won't harm you.'

Though she wanted the weapon, likely he was right. The

folk had not bothered to open their doors when she'd needed fire. It hurt to think that they, like her husband, did not want to know her.

'It is late.' He extinguished two of the lamps and stood, donning his cloak. 'I must return.'

She wanted to sigh with relief. And yet, she felt guilty for sending the other family away. It wasn't right for her to use this hut alone, when others had the need. But she didn't voice her feelings. At dawn she would find a way to reach the mainland.

Isabel extended her hand in friendship. 'I bid you goodnight.'

Patrick didn't move towards her, nor did he take her hand. She could almost feel the heat of his body, though he stood across the room. He took a long moment, his gaze memorising hers. She found herself drawn to his mouth, to the rigid jaw and the way he held himself back.

Though her hand fell away, she sensed another fight within him. A rush of unexpected feeling pressed through her skin.

'Goodnight.' The door closed behind him, and Isabel released a tremulous breath.

Patrick MacEgan was far more dangerous than she'd expected.

For the first time in her life, she could not plan the future. The idea of remaining prisoner upon Ennisleigh frustrated her. She needed to know what was happening, and she hated being idle.

A heaviness gathered in her chest, and she closed her eyes, trying not to despair. The first step was to get off the island.

Ruarc MacEgan itched for a fight. He wanted to unsheathe his dagger and bathe it in the blood of the Normans. Belenus, what had his cousin Patrick been thinking, opening the gates to them? Did the king not realize the enemy intended to weaken them and take over the *rath*? Even a simpleton could see that.

He watched them, waiting for one of the soldiers to make a move. They had finished eating and their faces were flushed from drink. Good. Let the mead dull their senses, make their reflexes slower.

He moved alongside the benches, searching for a target. When he reached the last Norman, he bumped against the man, sending him sprawling to the floor.

As he'd hoped, the soldier jerked to his feet and drew his knife. Ruarc dodged the slash of the blade, while around him he heard the cheers of his kinsmen. He let the Norman move in closer, biding his time. The ivory hilt warmed within his palm while his blood coursed with anticipation.

A fist moved towards him, and he bent backward to dodge it. With no armour to weigh him down, he moved swiftly. His opponent wore chain mail, and Ruarc swung a kick at the man's legs, hoping to trip him.

Instead, the Norman blocked the kick. A vicious pain sliced through his arm when he missed a step. Ruarc waited for an opening to bury his blade in the Norman's chest. He circled the enemy…waiting…

'What in the name of Lug do you think you're doing?' Trahern bellowed. Ruarc fought to stay on his feet, but the giant shoved him backward, slamming a fist into his jaw.

'Fighting,' he remarked drily.

'Not any more.'

The Norman soldier offered a cocky grin, swiping blood from his lip.

Bastard. He'd have won the fight if Trahern hadn't interfered. But Ruarc kept his temper and stared hard at the enemy.

He would have his chance for vengeance and soon, if he had his way about it.

Ruarc wiped the stinging cut on his arm and strode outside. Muffled sounds of conversation, and the faint cry of a child came from the circle of huts.

He shoved the door open to his own dwelling. There were no sounds of welcome within, only a gasp of fear. He raised the oil lamp and saw the face of his sister Sosanna. Pale and frightened, she breathed an audible sigh of relief when she saw it was only him. Her matted fair hair hung uncombed about her shoulders. She had not changed her gown either, he noted.

A hard ball gathered in his stomach. She hadn't been like this before.

With a tentative smile, Sosanna rolled over and returned to sleep. She didn't speak, just as she hadn't spoken a word in all these months. No one knew what had happened to her during the attack, but Ruarc blamed the Normans. Their father had died in battle, along with his youngest sister Ethna. Ethna had tried to flee from the battle grounds, only to be trampled to death beneath the horses.

He'd found her broken body and wept for her. And for Sosanna, he held fast to his bitterness. One day, he would learn what they'd done to her. And if the gods had mercy upon her, they would heal the invisible wounds.

The others had suffered losses. But instead of fighting back, instead of seeking vengeance, Patrick had taken a Norman bride. A traitor, he was. One who deserved to lose his power.

He could not bring himself to call the MacEgan his king. Though Patrick had won the people's support, already Ruarc could envision his cousin's throne crumbling.

He intended to see to it personally.

Chapter Six

'Sir Anselm wishes to speak with you,' Bevan informed him. Patrick stepped outside the chapel, the air clinging with incense. He'd prayed for guidance at the dawn Mass. But the Latin rites had brought no comfort.

Outside, he surveyed the remains of the *rath*. The palisade wall needed repairs from the fire damage. Though they had made some progress, it was not enough to keep the tribe safe. Below the gatehouse, several vulnerable areas showed signs of crumbling.

Weariness etched heavy lines upon his men's faces. They looked as though they hadn't slept, like himself. He had returned to a quiet Laochre that night, the fortress silent yet watchful. Though he had slept in his own bed, he had found himself studying the space beside him. He still did not feel married, much less to a Norman bride. It should have relieved him to be gone from her side, yet he found himself wondering about Isabel. He didn't remember sleeping, only staring at the walls and praying that the fragile peace would hold.

As he crossed the courtyard, knots of tension tightened every muscle. A few tribesmen had fresh cuts with swollen eyes and knuckles. Though he hadn't seen any disagreements, it was clear that all had not been peaceful while he'd visited Ennisleigh.

'What happened?' he asked, nodding towards one of the men.

Bevan pointed towards Ruarc's dwelling. 'Ruarc started a knife fight, and though Trahern broke it up, a few of the others started a skirmish later.'

'Any broken bones or more serious injuries?' he asked.

Bevan shrugged. 'None that I am aware of. But I bloodied a nose or two, myself.'

'You shouldn't have done that.'

His brother's face grew taut. 'They deserve far more than that, and well you know it.'

'Now is not the time. Call the men together and bring the Norman soldiers in. I wish to address all of them.'

Though he trusted Bevan implicitly, his brother despised the Normans, his temper threatening to lash out. Yet Patrick needed every loyal man to protect Laochre, and Bevan was one who would fight to the death for their tribe.

He didn't know what he would say to the men yet, but the Normans had to understand their limits. At the moment, they bowed to Sir Anselm's authority. Though the Norman knight had behaved with dignity, Patrick wanted Sir Anselm's oath of allegiance. Only then could he command the Normans and keep them separate from his men.

Patrick entered the Great Chamber, going over the words in his mind. In the privacy of his chamber, he changed into a more formal tunic and trews. Though he had not taken care with his appearance before, today he had to assume the role of king. If he could not control the situation, his tribe would weaken even further.

He wore the blue cloak given to him by his father. Though it held the bright colour and silver threads embroidered by his mother's hands, it weighed upon his spirits. Often he doubted himself. He didn't know how to be the quiet, resolute leader his forebears had been. He understood the use of a sword easier than the use of a crown.

But the people had chosen him. Whether he willed it or no, he had to accept the responsibilities that came with the kingship.

A knock interrupted his thoughts. His brother Trahern stepped inside. 'The men have assembled. Both the Normans and our tribesmen await your orders.'

Patrick gave a nod of acknowledgement. He opened a chest at the far end of the chamber and removed the ceremonial *minn óir* and arm bracelets. Beside the diadem rested a silver circlet and silver torque set with amethysts. It was meant for his queen. Isabel would never wear them. He'd sooner see the jewels destroyed than give them to a Norman.

'I've not seen you wear that since your crowning,' Trahern remarked, pointing to the golden diadem.

Patrick set the *minn óir* upon his head. 'It has its purpose. Today the Normans must accept me as their king.'

'You look fetching,' Trahern teased. 'Will you wear golden balls in your hair as well?'

Idiot. Patrick hid his grin and swung a light fist at his younger brother, connecting with Trahern's shoulder. Trahern pounded him on the back, his laughter easing the tension.

'Go and make yourself pretty,' Patrick advised his brother. 'You look like a swineherd.'

Trahern wore a faded saffron tunic and brown trews. Mud caked his boots. 'But I am not the king, am I? It's you who must make ceremonial speeches and give commands.' He shuddered, leaning against the door frame.

'Would that I could command them to leave.'

'You can feed them a feast to remember,' Trahern suggested. 'It may put them in a pleasant mood, as well as our own folk. We've not had fresh meat in a long while. Or good bread. Do you suppose your new wife knows how to prepare better food?'

'She'd sooner poison us all, I imagine.' But he remembered the quiet night of conversation they'd had, and the way Isabel had silently filled his goblet without being asked. With her hair falling over her shoulders and the innocence in her eyes, she possessed a simple beauty. Patrick closed his eyes. She was not, nor would ever be, his queen.

'Give the orders for a feast,' he commanded his brother. 'And have Huon bring my horse.' Once he had finished donning the royal finery, Patrick moved through the narrow hallway and down the spiral stairs.

Inside the Great Chamber, his tribesmen had gathered together. Men and women alike stood at both ends of the Chamber as if awaiting instructions. A few of the smaller children chattered, breaking the silence, only to be hushed by their mothers. The men raised their knees in a gesture of respect.

He crossed the Chamber and stood at the threshold, looking back at them. None of the Normans were present. 'Come. What I have to say must be spoken to everyone dwelling at Laochre.'

From the sullen expressions on their faces, his folk appeared more like stubborn children than grown men and women. But they obeyed, following him outside.

The Norman soldiers stood at the opposite side of the *rath*. Some of them were seasoned fighters, others barely past the age of his younger brother Connor, who was nine and ten. Patrick expected Connor to return from his travels at any moment, for he had finished his fostering two years ago.

He mounted his horse, leading Bel to the centre of the ringfort. 'There will be no fighting this day.' He let his gaze fall upon each man, woman, and child. 'Not from my people.'

He turned to the Norman commander Sir Anselm. 'And not from yours. Anyone who attempts to break the peace will suffer the consequences.'

Silence descended over the people, and rebellion brewed. He could feel their resentment, but it did not sway him from his decision.

'Trahern,' he called to his brother, 'begin pairing them up. One tribesman to each Norman.' Trahern's eyes lowered, but he did not disobey.

'As a penalty for fighting, you will spend this day working alongside each other. Each man will be assigned to a section of the palisade wall or to the main fortress. You will begin the repairs today.'

A few of the Normans glared at him, defiance written upon their faces. But when they looked to their commander, Sir Anselm gave a silent nod. Though the knight had done nothing to undermine his authority, frustration seethed within Patrick. This was his fortress, and he could not have the men looking to Anselm for commands.

He stood back, watching as Trahern matched the men together. The Norman forces outnumbered them, and when a score of men remained, Patrick said, 'Bevan and I will take the rest.'

'What should we do?' a woman asked. 'Shall we work upon the thatching?'

'No,' he answered. 'Slaughter several of the sheep and begin preparations for a noon feast for the men. Those who accomplish their repairs will be rewarded. Those who continue to fight will go hungry.'

With the message delivered, he ordered the remaining Norman forces to follow him. Bevan walked among them, with unshielded hatred in his eyes. Though his brother had threatened to leave, Patrick was grateful he'd stayed. The only men he trusted at the moment were his brothers.

He led the men towards Baginbun Head, in clear view of Bannow Bay where the Normans had landed last season. Patches of new spring grass shifted in the breeze while the sea tide swept over the sand. Reddish-brown rocks lined the edge, as though the earth had absorbed the bloodshed from the invasion.

He drew Bel to a stop when they reached the summit of the hill. 'Do you remember the battle?' he asked the men, his voice grim. Upon their faces, he saw their memories. More than one man held the hollowness of grief from those who had died.

'Our men killed one another last summer. We won't ever put that behind us.' Even now, he relived the moment when he'd seen his brother Liam fall, the sword cutting him down. He blamed himself still.

Patrick raised his eyes to the men. 'And I know that both sides would like nothing more than to kill each other now.' His hand moved to the hilt of his sword, palming the familiar ruby. 'But though we may be enemies, I ask that you live among us in peace until the end of the harvest.' He said nothing of Thornwyck's intended visit, nor his own plans to send them back to England.

He turned to Sir Anselm. 'And I ask for your oath of allegiance.'

The Norman knight's face turned rigid with anger. His hand moved towards his sword, as if to defy the order. Before he could speak, Patrick added, 'I am king of these lands. I have wed Thornwyck's daughter, and if you are to live among us, you must accept our laws.' He rode closer to Anselm, meeting the knight's gaze with his own hard stare. 'I won't tolerate disobedience. Or disloyalty.'

He addressed the remainder of the men. 'Each of you has a choice to make. If you refuse to give your oath, you will live outside the *rath*. We will provide you with nothing.'

'And what if we choose to take what we need?' Anselm asked, his dark eyes glittering.

'Then the battle will begin anew.'

He didn't want war, but neither could he allow the Normans to take dominion over Laochre. Though he knew not if he could gain their obedience, there was no alternative.

This was, quite possibly, the worst idea she'd ever had. The water was brutally cold, like knives against her skin. Isabel's teeth chattered, her limbs half-frozen as she struggled to reach the opposite shore. The waves battered at her arms and face, filling her mouth and nose with salt water.

She clung to a broken segment of the palisade wall that she'd used as a makeshift raft, forcing herself to keep swimming. The stout limbs were tied together in a rectangular shape, but they would not support her weight as she'd hoped. She had placed a small bundle containing her gown upon it, but even that was soaked.

Isabel had made up her mind this morning that she would see the mainland and fortress for herself. She had not yet seen the extent of the damage, and she needed to know the truth—not to mention she was dying of boredom.

The problem was, she could not find where the islanders kept their boats. None were visible along the shoreline. She didn't know how Patrick had reached the opposite side a few nights ago, and so she was left with no choice but to form her own vessel.

The mainland had seemed so close, and yet, with each stroke, her arms felt heavier. If she drowned, she could imagine the souls of the dead laughing at her idiocy.

Well, she'd come this far. She had no choice but to reach the shoreline. With one arm grasping the raft, she continued swimming.

It seemed like hours, but eventually her feet touched bottom again. She staggered upon land, her shift clinging to her body. The late afternoon sun offered no warmth at all.

She couldn't remember ever being this cold. Shivers coursed through her, and she clutched her arms, unable to feel anything in her fingertips. Perhaps her husband would find her dying body here, frozen.

From inside the bundle, she pulled out her shoes. Her fingers trembled as she tried to put them on. Though she hated the thought of donning a wet woollen gown, at least it would protect her modesty. The clammy fabric weighed down upon her, offering no warmth.

A fire. She dreamed of a roaring fire and warming herself before it. The thought elevated her spirits, and she trudged up the bank until she reached the rise of the slope. Shielding her eyes, she nearly groaned when she saw the distance to the ringfort.

But at least she'd found it. The fortress of Laochre dominated the landscape, with even fields of seedlings dotting the hills with new green. Beehive-shaped stone cottages with thatched roofs encircled the structure, while a wooden palisade wall protected the inhabitants. Beyond the wall, a large ditch and embankment offered further defences.

When she reached the fields, Isabel pressed her hands to her mouth. At a closer view, she saw the blackened walls and the crumbling homes. She had imagined a place of grand wealth, a fortress worthy of a king.

But this…

The desolate ringfort had been brought to its knees by her father's forces. She could almost smell the smoke, hear the screams of those who had died. It hurt to look at it.

And she suddenly realised why her husband hadn't wanted her to see it. This was not the glorious kingdom of a warrior, but the dying remains of a tribe. Isabel tried not to imagine the women and children who had suffered. She huddled with her arms wrapped around her middle, struggling to think.

Seeing it brought back all the harsh memories of the destroyed village and the crying child. She hadn't acted then, and she carried the guilt upon her conscience still.

The weariness in her husband's eyes, the unseen weight upon his shoulders, became evident. She felt it as though it were her own. Could she help him in this task? But her stoic husband would likely refuse any assistance, particularly from herself.

With each step forward, she understood the decision she had made. She was going to stay here, because it was the right thing to do. She couldn't abandon those who had lost so much, not when she had married their king. Even if her marriage remained a distant arrangement, she was needed here.

Isabel moved towards the ringfort, passing through the underbrush and beyond small groves of trees. She stopped to rest, still shivering violently. Only the thought of a fire and her own stubborn refusal not to die kept her moving.

In the distance, she heard men's voices. It was too late to hide, and so she squared her shoulders.

Behave like a queen, she instructed herself. She tried not to think of how bedraggled she looked. Nor how angry Patrick would be when he discovered her escape.

Men surrounded the palisade wall, ripping away broken limbs and binding new ones in their place. Her father's men worked alongside the Irish. Now and then she heard the lilting tones of the unfamiliar language, but not once did she hear her own tongue. The Normans held their silence. One stared at her, and Isabel's throat went dry at the caged hostility in his face. It felt like she were stepping into the midst of a battle. Her husband didn't want the Normans here. And now she wondered if she'd made a mistake.

Isabel turned her gaze away from the man, moving towards the gatehouse. She nearly screamed when a boy's face loomed before her, out of nowhere.

'Ewan,' she gasped. 'You startled me.'

The boy grinned, his gamine face delighting in the trick he'd played. His shaggy blond hair curled around his ears, and he jumped down from the wooden ladder. 'Come.' He grabbed her hand and led her inside the ringfort. 'Before he finds you.'

Isabel didn't have to ask whom he meant. She wasn't entirely eager to face Patrick. Like as not, he'd drag her away and force her back to Ennisleigh again. She obeyed Ewan, following him through the gates.

The interior of the ringfort was as bad as the exterior. Blackened by fires, destruction surrounded them. She shuddered at the sight, her own nerves gathering strength at the thought of what Patrick would say. Then she stopped short when she spied a child.

A young girl stood nearby, so thin Isabel could see the sharp angles of her bones. Pale and weak, the child stared with curiosity. And she wasn't alone. Other children, frail with hunger, eyed her and Ewan with interest.

Her resolve to help them only strengthened. No child should have to suffer, especially not from hunger. Whether Patrick wanted her help or not, she wasn't going to stand aside.

'What happened to them?' she asked Ewan.

He didn't seem to understand her question at first. Then comprehension dawned. 'The Normans destroyed our winter stores. Laid siege, they did.'

Isabel expelled a breath. By the Blessed Virgin, how could her father ever believe the two sides could be brought together? The answer came quickly enough: he didn't. He expected the Normans to conquer the Irish. And what of herself? Was she supposed to govern them as their queen, ignoring their suffering?

No. She couldn't turn aside and pretend she didn't see what was happening. As lady of these lands, she knew her duty was to protect the weak.

With her family's wealth and her dowry, she could restore their fortunes and blot out the evidence of hunger. Her mind hearkened back to their wedding day. Patrick had warned that his people would die if he didn't wed her. She hadn't wanted to believe him, thinking that her father would never make such a terrible bargain. But seeing evidence of the conquest made it clear Patrick was right.

Ewan stopped in front of an empty storage hut. 'You could wait here. No one will see you.'

'That isn't why I came,' Isabel admitted. She had no intention of hiding herself. Though she had no idea how she would begin taking her proper place, she would find a way.

'I think you should stay here until Patrick comes,' Ewan warned, his adolescent voice cracking. 'They cannot speak your language.'

He tried to pull her inside the hut, but Isabel stood her

ground. 'I'm not afraid of them.' Perhaps if she said the words aloud, they would become true.

Ewan seemed about to protest again, but a male voice called out him in Irish. 'Wait here,' the lad said. 'Trahern has asked for me.'

Isabel nodded. 'Go on. I'll be fine.' And yet, at the moment, she felt terribly isolated and afraid. She waited until Ewan had disappeared, and then studied the remaining huts.

The rich scent of roasting mutton filled her nostrils, and she decided to enter a large stone hut that appeared similar to her father's kitchen. A group of women spoke Irish to one another, their voices mingling in pleasant conversation.

For a moment Isabel hung near the door, forcing away the shyness she felt. This would be so much easier if she could speak their language. She only knew a few words, hardly enough to converse.

This is your duty, she reminded herself. *These are your people now.* She stepped inside the hut. 'Good morn to you,' she said.

Their conversation ceased. No one smiled, no one offered any word of welcome. Instead, the women turned their backs on her.

Isabel moved to stand beside the fire, not looking at anyone. They worked in silence, keeping their distance. The roasting meat sizzled over the open flame, the fat catching fire. Isabel found a heavy cloth and turned the spit over the fire, while the warmth of the flames dried her sodden gown. She had never performed such a task before, but it seemed better than letting the meat burn.

The women's infuriated looks made her wary. She decided to attempt speaking Irish, hoping that she would not sound foolish.

'I am Isabel,' she said. Her voice came out weaker than

she'd wanted, but at least she'd managed an introduction. She forced a smile on to her face, feeling all the world like an outsider.

At their blank expressions, she repeated her name again. 'Isabel.'

A red-haired woman glanced at her peers. 'Alannah,' she replied. Rapidly she spoke to the other women, and even as they stared at her, they made no gesture of welcome.

Isabel struggled to remember a simple greeting, but could not recall any of Patrick's words. She acknowledged the woman with a nod. None of the others offered their names.

Alannah's attention narrowed upon Isabel's damp gown. She voiced a question, pointing at the fabric.

'I swam,' Isabel explained, making swimming motions with her hands.

Their eyes widened, and one of the women giggled. Isabel did not return the laughter, but instead pretended as if she didn't hear them.

They talked amongst themselves, and no doubt it was about her. Isabel vowed to learn their language as quickly as possible. She could never be mistress here unless she learned to talk to the people.

The thought sobered her, for it was going to be much harder than she'd thought.

She warmed herself by the fire, her spirits sinking. Everything seemed so different here. Her husband preferred to exile her, rather than to help her fit in. She stared into the flames, thinking of the night in the cavern when he'd drawn close to her. He claimed he would never touch her, and though she should feel grateful, now it made her even more aware of her loneliness.

The women began chopping vegetables for the noon

meal, so Isabel moved forward and stood among them. As soon as she did, they moved away. She mustered a smile. 'You aren't going to make this easy, are you?' Since they didn't intend to speak with her, it meant nothing if she spoke her opinions.

Seizing a carrot, she looked around for a knife. They eyed each other, as if trying to decide what her intentions were. She motioned to them as if chopping the carrot; finally, Alannah handed her a dull blade. Isabel scraped the skin from the carrot, behaving as though nothing were wrong. She had watched the servants prepare vegetables a thousand times before, but she struggled with the task. The knife slipped and knicked her finger. Every pair of eyes watched her.

'I suppose queens aren't supposed to work, are they?' she muttered. 'But since I haven't anything else to do, I might as well be useful.'

After she had peeled three carrots, they stopped staring and resumed working. Once or twice, the women's gaze shifted upon her.

Isabel strained to catch a familiar word, but the language was too difficult to understand. Now and again, she heard a name, but that was all.

She kept her gaze lowered and caught another woman staring at her from the shadows. The woman had an unkempt appearance to her. Her long fair hair hung in greasy ropes around her dirty face. The gown she wore was stained and the hemline frayed.

The woman reminded her of a wild animal, too afraid to draw near. Isabel offered a slight smile, but she did not return it.

'Isabel,' she said, pointing to herself. The woman moved far away, huddling against the corner of the hut.

At her questioning look, Alannah named the woman.

'Sosanna,' she said, pointing. Isabel wondered why the woman had not answered for herself, but the others seemed wary.

Outside, Isabel heard the sound of men's voices. Her husband's voice issued orders, and she caught a few men muttering protests in her own language.

What was happening?

Isabel moved stealthily to the entrance where she saw rows of her father's men lined up. Beside them were the Irishmen. The two groups stood in sharp contrast. The Irish wore no armour, their rows uneven. Some stood openly glaring at the Normans. More than a few had raw sores upon their faces, bruises forming.

Patrick strode towards the Normans, rage creasing his face. 'When I give orders, you are to obey them. If you expect us to feed and house you, then you must help us complete the task of rebuilding.'

'We'd have been better to burn it to the ground,' one Norman remarked beneath his breath. 'At least then we wouldn't have to live here.'

Isabel couldn't believe the soldier had the courage to voice such insolence. How could Patrick let him speak in such a way? His disrespect was unacceptable.

She took a step forward from the hut, staring at the men. Her stomach clenched at the thought of interfering. This was Patrick's battle, not hers. And yet, she felt an obligation to speak, despite her apprehension.

Isabel moved to stand before the men, aware of her dishevelled appearance. Though she didn't know many of the soldiers, she recognised a few faces, including her father's captain Sir Anselm.

'What of your families?' Her voice came out hardly above

a speaking tone, but a few glanced in her direction. 'Would you have them sleep on the ground when they arrive? If this is to be your home, it is not unreasonable to ask for your help in rebuilding it.'

Behind her, Patrick moved in. His hand curled around her upper arm like a steel manacle. 'Go inside the Great Chamber.' His voice held a tangible threat, but Isabel refused to back down.

'My father has arranged for a truce between our people,' she said to the Norman soldiers. 'You won't be going back to England.'

'Trahern.' Patrick nodded to his brothers. 'See that the men are fed. Our men first, then the Normans. Any man with cuts or bruises from fighting will not eat.'

His words startled Isabel. Would he really deny the soldiers food? Surely things weren't that bad.

Her husband's grip tightened over her arm, and he half-dragged her to the building. Isabel didn't fight him, not wanting to make a public spectacle. But she intended to discuss several matters with Patrick, especially the treatment of her own people.

Inside the entrance, he closed the door. 'What are you doing here? I gave orders for no one to bring you to the mainland,' he demanded. His grey eyes blazed with untold fury. Dark hair framed an angular face, his mouth a harsh line.

'I brought myself.' She raised her chin. 'And I swam, if you must know. It was rather cold.'

'Have you lost your wits? You might have drowned.'

'No. But you have lost yours if you believe those men will obey your orders.' She placed her hands on her hips, meeting his anger with words of her own. His methods would only result in more conflict and anger.

'They will obey, or they will not eat.'

'And that will make them respect your authority?' Isabel could not believe he would be that cruel. 'Denying them food will only breed more hatred.'

'If you've finished, I am taking you back to the island.'

'I have not.' She poked a finger at his chest. 'I am your wife, and I belong here. Not buried upon an island far away from where I'm needed.'

'You aren't needed, Isabel.'

'That's where you're wrong,' she insisted. 'If you intend to bring the Irish and the Normans together, I can help you. I know these men.'

'Bringing the Irish and the Normans together was never something I wanted.' The coldness of his tone sliced at her heart. What did he mean, it was never something he wanted? Wasn't it the reason for marrying her? To heal the strife and end the battle?

'What's done is done,' she said softly. 'We must make the best of it. Including our marriage.'

Patrick shook his head. 'We have an arrangement. Not a marriage.'

She straightened, feeling the tenebrous anger exuding from him. Though he made no move to touch her, the brunt of his frustration was tangible. His fists clenched, but somehow she sensed that there was more behind it. He held the burden of an entire tribe, struggling to keep his people alive.

Isabel took a step forward and touched her hands to his fists. He froze, startled by her gesture. 'I've done nothing wrong. You've no cause to despise me the way you do.'

His hands relaxed their grip, but he did not move away. 'You aren't very good at following orders.'

She shrugged. 'That may be. But do you truly wish for our marriage to be so distant? We could be friends.'

The mask of distance shadowed him once more and he moved his hands back. 'It can be no other way.'

'Why?' She couldn't understand what was wrong with her. 'Am I not fitting to be a wife?'

He lowered his gaze. 'Someone else's wife, perhaps. But you were never meant for this.'

A heaviness gathered in the pit of her stomach, and she didn't know what to do. Tears pricked at her eyes, but she refused to lower herself by begging. If he didn't want her, so be it.

'Dry yourself by the fire., I'll come for you soon.' A moment later, warmth covered her shoulders. When she looked up, Patrick had gone. Across her shoulders, he'd draped his own cloak.

The heat from his body clung to it, along with the spicy scent of him. An angry tear broke free, sliding down her cheek. Isabel let the cloak fall to the floor and cursed herself for ever thinking she could be a part of the tribe.

Chapter Seven

If his mother were alive, she'd flay his hide for treating a woman this way. As Patrick hammered pegs into the palisade wall, he took out his frustration upon the wood. Isabel had asked for peace between them. Friendship, even.

Though her request was innocent enough, he couldn't see them becoming friends. Their lives were too different.

He glanced up at his dwelling and saw her standing at the entrance, his cloak wrapped across her shoulders. Even soaking wet, she carried herself like a queen. She reminded him of one of the ancient female warriors, fearless and bold.

He still could not believe she'd swum the channel. A more reckless move he'd never seen.

And Christ's bones, she captured his attentions. Though he knew he would never share her bed, it didn't stop him from desiring her. The innocence of her touch had sent need blazing through him. Deep mahogany eyes stood out against her gentle face and the shining gold of her hair. Her mouth tempted him like Eden's fruit.

Patrick hammered another peg and split the board. Cursing, he tossed the wood aside.

'Brother, you should not be doing such work,' Trahern cautioned. 'You are the king. It is beneath you.'

Patrick knew it, but he'd be damned if he stood on ceremony. He'd only been a king for less than a year, and it struck him as arrogant to stand back and watch the others sweat and toil.

'I've a need to do the work.'

He picked up his mallet and slammed another peg in place. Only an hour ago, the Normans had given their oath of allegiance while they stood near Baginbun. Even Sir Anselm.

Though each man had pledged himself, Patrick had not missed the fury and resentment in their eyes nor the bruises from recent fighting. It was a small step forward, but he didn't trust any of them. His reward, in return for their oath, was the promise of permanent living quarters for the men. He supposed that was why the men had agreed, for all seemed tired of living within tents. And, he suspected the words meant little to them. Their hearts were loyal to Thornwyck and their countrymen, not the MacEgan tribe.

Trahern glanced in the direction of the donjon where Isabel stood. 'I thought you said she was going to stay on Ennisleigh.'

'She was supposed to. The woman swam across the channel.'

Trahern expelled a low whistle of admiration. 'Not something I expected from a noblewoman. I'll admit it, she has courage.'

'She won't listen to orders. I swear by the gods, I'll have to chain her down for her to obey.'

Trahern chuckled. 'Were it me, brother, I'd chain her to my bed.'

The thought of Isabel lying naked upon his bed was a dangerous one. His imagination could think of several things he'd like to do. Gods, he needed her to remain on Ennisleigh, away from his sight. It was easier not to think of her, nor to be tempted by her. 'I'm taking her back to the island after she's dried her wet clothing by the fire.'

'Why send her back? She's done no harm.'

For if he didn't send her far away, he didn't trust himself not to claim what rightfully belonged to him.

'I don't want her becoming part of our tribe. After Lughnasa, I'm setting her aside. We'll have driven the Normans out by then, and Thornwyck as well.'

His brother's face turned troubled. 'I hope you're right. But you married her upon English soil. It won't be easy to divorce her.'

'With enough gold to bribe a Church council, anything can be done.' Patrick didn't concern himself with the Norman politics. 'We both know it's best for our people if a tribeswoman is our queen.'

'Is that what you want?' Trahern asked quietly.

His brother seemed to see past his words, as if knowing how much he desired Isabel. 'It is the good of our people we speak of.'

Trahern picked up another mallet and joined him in the repairs. 'Does she know the marriage is not permanent?'

'No. And there is no reason to say anything yet. Let her believe what she wants. I vowed I'd give her freedom. And so she shall have it, upon Ennisleigh.'

Trahern shook his head. 'I've a feeling your new bride will have a lot to say.'

'I will speak with her this night.'

'You should do more than talk, brother. It might ease that foul mood of yours.'

His brother's hint did not go unnoticed. But he would not share Isabel's bed. There could be no child between them. He wanted nothing to bind them together after they separated.

And, it was more honourable to let her go as an untouched maiden. She could make a suitable marriage to a Norman lord and go to him as a virgin bride. He clenched his fists, his irrational temper darkening at the thought of another man touching her.

'I need to take her back.' Patrick set down the mallet, testing the strength of the palisade wall.

'A word of advice, Patrick.' Trahern leaned against the fence, his green eyes amused. 'Take the chess pieces with you.'

'Why?'

'You need to keep up appearances. At least, for now, make it seem that you are sharing her bed.' Trahern winked. 'And the chess board will give you something to do on those long nights with her.'

Patrick handed his brother a replacement post. 'It sounds as if you're the one who needs a woman.'

As he strode towards his wife, Trahern called back, 'I wouldn't complain.'

He sent Trahern a look of death. 'Gather supplies to send to Ennisleigh. She needs food and mead for the next sennight. Load them on one of the horses and I'll bring them along.'

At his brother's teasing, Patrick's temper had softened. When he returned to the donjon, he found Isabel back inside the Great Chamber. She had found a broom and was sweeping cobwebs from the corners of the room. Her damp hair spilled down her back, and it made her seem as if she'd just come from a bath. She appeared vulnerable, and utterly alluring.

He gritted his teeth, forcing his attention away from her face. 'It is time to go. Are your *léine* and overdress dry?'

Isabel lowered the broom and shrugged. 'Well enough.' She turned and studied the interior of the Great Chamber.

'You should take down that wall there, and open the chamber up. Then you could bring everyone inside for a gathering.'

'And why would I want to do that?'

'You could make this place into one of the most powerful castles in Erin. It has wonderful potential.'

'It's a *rath*. Not a castle.' His ringfort was half the size of the Norman structures he'd seen, and he had no intention of copying their designs. Her idea of changing the interior caught him by surprise. He struggled to envision the changes she was suggesting. 'We've no need to alter the structure.'

'I disagree. You could not defend it during your last attack.' She ran her hands across the wooden surface, nodding to herself. 'You've seen my father's castle. If you change the design of this, it would give you more space.'

'And it would diminish the inner bailey. I won't infringe upon my people's homes, even if it is my land.'

'I didn't say that. Widen the fortress. There is room. And when you finish the palisade walls, whitewash them. From a distance, it will appear like stone and your enemies will stay back.'

Though her suggestions had merit, he didn't like her insinuation that the fortress was vulnerable to more attacks. 'We've no need to make such changes. We'll repair what we have and train the men to become better soldiers.'

'The bones of this dwelling are strong. Can't you imagine it? Tapestries hanging on the walls. Musicians. Dancing. Feasting.' She smiled at the thought.

'I am not replacing my home with a Norman fortress. The *rath* has stood for centuries.'

'Until last summer,' she said quietly. 'More Normans will come. The Earl of Pembroke won't rest until he's taken more territory.'

Patrick knew it. But he could never tear down the walls

built by his grandfather before him. They had withstood Norse attacks and countless invader assaults before this time.

'We must be ready for them,' she said.

We. She spoke as though she intended to fight among them.

'Why would you wish to stand with us? Would you betray your own father?'

Her expression faltered. For a moment he saw a flash of uncertainty.

'I hope it would never come to that.' She tried to muster a smile, but her mouth tightened. 'And my father has no need to attack Laochre again. As your wife, I—'

'He believes you are my queen,' Patrick said. And it could not have been further from the truth. He'd tried to keep Isabel away for her own protection. Sooner or later the attacks would begin again. And he feared the Normans would turn on them.

Isabel tugged at the cloak around her shoulders. 'I know why you wed me. But I don't understand why you won't let me help you. I have a duty to these people. I can't stay behind on Ennisleigh.'

Though her gesture was a woman's plea, she conjured up unwanted desire. He tensed beneath her touch. What was the matter with him? She was a Norman.

Isabel drew close to him. Her hair hung down, the faint scent of salt clinging to her. He found himself staring at her mouth. Soft and full, her lips fascinated him.

She's your wife, his body argued, *and a beautiful woman.*

'I don't want you hurt,' he said.

Liar, his conscience accused. He didn't want to be tempted by her.

'It is time to leave.' He extended his hand, turning away to break the spell she had cast.

'Wait.' Her eyes lowered, and she took his hand. 'I saw the

children today.' Her fingers joined with his, and the softness of her skin distracted him. 'You wed me to save them.'

He wanted to pull away, but the touch of her hand seemed to burn through his skin. 'You knew that on our wedding day.'

'But I never understood you.' Her eyes filled with compassion, and he grew uncomfortable. She didn't understand, couldn't understand what had happened to his people. It was beyond anything she had ever experienced.

'I want to help them,' she said. 'You never sent for my dowry, did you?'

'I've no need for household goods.'

'What of the gold and silver?' she asked. 'I could help replenish your supplies.'

He didn't want anything from her or her family. Though she made the offer in good faith, he couldn't accept it. It was his responsibility to provide for his people, not hers. He'd not let her become involved, particularly since their marriage was not permanent. He wouldn't use her that way.

'There is no need for your dowry.' He took several steps away from her. 'We are leaving now.'

'If you take me back to Ennisleigh, I'll only swim back again.'

He didn't doubt she would make good upon the threat. Instead, he tightened his grip upon her hand. 'Trahern suggested I chain you down. The thought did occur to me.'

'Try it, Irishman, and you'll be sorry for it.'

As he guided her outside, he didn't miss the stares from his people. The women's expressions were filled with hate, while his men regarded her with suspicion.

No one smiled, no one spoke. Isabel kept her chin raised, feigning indifference. But he saw the slight tremble in her hands and the way she did not look at anyone.

'Is that our queen?' a young child asked, pointing.

His mother shushed him, murmuring, 'No. She's a Norman like the others.'

Patrick did not correct the woman, for she had spoken his own thoughts. Though Isabel was now his wife, she was still one of the enemy. And he needed to remember that instead of feeling pity for her.

He needed to place her back upon Ennisleigh, away from his people. And, most especially, away from himself.

Ruarc stopped outside his home, a strange sound coming from within. His hand automatically went to his dagger as he opened the hide door.

Sosanna knelt beside a low wooden table, her shoulders huddled as she wept. Her tears brought Ruarc to her side immediately.

'What is it? Should I send for a healer?'

She shook her head and rested her cheek on the cold earthen floor. Her hand moved to her stomach, but she said nothing.

He helped ease her to her pallet, and it bothered him to see her so pale and fragile. It was as though she were dying and he could do nothing to stop it.

Her *léine* hung down, and she wore no girdle about it. Ruarc frowned, studying his sister closer. Without a warning, he moved his hand to her middle.

Horror creased her face. Ruarc couldn't conceal his shock, couldn't breathe. By the gods. She was carrying a child. From the size of her stomach, she would give birth by the end of the summer. How had he been so blind as not to see it?

'Who did this to you?' he asked, unable to keep the rage from his voice. 'Tell me the name of the bastard, and by Lug, I swear I'll slit his throat.'

His sister said nothing. She didn't have to. Already he knew that one of the Normans had hurt her.

'Sosanna?' he asked, softening his voice.

A tear slid down her cheek and she turned from him. Huddled amongst the furs, she would not speak.

Death was too good for any of the Normans. Ruarc strode outside, his fists curling up. It took only seconds to find an enemy soldier. Blood seemed to swim before his eyes, and he released his rage, snapping the man's head backward with a punch.

Taken by surprise, the Norman hesitated a fraction before retaliating with his own strike. Ruarc dodged the blow and pounded at the enemy's ribs.

He'd passed beyond all reason. All he could think of was hurting the unknown man who had harmed his sister. One of these men had taken away his sister's voice and her pride. And they would pay dearly for it.

He tasted blood, enduring bruises, but getting in a few solid punches of his own. Lug, if he had a sword, he'd love to slaughter them all.

Another Norman joined in. Ruarc struck a kick to the man's gut, spinning to punch another. A rib cracked, and Ruarc dove at the first man, slamming his fist into the Norman's jaw.

Then something hard struck his head. His vision blurred, and he dropped to the ground. Dimly he was aware of his hands confined, his body dragged across the ground. They forced him to sit with his back against a post. Leather bindings tightened across his wrists as his kinsman regarded him.

'You will remain here until your king returns,' Bevan MacEgan commanded. 'And I don't think that will be until tomorrow's sunrise. You'd best pray that the gods show mercy upon you. For Patrick won't.'

Ruarc raised his eyes to Bevan's. 'They hurt my sister. And they should burn for what they did to her.'

He saw the flash of recognition in Bevan's eyes. Of all the men, his cousin understood. He'd lost his own wife Fiona to the invaders.

'She deserves vengeance,' Ruarc said beneath his breath. 'None of them should be alive.'

Bevan rose, crossing his arms as he regarded the Normans. From inside Ruarc's hut, Sosanna emerged. Her cheeks were wet with tears, her hands clenched around her middle. There was nothing in her eyes, save resignation.

'I agree,' Bevan said quietly. 'The Normans have much to answer for.'

Isabel held on to the edges of the wooden boat as Patrick rowed towards the island. She felt like a child facing punishment from a parent. Her husband's face held the creases of deep rage.

'I cannot believe you swam that far,' Patrick said, his arm muscles flexing against the pull of the tide. Crimson streaks of sunlight rippled upon the water. The sea had grown calm, a contrast to her husband's temper. 'You could have drowned.'

'I could have, yes.' She managed a chagrined smile, though it did nothing to soften his gruffness. 'I realised that when I was halfway across. By then, it was too late to turn back.'

'Don't do something that foolish again,' he warned. His oars sliced through the water, drawing them closer to the island.

'Next time, I'll borrow a boat.' If she could find one, that is. She had no desire to experience such cold water again.

'There won't be a next time.'

Isabel was growing tired of his high-handed ways. His orders were from an effort to control her, not concern for her safety. 'Do not be so sure of that.'

Shadows silhouetted his face. He stopped rowing and let the oars rest upon the wood. 'What are you trying to prove, Isabel?'

She tucked her hands between her knees, suddenly aware of the intensity of him. His steel-grey eyes held such anger. The lean planes of his face held no sympathy, nothing but a fierce warrior.

'I won't be commanded by a man who chooses to exile me.'

'Won't you?' He rested his forearms upon his knees, the leather bracers emphasising the deeply cut muscles.

'No.' Behind the weight of responsibility, he was a handsome warrior. What would he be like if he weren't so angry? Isabel hadn't missed the way the Irish women had watched him.

'Were you betrothed to anyone before you wed me?' she asked.

Patrick shook his head. 'Why do you ask?'

Because the women had stared at him as though he were a delicious cake dripping with honey. 'You aren't terribly ugly,' she offered. 'And you are a king.'

'Not terribly ugly?' His mouth twitched. 'And here I thought I was a barbarian monster.'

She nodded her agreement, and his lips curved upwards.

He let the boat glide through the water, and his intent stare made her shiver.

Isabel changed the subject. 'Erin is very beautiful at night.'

'It is.' His mouth softened. Grey eyes fixed upon her, his voice rich and seductive. 'Very beautiful.'

Colour flooded her face. Isabel forced herself to look away. With the darkening sky above them and the sea all around, everything seemed to fall away.

What would it be like for him to kiss her? She covered her mouth with her hands, willing the sudden thought away. Her father's threat haunted her. He wanted her to bear Patrick's child. What would he do when he learned she was still a virgin? He'd sworn to come only a few months from now at harvest time. Would he demand a ceremonial bedding? She would not put it past him to humiliate her in such a way.

'I know you did not wish to wed me,' she began, not really knowing what to say. 'But I meant what I said earlier. I'd rather we be friends.'

The awkward silence stretched further when Patrick picked up the oars and began rowing again towards the shoreline. 'Trahern wants me to stay with you tonight to keep up appearances.'

It wasn't precisely what she had in mind, but it was better than nothing. If they shared a meal and conversation, she might uncover what sort of man her husband truly was. He wore the mask of a king at every moment.

'It is a great sacrifice,' she said drily, 'having to spend time with me.'

'More than you know,' he muttered.

Isabel dipped her hand in the sea and flicked a palm full of water at his face.

Patrick's face darkened. Droplets of salt water slid down his bristled cheeks. 'That was a childish thing to do.'

'That was not a nice thing to say,' she retorted.

Seconds later, a splash of frigid water struck her own face. Patrick's wet hand proclaimed his guilt and wickedness gleamed in his eyes.

'Don't start this.' Isabel set her hand back in the water as a threat. 'There's already one war between us.'

Before she could move, he trapped her hands in his. The weight of his body moved her astern. His thighs surrounded her legs, his chest invading her space.

A trickle of water slid down his neck and dripped upon her skin. Her nipples tightened at the cold sensation. With his dark hair framing his face, her attention moved to his mouth again. His firm lips captivated her.

The rocking of the boat moved his body against hers, and she felt the evidence of his desire. The shocking sensation heated her skin, her body needing to be closer to him.

Though she didn't understand why, he pulled her arms around his neck. She clung to him for balance, her heartbeat pounding against her chest. No longer did she feel the chill of the water. Instead, her body burned in a way she didn't understand. She wanted to feel his skin upon hers, and she flushed at the thought.

He wasn't going to kiss her. She could see it in his eyes. He was fighting against it.

But he didn't let go of her. His hands caressed her back, holding her away from the hard wood of the boat. A secret part of her ached to welcome him. She wanted his hands to move over her, caressing her. She needed more than this, and yet he held himself back.

Embraced in his arms, she pressed her breasts close to him, her body trembling. Her mouth parted, wishing for what he would not give.

Then she lifted her face and kissed him.

Chapter Eight

Need roared through him at the soft touch of her mouth. The innocent taste of her sent him reeling. Patrick plundered her mouth, tasting her forbidden sweetness. Caveats coursed through his mind, but he ignored them. He wanted to kiss this frustrating woman, to drive her from his thoughts.

Though he didn't know what had possessed her to kiss him, he wasn't going to let her go. Not until he exorcised the craving for her.

His mouth moved over hers, and he felt her shuddering. Deliberately he softened the kiss, nipping at her lower lip. She opened to him and he slid his tongue in her mouth.

The sensation mimicked the sexual act he was denying himself. Her tongue met his, and Lug, his body hardened into stone. Right now he could think of nothing better than to remove her clothes and make love to her in the boat.

He kissed her cheek, the tender spot behind her ear. Then a gasping cry spilled from her lips when he kissed the softness between her neck and shoulder.

'Patrick,' she whispered. He forced his mouth away from

her delectable skin, and he kissed her lips again to silence her. He wanted nothing to interrupt this moment.

Sunset bathed her body in golden rays while the boat moved in the gentle rhythm of the tides. Her hands slid beneath his tunic, caressing his chest. By the gods, she was taking his honour apart. Even now, he rationalised that there would be no true harm in making love to her. He could still set her aside later, and she could marry another.

But if there was a child, he'd be forever bound to her. He couldn't break the vow he'd made, never to let her bear a child of his blood. If he succumbed to this temptation, he might as well surrender everything to the Normans. Never did he want the tribe to fall into their hands, nor lose what his kinsmen had died for. And giving Isabel a child was rewarding Edwin de Godred for his conquest. He couldn't do it.

'I'm sorry.'

Isabel's lips were swollen from the kiss, and she touched her throat as if afraid of him. And well she should be. At the moment his control was about to snap.

'I shouldn't have done that,' she whispered.

'No, you shouldn't.'

At the harsh words, she closed her eyes with embarrassment. He could see that he'd hurt her feelings, but could not bring himself to soothe her.

Patrick glanced behind him and saw how close they were to shore. Without thinking, he jumped over the side of the boat, extinguishing the evidence of his lust in the waist-deep water. The frigid waves cooled his desire instantly, a welcome respite.

He guided the boat on to the strand, helping her step on to the sands. Dragging the vessel beyond the tide's reach, he gathered up the two large bundles of supplies and strode up the path towards the ringfort.

Isabel remained behind him, still standing where he'd left her. The breeze lifted her hair, billowing the *brat* from her shoulders. Like a legendary goddess, she appeared born of the sea. The water swelled to touch her ankles, but she stepped away.

He forced himself to walk up the hill, entering the *rath*. Eventually her footsteps sounded behind him. He walked to the stone hut they had shared last night and pushed open the door, dropping the supplies inside the entrance. It took time to kindle a fire, but he coaxed a small flame and fed it with tinder. At last he added the peat bricks.

He heard the door close, and Isabel stood at the entrance watching him. In the dim light, her golden hair gleamed. With graceful steps, she neared the fire.

Gods above, he didn't know how he would endure a full night, knowing that she was within reach of him.

'What food do we have?' Isabel asked, kneeling beside the supplies.

'I have no idea what Trahern packed. I told him to send enough for a sennight.'

He stood warming himself while she untied the bundles. A moment later, he heard her cry out with joy. Had Trahern packed a bit of mutton? Or roasted fowl?

'A comb!' Isabel revealed her prize, smiling as though she'd been handed a treasure. He hadn't thought of such a simple need, and he frowned. His wife held it out as though Trahern had sent her a sack of gold pieces.

'What of the food?' he asked.

'Oh, there's bread and dried apples. Some meat, too.' Joy brightened her eyes. 'But, oh, the comb. Thank the saints.'

She knelt beside the fire, dragging the carved antler comb through her hair. Gently, she untangled the strands, pulling her hair over one shoulder.

What would it be like to touch that hair? Silken, like spun sunlight, he supposed. It fell to her hips, and he pictured her lying upon the pallet wearing nothing but her hair.

He prayed Trahern had packed the chess set. For otherwise he'd need another swim this night.

The wind bit into his bare chest as Ruarc fought the leather bindings. Bevan had left him there alone, bared from the waist up. Blood caked his wrists from where he'd fought against the restraints. His face had swollen up, his lips cracked.

He didn't care about any of it. But he feared for his sister. Earlier, Sosanna had come to see him. She'd touched his head, then his cheek. She shook her head as if to reprimand him. Then sadness filled her eyes. Moments later, she'd walked outside the ringfort.

Ruarc had called out for her to stop, but she behaved as though she hadn't heard him. He'd called out for his friends to go look after her. But they ignored him.

One of the Normans, Sir Anselm, had followed Sosanna. *Críost*, but he had to break free from this damned post. For all he knew, the captain might have been the man to hurt her. He couldn't let that happen again.

He gasped as a shooting pain lashed up his arm. His efforts had only drawn the bindings tighter. A few of the Normans glanced at him, but they spoke amongst themselves in an unfamiliar language.

His voice was hoarse from calling out. At last, Bevan emerged from the Great Chamber and approached the wooden post. He held out a horn of mead and tilted it so Ruarc could drink.

'My sister,' Ruarc urged. 'She's gone. Send someone after Sosanna.'

'We did earlier. She went out to the fields with some of the other women. She's well enough.'

He relaxed a little at that. 'Send one of the women to look in on her for me.'

Bevan nodded. The scar upon his face drew tighter. 'I will tell Patrick about the child.' His voice held vengeance in its tone. 'We will discover who did this to her.'

'I want him dead.'

'I can understand your wish. And I might have done the same, were I in your shoes.'

Bevan unwrapped a piece of bread and shoved it in Ruarc's mouth. 'Eat. And don't tell Patrick I gave you anything. Otherwise I'll be the one tied up tomorrow morn.' With a grimace, Bevan disappeared back inside the Chamber.

Ruarc bowed his head, steeling himself for the long night ahead. Silently he prayed that his sister would be safe.

'Your move.' Patrick slid his pawn forward and waited for Isabel. His wife sat across from him, a low table between them. Her brow furrowed with concentration.

He'd barely won the last game. Isabel had played well, and he didn't know when he'd had to use such strategy. Even so, she distracted him with the way she leaned upon the table, revealing the curve of her breasts.

Worse, he remembered the taste of her. Even the sensuous fragrance of her, like honeysuckle. Were she a tribeswoman, he'd not be spending the night playing chess. No, he'd lay her down upon soft furs and watch her tremble as he loved her.

'Check.'

Check? Damn, she'd moved the rook instead. Patrick glared at the board, moving the queen to a safer square.

Several moves later, the game was hers. Delighted victory creased a smile upon her lips.

'Care to play again?' she asked.

He did want to play. But not with a chess board. 'No.' He stood up and stretched, pushing thoughts of her away. He had responsibilities to his tribe, above those to his wife. Why had he come here? He was playing chess with Isabel instead of remaining with his men. Worse, he'd enjoyed the challenge.

It was the first time in several moons that he'd relaxed with a game. She was a worthy opponent, and her ruthless style of strategy challenged him.

He liked that.

Guilt forced the thought away. Her father had killed his men, destroying his family life. He didn't deserve to be here with her, not when he shouldered the blame for their loss.

His trews had not fully dried from the seawater, so he went to stand beside the fire. Musky peat permeated the interior of the hut.

'Patrick?' she asked. Isabel's silken voice conjured up visions of her lying naked before him. He closed his eyes, unsure of what she wanted. Behind him, he heard her approach. Her palms touched his upper arms. Though it was an innocent gesture to gain his attention, her forbidden touch inflamed him.

He stifled a groan. 'What do you want?'

'I don't know. But we—we could talk,' she stammered. 'Or if there's any chamomile I could make some tea for us.' Her fingertips stroked his skin, arousing him with the barest touch. 'I'd like to know you better.'

'It's better if we don't.' He hid his face from her, his control barely holding on. He didn't need to be anywhere near Isabel de Godred. It had been far too long since he'd known the sweetness of a woman's arms, and he wasn't thinking clearly.

'Stay away from me, Isabel.' Her hands fell away, and he spun to face her. 'I've left you alone for several nights now. I have my limits.'

She blanched at his honesty. Was she truly that innocent, not knowing what her touch did to him?

'I thought you might wish to remove your wet clothing. It cannot be comfortable.'

His gaze sharpened upon her, and she flushed. What game was she playing? Was she asking to share his bed? She knew better than to pursue that path.

'It is better if I remain clothed.' And better if he left the hut and stood in the frigid water for the next hour. His trews strained while he tried to master his unwanted response.

'I am your wife,' she whispered. 'There is no need to suffer discomfort because of me.' She shivered, covering her breasts with her arms.

You have no idea, he wanted to say. But his discomfort had nothing to do with the damp wool; rather, it was the vicious desire that curled inside him, wanting release. He tightened his resolve.

'If it bothers you, I won't look,' she promised.

He did smile then. 'You'll want to.'

Isabel had never seen Patrick smile before. Sweet saints, he was handsome in a wild manner. His slate eyes darkened with promise. Instead of terrifying her, she wanted to draw nearer. The low firelight offered complete privacy, and for a moment she felt the desire to know this man.

He was a stranger, intelligent and fiercely loyal to his people. She admired that, even as he frustrated her.

She sat upon a low tree stump carved as a stool and turned her back to him. There was no need to look. Already she knew he would have powerful thighs, moulded with tight muscles. As for the rest of him…she supposed her imagination would not do him justice. The thought burned her cheeks with embarrassment and a slight touch of anticipation.

The straw pallet crackled beneath his weight. Isabel cupped her face in her hands. So long ago, he'd said that he wouldn't bed her. And he'd kept his word.

Though she hadn't questioned it at the time, she knew it was expected that she bear him a child. And he didn't seem impervious to her any more. He'd responded to her impulsive kiss in the boat, offering her a glimpse of the dark pleasure awaiting both of them. The hunger within him sent her senses into disarray.

But then he'd broken away, preferring to walk through frigid water than spend another moment with her. She had wanted to die of embarrassment, even as she desired him.

Now, she wondered if she'd misunderstood his rejection. He wanted her to stay away, claiming that he had his limits. Was it because he wanted her? Was he keeping his distance out of misguided honour? She didn't understand his reasons for keeping her a virgin.

The unbearable loneliness weighed down until she craved human companionship. Behind her was her naked husband, awaiting her in their bed. Her gown felt heavy, the rough fabric coarse against her skin. Beneath it she'd continued to wear her shift, though the women here wore no such garment.

Did she dare offer herself to him? Or would he turn her away once more? She reached for the horn of mead and took a long drink to fortify her courage. Saints, she hungered for his touch. It was strange to feel these longings for the man she'd once feared. Rising to her feet, she turned to Patrick. His naked back faced her, his lower half obscured by a woollen blanket.

He'd kept his vow not to touch her. She knew it was because of who she was. But was he beginning to change his mind? After their water fight and the chess game, he didn't seem to hate her.

Why, then, did he continue to push her away? If she came to him as a wife, offering herself, would he surrender to what they both wanted?

She prayed for courage, for alone she could never do this. Her father's bargain would be completed, once Patrick took her virginity. And no longer did she fear her husband.

Without speaking a word, she raised the gown above her head and dropped the garment upon the floor. He didn't see her, still facing away.

Barefoot, she walked towards the pallet. Her nipples rubbed against the linen shift, rising with a need she couldn't describe. She breathed deeply, then removed her shift so she stood naked before him. 'Patrick?'

'What is it?' He rolled over, and, when he saw her, his eyes deepened with hunger. Isabel knelt upon the pallet, touching his black hair. His grey eyes held hints of blue, traces of green.

He captured her wrist, trapping it upon his face. Dark bristles of his unshaved beard abraded her palm. 'What are you doing, Isabel?' His mouth moved against her pulse as he spoke.

'In a few weeks, my father will demand proof that I am no longer a virgin.' Goose flesh rose upon her skin beneath his hot gaze. 'I'd rather finish our agreement now.'

He never took his eyes off her bare skin, though he did not touch her. A muscle tightened in his cheek, as though he were trying to curb his needs. 'You don't want this, Isabel,' he said in a low voice. 'And neither do I.'

She didn't know what to say. Humiliation stung her

feelings, and she rapidly donned her shift. Hot tears gathered, but by God, she would not weep before him. She had mistakenly let herself be blinded by the kiss earlier.

She was stupid to think that he would change his mind. Like as not, he did not find her appealing. Damn him for it.

'Isabel,' he said, his voice rough with sympathy.

'No. Don't say it.' She put on the hideous gown and sat as far away from him as she could. Anger and mortification slashed her self-worth. Twice she'd lowered herself this night.

She wanted to ball herself up on the floor and weep bitter tears. By the bones of Saint Peter, if he did not want her, so be it.

She heard him getting dressed, but did not turn around. Moments later, she sensed him standing behind her. Then a warm hand cupped her jaw.

Isabel shoved him away. 'Leave me alone. You made it quite clear that you do not want me.'

Patrick did not refute her words. His silence cut her confidence into shreds. 'It is better this way, *a chara*. Trust me.'

'Go back to your fortress,' she said stonily. 'I've no wish to set eyes on you again.'

At dawn, Sir Anselm waited atop his horse, watching the young woman from the shield of trees by the cliffs. Sosanna, they'd called her. He'd seen her out walking last night, but she'd returned home within an hour.

Now she had left her home once again. He didn't know what had brought her out this far alone, but it did not bode well. His instincts warned him to keep a close watch over her.

He'd seen the frustration and worry upon the Irishman's face. Though he was gladdened to see Ruarc punished,

Anselm wanted the man whipped for his disobedience. More than one of his soldiers had grumbled about Ruarc's fighting.

Yet Anselm recognised the tribesman's fear for his sister. It was why he'd followed the woman a second time. For he sensed what she was about to do.

He dismounted and strode towards her. She stood near the edge of a ragged granite outcropping, staring down at the frothy black waves below.

'Hello,' he greeted her.

Panic widened her eyes, and she took a step closer to the edge. Anselm raised his hands, showing he carried no weapons. 'I won't harm you. My name is Sir Anselm Fitzwater.'

The confusion on her face reminded him that she could not speak his language. He couldn't speak a word of the Irish tongue either.

Her hand moved protectively to her stomach, and she took another step. Anselm wanted to curse. At this distance, he couldn't stop her from walking off the edge. If she killed herself, he had no doubt Ruarc would incite a war between both sides. King Patrick had given rigid orders to maintain the peace. But there was only a fragile chance of success.

He took a gamble and sat down, picking a strand of grass and twirling it. 'You can't understand me, I know, but I would be grateful if you'd come away from the edge.'

She paled and sent another frightened glance towards the water.

Anselm kept talking, a soft stream of conversation that moved from one topic to the next. While he spoke, he studied her. Beneath the dirt and her dishevelled appearance was a strikingly attractive woman. With high sculpted cheekbones and lips the colour of ripening summer cherries, he tried to envision her former beauty.

The advancing pregnancy swelling against her blue gown provided an explanation for her actions, yet he didn't believe her tribe would cast her out for it.

He didn't know how much time had passed, but she seemed to be less afraid of him, so long as he kept his distance. He beckoned for her to come back with him, and she shook her head.

'Ruarc,' he reminded her, holding up his wrists as if bound. At the mention of her brother, she whitened. With a glance at the cliffs, sadness touched her countenance.

'Come.' He strode towards the grove of trees and led his horse out. 'Do you want to ride?' He tried to make his meaning clear with gestures, but Sosanna shook her head.

'As you like.' Anselm waited until she started walking. He led the horse by the reins, whistling slightly. Slowly and reluctantly, she followed him, keeping a large distance between them.

He only breathed easier when she was far from the cliff. There was something fragile about the woman, and though he suspected what had been done to her, he did not want to believe his men were responsible. They were too well trained, too disciplined.

He glanced behind him to see where she was. Sosanna had stopped walking. In her eyes he saw terror. He followed her gaze and saw a small group of his men training.

One of the cavalry soldiers spurred his horse forward. Though the man only wanted to speak with him, Anselm raised his hands to stop him.

It was too late. Sosanna whirled around and began running. Anselm cursed and took off after her. He mounted and urged his gelding faster. Almost there.

Seconds later, she stood at the cliff's edge. Her eyes wild with fear, she leaped off.

Christ's blood. Anselm charged his horse forward, halting

at the edge. Her blue gown billowed out in the water. He didn't stop to think but threw off his helm and dove into the icy sea. The water hit him with the force of a stone. Thank God he hadn't worn chain mail armour. The weight would have dragged him under.

Anselm swam towards Sosanna, reaching for her prone body. He didn't even know if she was alive. She did not respond when he touched her. Was she breathing? He fought to swim to shore, while keeping her above water.

When they reached land, he staggered across the sand, laying her body upon it.

'Breathe,' he pleaded, rubbing her cheeks. He didn't know how to save her. And, sweet Christ, she was so pale. Beneath his breath he murmured a prayer.

God answered him, for a moment later, she coughed up the water, her frail body shaking with the effort.

He held her hair back, stroking it while she inhaled gulps of air. And when she stopped, he held her close. It felt as though he had been the one to nearly drown.

She closed her eyes, and he picked her up. If he took her back to Laochre, Ruarc would find out. The young hothead's temper would undo any peace between the two sides. He had to help Sosanna, but not at such a cost.

Anselm scanned the area and saw a small boat beached out of the tide's reach. And he knew exactly where to take her.

Chapter Nine

Isabel's arm muscles ached, but she set another stone on the wall. For half a day she'd worked at replacing the exterior of the ruined palisade. Though the walls were made of wood, there was enough limestone upon the island to build three donjons. And she was tired of living in someone else's cottage when she had her own shelter, dilapidated though it was.

Sadly, her stone wall was only two hands high.

The work helped take her mind off Patrick. She longed to pound his skull with one of the rocks, for he still refused to see her as a wife and not a Norman. What more did she have to do?

Around her, she saw the faces of the islanders watching her. No one spoke, but they watched her labour, taking turns to stare at her while performing their own chores. She felt like a travelling minstrel, offering entertainment.

She backhanded her brow, wiping the perspiration away. A slight motion caught her attention. A young girl of possibly ten years stepped forward, her blonde hair twisted in a braid. She wore a grey *léine*, and her feet were bare.

The girl spoke a lilting mix of Irish, words Isabel could

not understand. But she did understand the clay mug the girl held out.

'Thank you,' she said, accepting the drink. The ale was not cool, but it was the first time anyone had offered her hospitality. She gave the mug back after she'd finished, offering a slight smile. Gesturing towards the pile of stone, she asked, 'Would you like to help?'

The girl glanced back at her mother, who shook her head. Isabel hid her disappointment. Instead she continued her work, setting stone upon stone.

She stopped for a few bites to eat when the sun reached its summit. It was at that moment she heard excited voices. Many of the children scampered through the entrance to the ringfort, chattering about something.

Isabel rose and saw Sir Anselm carrying a young woman. Both of them were soaked to the skin. She didn't stop to wonder why he'd come to Ennisleigh, but raced forward. At the sight of the woman's pale face, she recognised her. It was Sosanna, the silent woman from Laochre.

'What happened?' Isabel asked.

'She jumped from the cliff,' Anselm replied grimly. 'Her brother is one of the Irish rebels. If he finds out what happened to her, he'll blame my men.'

Isabel understood. 'Bring her inside the hut. Help me build a fire, and we'll look after her.'

The islanders followed Sir Anselm, hovering around the entrance to the hut. Isabel sent him in first and then stopped the people at the door.

'Don't worry,' she said. One of the women stepped forward, gesturing that she wanted to come inside. It was the mother of the girl who had brought the ale.

Isabel realised they would not believe her intent to help

Sosanna unless they saw it for themselves. She beckoned to the young girl's mother and her daughter. 'Come and help me.'

If they worked together, perhaps the woman might begin to trust her. Pushing open the hide-covered door, Isabel waited.

The woman went inside without hesitation, and Isabel left the door open. Anselm had laid Sosanna upon a pallet.

Isabel introduced herself and the Norman knight. She learned the child's name was Orla, and her mother Annle.

Annle knelt beside Sosanna. Her hands moved with the expertise of a healer, checking Sosanna for broken bones or other injuries. Isabel sat beside her, silently offering prayers for the girl's life and that of her unborn child. 'When did this happen?' she asked Sir Anselm.

'This morning, just an hour ago. I saw her leave and followed.'

'Does anyone else know?'

Sir Anselm shook his head. 'I don't think so. They'll know she's missing and that I took one of the boats.'

'Will you go and tell Patrick? Tell him we are taking care of her on Ennisleigh.'

'Do you think that is wise? The king may blame me for the accident. I was the only person who saw her jump.'

'You had no reason to harm her. And all of us saw you bring her here.' She waved her hand. 'Go. We'll look after her now.'

He hung back, his eyes focused upon Sosanna. *He cares*, Isabel realised. For some reason the Norman soldier wanted to be assured that Sosanna would be all right.

'You may come and see her later,' Isabel said gently, escorting him out.

After he had gone, Annle helped her undress Sosanna. The unconscious woman did not respond, and her skin was frigid. Annle touched the young woman's stomach, and Isabel laid her hand upon it as well. They waited, and, in time, a small fluttering movement rippled beneath Isabel's hand.

She withdrew her hand, stunned that she could feel the unborn child moving. Never had she touched a pregnant woman before. Her mood grew sombre. Looking at Sosanna only taunted her with what Patrick would not give her. She refused to lower her pride again. When her father arrived and found her a virgin, Patrick could face the consequences then.

Isabel studied Sosanna, who lay frighteningly still. Annle drew a coverlet over the woman, warming her frail body. She motioned for Isabel to wait and stepped outside the hut. Isabel stoked the fire to keep it warm inside.

When Annle returned, she held a basket. She withdrew a mortar and pestle, along with a bundle of herbs, instructing Isabel with motions to grind the herbs. The mixture of comfrey and wintergreen were good for bruises, Isabel knew. She mashed the herbs and gave the mortar back to Annle.

Annle spread some of the mixture upon a swollen spot on Sosanna's arm. When all the minor cuts and bruises were treated, there was little more they could do except keep her warm.

The healer lifted a pot of water to the hearth and then reached back into her basket for vegetables. She handed a bundle to Isabel, making the signs for food preparations.

Isabel unwrapped a cloth package of peas and realised Annle's intention to prepare a pot of soup. She wished she could ask questions about what other vegetables were ready this season. Perhaps they had onions to add for flavour.

Her frustration intensified. In the days since she'd arrived in Erin, no one had offered to teach her the language. Well, perhaps it was time to start learning.

'What is the word for bowl?' she asked Annle, picking up

a carved wooden bowl. The woman's brows furrowed, not knowing what Isabel was asking.

'Bowl,' Isabel repeated.

'Babhla?' Annle asked.

Isabel held up the bowl. *'Babhla?'* When the woman nodded her head, Isabel brightened. Thank the saints. It was a beginning, at least.

She walked around the room, pointing towards each item and asking Annle to name them. Then she repeated them back. Though Annle seemed hesitant, she answered Isabel's queries.

Hours passed, and several of the islanders came to visit. Isabel strained to distinguish the different words, but the stream of conversation was lost to her, much as she tried.

Finally, Patrick arrived. His strong form seemed to fill the door frame, his dark hair falling upon his shoulders. A few cuts marked his face, and one hand was bound with a linen cloth, as though he'd been fighting. At the sight of Sosanna, he sobered.

Isabel could not understand all of his questions, but Patrick seemed satisfied with Annle's responses. Then, he dismissed everyone. Isabel got up to leave, but he stopped her. 'I want you to stay.'

'I thought it would be better if I left.' It was hard to look at him, for she kept remembering last night and her embarrassment.

Patrick removed his dark red cloak and moved to sit near Sosanna. 'What did Anselm tell you? Was he responsible for her fall?'

'She didn't fall. She jumped, and he went in to save her.'

At the doubtful look on his face, Isabel stood. 'You don't believe me.'

'I don't, no.'

Her jaw clenched. How could he not see the woman's pain? Couldn't he guess that she'd likely been raped? The child growing inside her was an everyday reminder of her suffering.

'Anselm brought her here,' she reminded him. 'He rescued her.'

'He should have prevented the fall.'

'And what was he supposed to do? Dive off the cliff and catch her?'

'She shouldn't have been out there alone.'

There was worry beneath the shell of anger, and Isabel ladled a bowl of soup, handing it to him. 'She's hurting, and it's more than just the child or her physical injuries. How long has it been since she's spoken?'

'Since last summer.' He blamed himself for not investigating the true reason behind Sosanna's refusal to speak. Ever since he'd brought the Normans inside the *rath*, she'd withdrawn even more.

Had he known about the child, he'd have brought her to Ennisleigh sooner. The man who had dishonoured her might be here among them even now. He ate the bowl of soup Isabel offered, hardly tasting it.

'Does the babe live?' he asked.

Isabel nodded. 'I felt it move not long ago.'

He was relieved to hear it. The shapeless *léines* Sosanna wore made it difficult to tell when the child would be born. But if Isabel had felt movement, it could not be very long now.

'Has she awakened since Anselm brought her here?'

'No.' Isabel remained near the hearth. 'But she did take some of the broth we fed her.'

'Good. Stay with her tonight, and I'll return on the morrow. Ruarc will want to see her.'

'Have you told him what happened to Sosanna?' she asked.

'I haven't, no.' So far as he knew, Ruarc was still confined. He'd continued the punishment this day, wanting to break more of his cousin's defiance. He didn't want Ruarc starting a war.

Then again, Sosanna was Ruarc's sister. He deserved to see her, and though Patrick was wary of the man's reaction, he had an obligation to arrange it.

'Sosanna shouldn't be around the others now,' he told Isabel. 'Except for Annle and you, I don't want anyone else near her.'

It would give the young woman time to heal, without having to face questions.

'You want me to take care of her,' she said, 'when you believe the Normans hurt her?' Disbelief shadowed her face. 'She'll scream at the sight of me.'

'Then don't speak,' he advised. 'Don't let her know who you are.'

'She has seen me already and knows I am Norman. I won't lie to her.' Isabel moved apart from him, feigning interest in a pot of simmering water. 'I've been here for almost a sennight now. And in that time you've kept me away from everyone.' Hurt glimmered in her eyes. 'I don't want to continue like this. I don't know your language, I don't know your customs.' She lifted a dipper of water and watched it pour back into the pot.

He wanted to say something to her, to explain it all. But how would she react, knowing that he intended to set the marriage aside, after her father had gone?

'Do you want me to take you back to England?' he asked.

'Don't be foolish. You and I both know that will never happen.'

He stood and approached her, taking the dipper away. 'And if I allowed it? Is that what you would want?'

She turned to face him. 'I want what every woman wants.

A family. A home of her own.' Sadness and regret crossed her face. 'A true marriage.'

Patrick didn't apologise. Though he was sorry she'd become a victim of this bargain, he could never grant what she wanted.

'You ask what I cannot give.'

'No.' Her voice held a note of sadness. 'I ask what you will not give. And I don't understand why.'

'Walk with me.' He didn't wait for an answer, but held the door open. It was best to be honest with her, though she might not like the truth.

Outside the afternoon had already waned into evening, a light breeze ruffling the tall grasses outside the ringfort. He led her to an outcropping of rock where the sea stretched before them. It was a favourite spot of his. It felt like looking out at the rest of the world. The rhythmic waves pulsed against the rocks.

'I know you hate my people,' she began. 'But I am not to blame for the past. And you're blaming me for my father's deeds.' She sat upon the grasses, leaning against a slab of limestone, and wondered why he'd brought her outside the ringfort. His mouth was set in a firm line, as though he were reluctant to speak.

Weariness edged his eyes, and though he held the powerful strength of a warrior, his face was angular and thin. At his brows, the long strands of hair held a slight curve, as though they had once been war braids.

'I told you that my brother Liam ruled over the tribe until last summer.'

Isabel inclined her head, remembering that his elder brother had died in battle.

'The people chose me to succeed him, though Ruarc also competed for the right to be king.'

'What of your brothers?'

'Bevan had no wish for it, after the deaths of his wife and daughter. And Trahern said it was my duty to take Liam's place.'

His arms rested against his knees, the leather bracers crossed. 'You and I are more similar than you might think. Neither one of us can control our destiny.'

Isabel didn't like the direction of his conversation. 'I don't choose to live that way. Every man has the power to lead his own life. Even you.'

'I am a king. My power belongs to the people.'

'You are more a servant than a king.'

'That may be. But I give what I must to help them.' He reached down and picked up a smooth stone, fingering it in his palm.

'What can I do?' she asked.

He tossed the stone away and shrugged. 'Look after Sosanna for a time.'

'And after that?' She sensed a reluctance in his voice, as though he were hiding something from her.

He stood, facing away from her. 'Isabel, this is no place for you. I cannot undo our marriage, for it gave my people their lives. But remain at my side until after your father leaves, and I'll help you gain your wish. I'll grant you a husband who will treat you with the respect you deserve and give you children.'

It was the last thing she'd expected him to say. Was he talking of an annulment? That, at least, explained why he hadn't bedded her. Once, she would have felt overjoyed. But now, her feelings bled. She straightened her shoulders, wishing she could push away the anger and sense of being spurned.

She rubbed her arms against the chill of the wind. 'Is that what you want?' she whispered. 'To be free of me?'

His grey eyes bore into hers. 'It would be best, yes.' Moving closer to her, he added, 'It's what you want as well, isn't it?'

'Of course.' Her voice did not ring with much confidence. Now she felt even more foolish for her attempt to consummate their alliance. He didn't intend to share her bed because he didn't intend to remain her husband.

'But the Church would never allow it,' she argued. Though she tried to keep her face calm, inwardly her thoughts tangled in despair.

'It isn't impossible.'

'Nearly impossible. My father—'

'He'll be gone by then, along with his soldiers.' Patrick's gaze shifted back to the sea, and a light clouded mist drew closer from the coast. The moisture dampened her lips, and she smelled the harsh scent of salt.

After everything he'd put her through, knowing that this was a temporary marriage wasn't as satisfying as she'd thought it would be. Instead, fear of the unknown future rose up to taunt her. Would she return to England? Stay here in Erin? 'How long am I to remain your wife?'

He lifted his gaze to hers. 'Until winter.'

'Where will I go?'

'Wherever you like.' He took her hand, stroking her knuckles with his thumb. 'I have many allies, chieftains and other kings. There are men who would not care about your heritage. They would see only a beautiful woman.'

Beautiful. The word cut her like a shard of glass, for he had never taken the time to know her. He would not allow himself to be her husband, for the burden of kingship overshadowed all else.

'I want something in return from you,' she said. 'If I am to live here for a time, I want my dowry sent to Ennisleigh. And something else.'

He shrugged. 'Ask.'

'I want you to send for the families of the Norman soldiers.' When he was about to protest, she set her hand upon his shoulder. 'Hear me out. The men have not seen their wives and children for nearly a year. My father would not allow any women to travel with the soldiers.' She blushed, for not even the camp doxies were allowed. 'If you bring their families, you'll gain their co-operation.'

He stood. 'You want me to make their lives comfortable.'

'Yes.'

Fierce anger darkened his expression, and she involuntarily took a step backward. His voice took on a deadly tone. 'They killed our people, Isabel. I am not about to make their lives comfortable.'

He would not forgive the Normans for his people's loss. Though the battle might have ended, the war was not over. Not in his eyes.

The easiest path would be to turn away from the MacEgan tribe, to be blind to the people's needs. She could live upon the island in peace, without any knowledge or care of what was happening to them.

But then, that was a coward's path.

He'd said she would never be a true queen. Perhaps he was right. Though it was the habit of kings to wage war, it was often the queens who built peace.

Was there any way to overcome the resentment festering from their losses? Though it might seem insurmountable, Isabel wanted to believe she could help.

If she could somehow bring the tribe back into prosperity and gain the help of her own people, they might come together. Instead of killing each other, they could live in peace.

But she wondered if it was worth it, to fight for a marriage that was destroyed before it had even begun.

Chapter Ten

The following morn, Patrick and his men watched as the Normans sparred outside the ringfort. Bevan stood at his side, analysing every move the men made. Though both he and his brother wore leather armour, they did not don the heavy chain mail armour of their opponents.

'They're stronger,' Patrick remarked, 'but slower. The armour weighs them down.'

'It does,' Bevan agreed. 'But our men should be fitted for chain mail. The weight would help them in training.' He met Patrick's glance, and he knew what his brother was thinking. Their speed would be even faster one day, if they grew accustomed to the extra weight.

'Have we the funds to make it possible?' Bevan asked.

'No.' Outfitting all of his men would be far too costly. And he needed the funds from Isabel's dowry to bribe the Archbishop and end their marriage.

If the Baron of Thornwyck had provided gold, that is. Patrick suspected that the dowry would be little more than blankets and a carved bridal chest.

'What did you pay as her bride price?' Bevan asked.

'I agreed to house and feed the Norman army.' He shot his brother a sidelong glance. 'More than enough for a queen.'

His brother grunted in acknowledgement. They watched the Normans move through practice drills, their movements precise and trained. Patrick had seen exercises like these before, but his greater concern was the reaction of his tribesmen. They were leaning back to watch, drinking cups of ale and joking.

It was sobering, to see the enemy's discipline exceeding that of his own men.

He strode forward and addressed his tribesmen. 'Unless you learn to fight against them and know their strategies, you'll never defeat them.'

Ruarc stepped forward. Red chafe marks lined his upper arms and wrists from where he had been bound. Dark circles ringed his eyes, but instead of exhaustion, fury tightened his features. 'We need no strategy to defeat them. Only an opportunity.'

Patrick lowered his voice. 'And you'll gain that opportunity soon enough.'

Ruarc gave a thin smile. 'I don't believe you. You're turning into one of them.' He glanced at his tribesmen. 'He married a Norman, and now he thinks they are better fighters than us.'

'They are better,' Patrick said darkly. 'While you sit around drinking, they grow stronger.'

'And what have you done?' Ruarc demanded. 'Nothing except invite them to live among us. They eat our food, take our supplies, and now you're building homes for them.'

'They won't be here for much longer,' Patrick replied. 'Your hatred blinds you.' His temper held by the barest thread, and at the moment, he wanted nothing better than to fight his cousin. The satisfaction of bruising Ruarc's pride was far too tempting.

'I'm not blind.' Ruarc drained the rest of his mead. 'But our tribesmen's eyes are opening. They're starting to see you as I do.'

'What do you mean?'

'You're a traitor to us.'

Patrick grabbed his cousin's tunic, but Ruarc reached out for his throat. In defence, he dug his fingers into the sores upon Ruarc's wrists. With a swift twisting motion, Patrick sent his cousin sprawling to the ground. 'You've caused enough trouble here. I should banish you.'

His men looked uncomfortable. He could feel their doubts and Ruarc's anger undermining his authority.

'Go on, then.' Ruarc rubbed his wrists. 'I'd rather leave this place than watch you betray our tribe.' The darkness of his cousin's hatred was palpable. 'What sort of king imprisons a man trying to defend his sister's honour?'

Patrick's expression hardened. He hadn't told Ruarc of Sosanna's attempted suicide. 'She is safe now.'

'Now?' Ruarc whitened, his fists curling. 'What happened to her?'

'She is on Ennisleigh and will remain there until she has healed.'

Ruarc expelled a foul curse. 'How badly was she hurt? If the Normans—'

'She is alive, and I'll take you there. Isabel is looking after her.'

'You let one of the *Gaillabh* take care of Sosanna?'

'I let my *wife* join the healer in tending your sister's injuries. Sosanna tried to take her own life.'

Ruarc's visage turned forbidding. With his palm curling over the *colc* sword at his waist, he unsheathed the blade. 'I could have saved her, if you hadn't imprisoned me.'

'Put your sword away,' Patrick warned. 'And it's Sir Anselm you should thank for saving her life.'

His cousin's face drew in tighter. 'You're right.' His voice was deadly quiet as he approached Sir Anselm. 'I should thank him.'

Before Patrick could move, Ruarc drove his sword towards the Norman knight. Sir Anselm defended the blow squarely, without any emotion. In contrast, Ruarc poured himself into the sparring match, releasing his battle rage in a driven, vicious fight.

Although Sir Anselm met every strike with a deflection of his own, he didn't make any moves to challenge Ruarc. Patrick watched his cousin growing tired, and though the Norman had several opportunities to end the fight, he did nothing to humiliate Ruarc.

His cousin's strength was undeniable, but the knight was a superior fighter. As the fight wore on, more and more men gathered to watch. A few of the Irish began chanting in Gaelic, encouraging Ruarc's blade. Patrick saw their faces, their desire to see the defeat of the Norman commander. They had pinned their hopes on Ruarc. Though he hadn't intended it, with each clash of steel, the gap between the men widened. He needed to stop the fight.

Sweat poured down his cousin's cheeks, his dark eyes filled with hatred. But Anselm calmly continued the battle, letting Ruarc expel the last of his energy.

Patrick scanned the crowd for a glimpse of one of his brothers and at last found Bevan. He strode towards him and said, 'We must stop them.'

'You can't. It's too late for that.' The hardness in Bevan's tone made him suddenly realise that his brother wanted Ruarc to win. He didn't want peace either, nor did he believe it could happen.

Instead, Patrick unsheathed his blade and stepped between the men, blocking his cousin's next strike. His muscles strained to keep Ruarc from releasing another blow.

'Enough,' he said quietly. To the commander he said, 'You fought well. For you and your men, I'll send a barrel of our finest ale.'

Then he turned to Ruarc. 'We'll go to Ennisleigh now. You can see to your sister's welfare.'

The burning ire upon Ruarc's face had not lessened. 'I want nothing from you.'

'Meet me at the shoreline if you want to see Sosanna.' Patrick walked away from the ringfort and heard his men grumbling amongst themselves.

'He's becoming one of them,' he heard a voice say.

'What do you expect?' another replied. 'He's wedded to a Norman.'

Patrick stopped short, training his gaze upon each of the men. 'Is there something you wish to say to my face?'

A few reddened, but no one spoke. Patrick stared back, his own tension gathering. Gods above, he'd given up everything for these men. And he could see them turning away from him.

He was among family and friends. Despite it all, when he looked into their eyes, he read the doubts. They didn't trust him, didn't understand what he was trying to accomplish. How could they defeat the Normans if they refused to learn from them?

When Patrick strode away, he caught sight of Sir Anselm. The Norman knight met his gaze with a steady look of his own. When the Norman inclined his head, the unexpected gesture of respect caught Patrick unawares.

Like a knife in his own heart, the twisted fact remained that he planned to betray the Normans out of vengeance. He intended to drive them out and kill them, once his men were ready.

Anselm could have shamed Ruarc before the others in that fight, but he had chosen not to. The commander had honed skills from countless battles. By refusing to attack, Anselm had lifted his stature in Patrick's eyes. Then, too, the commander had rescued Sosanna, risking his own life for hers. Why?

Patrick wondered whether he would have done the same, if a Norman woman had thrown herself into the sea. He thought of Isabel standing in Sosanna's place, and the answer came. Enemy blood or not, he'd have dived in to save her.

Isabel wanted to bring the men together, to make one tribe. Though he still did not believe it was possible, the idea of slaughtering the Normans seemed like an unnecessary waste of life. A coldness settled across his shoulders. Were his people right about him? Was he turning traitor without realising it?

Patrick refused the offer of a horse and walked the long distance towards the shoreline. When he reached the sands and waited beside the boat, he tried to dispel the unexpected guilt building within his conscience.

Somehow he had to rid Laochre of the Norman forces. He had to detach himself from them, to see them as the enemy once more.

If he didn't, his men would lose faith and he'd have nothing left.

Isabel laid more stones around the fortress, this time accompanied by the islanders' children. More often than not the boys threw rocks at each other instead of rebuilding the wall. But it felt good to be around people once more.

She listened to them speaking, trying to catch words that Annle had taught her. The children had giggled at her efforts to speak, but after a few corrections, they taught her to speak simple greetings.

When the afternoon sun rose high above the island, warming her with its rays, Isabel saw Annle approaching.

'How is Sosanna?' she asked.

Annle shrugged, which Isabel took to mean there was no change. Though Sosanna had opened her eyes once or twice, she hadn't spoken. Terror lined her face, and only when she touched her stomach and felt the reassurance of the unborn child's movement, did she grow calm.

Annle spoke slowly, gesturing towards the ringfort entrance. Isabel understood only a word or two, something about a boat and men. She wiped her hands upon her *léine*, and joined Annle. 'Is it Patrick?'

The woman nodded. Isabel shielded her eyes and saw the figure of her husband entering the ringfort accompanied by a dark-haired warrior she didn't recognize. Beside her, Annle murmured, 'He is Ruarc.' Though Isabel did not understand the rest of her words, she sensed that Ruarc was related to Sosanna.

Patrick moved with confidence, his gaze moving across each of the people. He wore leather armour over a forest-green tunic. His toned arm muscles seemed tight against the leather bracers upon his forearms. Around his upper arms he wore twisted bands of gold. Though they proclaimed his rank, Isabel was beginning to understand the truth. Her husband was both a king and a slave to his tribesmen. Never did he let down his mask, never did he let her see the man behind the king.

Most of the islanders greeted him, but even as Patrick spoke with them, his eyes searched for her. Guilt lined his expression in an unspoken apology.

Isabel turned away and continued her task of rebuilding the wall. It kept her busy without having to face him.

A shadow fell across her work, in spite of her desire to avoid him. 'How is Sosanna?' Patrick asked.

'As well as can be expected. Her child will be born by harvest time.'

'Lughnasa,' he murmured.

'Yes.' The mention of Lughnasa reminded her of her father. Edwin would return, expecting her to bear a child from this marriage. Isabel's throat closed up, for she didn't know what she would say to him.

'I've brought Ruarc to see his sister. He's a cousin of mine.'

The tone of his voice suggested a low opinion of the man. Ruarc had followed Annle inside the dwelling. 'You don't seem happy to see him.'

'He causes trouble among the men. I should send him away.'

'But you are his family,' she said quietly. She saw the indecision on her husband's face, and understood that Ruarc's place was more secure than her own.

His plan to end their marriage stung her pride. She found herself wanting to fight for her place here, for there was so much she could do to help the people. No longer did she want to be a nobleman's wife, content to supervise the estates and weave tapestries. She wanted to rebuild this place and to be a part of it.

'I dispatched a messenger to your father this morn. I've asked him to send your dowry.'

She acknowledged his words with a nod. 'Thank you.' Her attention was drawn to his hands and the skin that was darkening as summer neared. A flush suffused her, and her body wanted to draw closer to him. His black hair hung freely about his shoulders, his dark grey eyes piercing. He was a warrior king, not an ordinary man.

Patrick ran his hands along the stone wall and added, 'You've done well here.'

'It gives me something to do.' She reached to lift another

stone. Patrick took it from her and set it atop the wall. The light touch of his hands against hers meant nothing. And yet, she felt the warmth of his touch sinking beneath her flesh and into her heart.

'Go and see Sosanna,' she murmured. He hesitated a moment, capturing her gaze. Isabel forced herself to look at him, her heart beating faster.

After he left her side, Isabel clenched her hands together. Though it was a fruitless endeavour, she wished she could know this man better, to become his wife in truth. But whenever he looked at her, she no longer knew whether he saw an enemy or a woman.

She walked towards the edge of the ringfort. Beyond the stone wall, she stared at the cerulean sea. White clouds skimmed the horizon, and the bright sun should have made her feel better. Resting her chin upon her palm, she saw the stretch of green land up to the massive fortress of Laochre, the kingdom she would never rule.

Patrick was right. The people there did not want her as their queen. The uncomfortable silence and lack of welcome made that clear.

And she didn't know what to do now.

Ruarc entered the darkened interior of the hut, the only light from the glowing peat upon the fire. His sister's back faced him as she slept, her arms wrapped around her stomach.

He trod softly, almost afraid to awaken her. When at last he reached her side, he saw that she was staring at the walls.

'*Tá brón orm,*' he said softly. But he was afraid the words of apology were not enough. He'd been so consumed with thoughts of revenge, of destroying the outsiders, he hadn't looked past his sister's pain to see the truth. She carried a child created in violence.

He drew up a wooden stump and sat beside her. 'It's my fault. And though you might not wish to live, we will face this.'

Tears filled her eyes, and he took her hand. 'Do you want to leave Laochre? I could take you somewhere far from here.'

She shook her head, her hands covering her stomach. The silent tears cut him down. He hated the helplessness of not being able to take away her pain.

'I will help you,' he vowed. 'I'll find the bastard and kill him.'

She lowered her head and squeezed his palm. And he vowed that, no matter what, he would avenge his sister's honour.

Isabel's hands sank deeply into a wooden bowl filled with bread dough. One of the baked loaves cooled upon a low table while she kneaded the new batch. Annle had given her the yeast mixture and she'd been pleased with the results.

The mindless activity helped push her mind away from her crumbling marriage. Saints, she was such a cursed idiot for kissing Patrick. It had been better not to know what it felt like to be in his arms, to be tempted by desire.

She punched the dough, working out her frustration. Outside, the afternoon sun was sinking, the evening light fading. After reshaping the dough into a soft ball, she covered it with a cloth and set it near the hearth to rise again.

Footsteps neared the hut, and she looked up at the entrance. Patrick came inside, closing the door. His attention moved to the loaf she had baked earlier. 'Did you make the bread?'

She nodded. 'Would you like a piece?'

He shrugged as if it were of no matter, but his eyes devoured the loaf. She cut a few slices of warm bread, a light steam rising from the crust. When she handed it to him, his hopeful gaze made her want to smile.

When he bit into the crust, he closed his eyes as though he were experiencing a moment in heaven. Her husband liked fresh bread more than most men, it seemed.

Isabel watched him, fascinated by the way he ate. When he'd finished the piece, he took a step closer to her.

'Is it all right, then?'

'It's the best I've ever tasted.' His eyes glanced over at the loaf again, and she hid her smile.

'There's more, if you want it.'

The boyish grin that spread over his face caught her unawares. Handsome and more tempting than sin itself, Patrick MacEgan made her senses grow dizzy.

When he reached for the loaf, she took his hands. 'There's a price.' The impulsive words slipped from her mouth, and she had no notion of what she intended to ask in return.

No, that wasn't true at all. She wanted him to kiss her again, to feel his hands caressing her spine. She wanted to lose herself in him, to forget that she didn't belong here. The heaviness of disappointment cloaked her mind, for she knew he'd turn her away.

'What do you want?' he asked huskily. His thumb drew lazy circles over her palm, and she wanted so badly to say, *Kiss me*.

She didn't answer, her breath catching in her lungs as he moved even closer. His hand stretched over her waist, his touch burning into her skin.

'I don't know,' she whispered. Her mind closed up with wicked thoughts, of dreams that could never be. *He doesn't want you*, she reminded herself. *You mean nothing to him*.

'What price do you want, Isabel?' His hand rose over her flesh, raising her temperature by several degrees.

And when she looked down, she saw that he had claimed a second slice of bread. With victory clutched in his palm, a devilish smile spread across his mouth.

'You cheated.'

'Of course I did.' He tore off a piece of the bread, placing it in her mouth. 'But I'll share it with you.'

The bread tasted dry in her mouth, even as she sat beside him and shared the meal. She hadn't voiced a single one of her desires.

And perhaps it was better that way.

Chapter Eleven

Evening turned into night, and Patrick knew it was time to depart. Isabel had prepared a meal for him, even challenging him to another game of chess.

'I must go,' he said, reaching for his cloak.

'Afraid to lose again?' she taunted. 'I thought as much.'

He gave her a severe look, a warning that made most of his men uncomfortable. Isabel only smirked.

That was it. He sat down at the low table. 'One game.'

Her smile widened. 'Prepare to lose, King Patrick.'

'Not this time.' He set up the pieces, choosing white. Tapping one of the pawns, he considered his move.

'I want to make a wager on this game,' she said, removing her veil. With her fingers, she combed the long golden strands, letting the curls fall across her shoulders.

He wasn't about to let that opportunity pass. 'Done. If you lose, you'll obey every command I give for a single day.'

She lifted her eyes skywards. 'You truly are dreaming, if you believe you can beat me.' With her hands, she lifted her hair off the back of her neck, stretching sinuously.

'What do you want, if by some miracle of the fates, you happen to win?'

A softness came over her, her smile growing wistful. 'I want you to stay with me. I want a night with my husband.'

Her words pierced a blade of desire below his waist. Somehow he managed to respond. 'I can't share your bed, Isabel.'

'It's lonely spending the nights by myself,' she admitted. 'You needn't share my pallet. But I'd like to have your company.'

He moved his pawn forward two squares, feeling low. It had been a long time since he'd stayed a night alone with Isabel. To do so now was dangerous, especially since his body and mind had very different ideas about how he should live out his marriage.

Even so, he murmured, 'All right.'

Isabel let the shawl drop from her shoulders and reached out to cut another slice of bread. She leaned over the chess board, and he caught a tempting glimpse of her breasts. 'Would you like some?'

'You're cheating,' he said, accepting the bribe. The light bread was better than any he'd ever tasted.

'I don't know what you're talking about.' But she bit her lip as she pondered the next move. She worried it, twisting those delectable lips until he wanted to kiss her again.

Críost, she was doing this on purpose, using her body to tempt him from thinking about the game. Two could play this.

'It's warm in here,' he remarked, unlacing his tunic and raising it over his head. Bare-chested, he reached out and captured her knight.

Isabel's eyes widened, but a few moves later, she loosened the laces of her gown. When she moved her bishop out of his path, she bared a single shoulder.

'You're not going to win that way.' He fully intended to conquer the black queen, and he wasn't at all interested in what his wife planned to take off next.

'Check,' she replied.

Damn it, she had his queen cornered. He moved the piece out of her attack and a few moves later, he'd put her in check.

'Your move,' he reminded her.

Isabel stood. 'I'm thirsty. Would you like a cup of mead?'

'I want you to finish this game. I'm about to win.'

She shrugged and poured herself a cup. Sipping it slowly, she knelt beside the chess board. With her fingers, she loosened the ties of the gown even more.

'Your gown stays on,' he gritted out. *Concentrate on the game,* he warned himself. But curse it all, he wasn't all that interested in winning any more. He'd much rather spend this night with Isabel, kissing her again.

'Checkmate.' She leaned against her palm, smiling serenely at him.

How in the name of Lug had she managed that? But there was no escaping it. She'd won, without question. Again.

Patrick shoved the game board aside, letting the pieces fall where they would. Isabel had no time to react before he seized her waist and pulled her to him, devouring the mouth that had captivated him for the past hour. She tasted of honeyed sweetness, and carnal temptation.

Her hands moved across his chest, tracing the outline of his muscles. He jerked at the touch, then took her hands in his grip. For the thousandth time, he cursed the fact that she was a Norman. He wanted her in his bed, wanted to know her body intimately.

But it would only tangle matters further. If she were still a virgin, the Archbishop could easily dissolve their marriage.

If he gave in to temptation, it would double the amount of gold needed to bribe the Church.

With regret, he broke away. 'Goodnight, *a stór*.'

Her expression was dazed, a woman caught up in the same storm of desire he felt. But she managed a nod. 'Goodnight.'

He turned away, lying down upon his own pallet while she slept at the opposite side of the hut. He ached to feel her body against his.

And for the remaining hours until dawn, he chided himself for ever agreeing to this game.

In the faint light of dawn, Patrick watched Isabel pour water into a basin, sponging off her face and neck. Her fair hair hung unbound around her shoulders, and she wore only a shift. Droplets of water slid over her neck, and his body responded immediately. He wanted to lift her hair aside and kiss her, dragging her onto the pallet with him.

In the end, he'd dragged himself outside, dousing his own face with water to clear away the unwanted desire. The cold morning air chilled him, and he blessed it for cooling his ardour.

He was about to leave the ringfort when he heard the dull clanging of the tower bell. His eyes narrowed upon the dark swathe of smoke rising up from the mainland, a visible signal from Laochre. He expelled a curse and began to run.

'What is it?' Isabel called out from behind him.

'An attack on our fortress. Likely the damned Ó Phelans, raiding our cattle.'

'What should we do to help?'

'Stay here. Ruarc and I will take care of Laochre.' He saw his cousin already running towards him, to the boat awaiting them on the strand. Within moments, they had pushed the boat into the water, boarding the vessel as it cleared the shore.

Isabel stood behind while a few of the islanders grabbed spears and other weapons, moving down to the rocky side of the island. Moments later, they emerged with boats from within a small cavern of rock. She hadn't noticed it before, since she'd been searching closer to the sandy shore. But at least she knew where they kept their boats, and she could travel to Laochre without swimming.

As Patrick rowed towards the opposite shore, she caught his gaze. For the first time, she was afraid for him.

Foolish, she was, to let herself worry. It was a cattle raid, nothing more. Skirmishes such as these never took a man's life. He wanted her to remain behind and do nothing. But her nerves prickled at the thought of Patrick becoming injured.

Last night, she had almost broken through to him. She didn't know what else to do, but he had wanted her. No longer did she doubt it. What she couldn't understand was why he continued to keep her away from him. It frustrated her beyond all being. She was his wife, and by the saints, she'd had her fill of this. The only way to convince him to accept her as a MacEgan was to fight for her place.

She whirled around and strode back to the ringfort, her mind working rapidly. Without a moment's hesitation, she opened the door to the storage hut containing weapons. Battle axes, maces, bows, spears and knives lined the wall.

Isabel studied the supplies and chose a bow hanging from a wooden peg. The familiar curve of the wood and the taut bowstring kindled a wave of unexpected homesickness. She hadn't touched a bow since she'd left England, and none of the islanders knew she could use it. She suspected Patrick would not let her near a weapon for fear of her loyalty.

Annle entered the hut. 'No.' She voiced a fierce argument

in Irish, but Isabel couldn't understand much beyond the command to stay.

'I can use a bow,' Isabel said, gesturing towards the weapon, 'and I'm not going to stay here while they attack my husband's fortress. I have to help them.'

She swung a quiver of arrows over her shoulder. The light weight evoked such strong memories, of the times when she'd gone hunting alone in the forest. Her common sense warned that she'd only killed deer and small game, never a man.

Isabel's fingers tightened upon the bow. She could easily strike her mark, ending a life. The question was, did she want to? Entering this battle was more than simply helping them against an enemy. It meant facing danger herself.

By now, the men would have reached the opposite shore. She knew Patrick was a strong fighter, from the deeply carved muscles and the confidence with which he moved.

Even now, he wouldn't want her to come, wouldn't want her to join in the fight. It was the greatest of risks, to demand her place among them.

But there was no other choice.

Battle cries cut through the sounds of horses and terrified cattle. Patrick ran alongside Ruarc, enraged at the sight of the signal smoke rising from the top of the round tower. The Ó Phelan chieftain and a dozen men had gathered outside the ringfort.

Early morning sunlight crept across the land, illuminating the shadows and revealing the position of the men. Patrick quickened his pace, furious that they would dare a raid during the daylight hours. His men had done their share of raiding amongst the other tribes, but always in the dark of night. This was a greater insult, implying that there was no means of stopping their attack.

As they closed the distance, the last grove of trees stood between them and the enemy. He paused near the edge, motioning for Ruarc to keep silent. For a moment they could set aside their differences. This was a confrontation both of them needed to win.

He raised his hand, asking Ruarc to wait. Ahead, he saw Trahern and Bevan fighting, along with a small handful of his tribesmen. Where were the Normans? He saw no sign of Sir Anselm or any of the others.

A sense of foreboding nettled his stomach. As a combined force, there was no question that victory was within their grasp. But the Normans were nowhere to be seen. He'd thought Sir Anselm would stand by them and help fight off the Ó Phelans. Now he knew it was not so. A resigned bitterness settled in his gut. The enemy lines hadn't blurred at all. Any understanding he'd felt towards the soldiers disappeared.

Ruarc signalled his intent to flank the Ó Phelans around the right. Patrick moved left. A roar emerged from his throat, as he drew his sword and met the blade of one of the Ó Phelan men. The impact reverberated through his arm, and he released his rage, fighting on behalf of his people.

Their chieftain charged him, and Patrick blocked the blow. Donal Ó Phelan was a tall, thin man with hair that hung down his back and a black beard reaching to his chest. Golden earrings adorned his lobes along with a torque about his throat.

'Hiding behind the skirts of your men, are you, King Patrick?'

The deliberate use of his rank sounded like a taunt. 'You don't want this fight,' Patrick warned. 'The Normans are within the walls.'

'They are fighting for you, are they?' Donal looked around in mock surprise. 'Well, where are they, then?'

Patrick swung his sword, releasing the brunt of his anger. By God, it felt good to wield a blade against an enemy. He thrust his weapon forward, not missing a step even when the Ó Phelan blade skimmed his arm. Blood trickled down to the leather bracers, and Patrick struck hard. The force sent Ó Phelan stumbling backward. The chieftain grunted, but Patrick held steady, waiting for the man to strike again.

A moment later, an arrow pierced Donal's shoulder. The chieftain roared with pain, echoed by one of his men who caught an arrow tip in his hand.

Though Patrick didn't know who had shot the arrows, he seized the advantage. 'Leave our lands before the next arrow takes your heart.'

The chieftain's face blackened. 'What coward attacks from the forest?' He turned to the trees and barked, 'Show yourself!'

A woman emerged from the grove, mounted upon one of their horses. She held an arrow knocked to the bowstring. Though she kept her face and head covered with a *brat*, Patrick recognised the hideous brown *léine*. It could only be Isabel.

He wanted to strangle his wife. How could she even think of joining them, risking her life among an enemy tribe? If she had ventured further, the men wouldn't have hesitated to cut her down, woman or not.

'Who are you?' Donal Ó Phelan demanded.

She lowered the *brat*, revealing braided golden hair and a face that had come to haunt him. '*Tá sé Isabel MacEgan.*'

The sound of his wife speaking Irish stunned him. He hadn't known she could understand any of their language. When had she begun to learn?

And then it struck him—she'd called herself a MacEgan.

Though it was wrong, a curious sense of satisfaction and pride filled him. She had shown more courage than most women, facing down an enemy tribe as if she were one of them. As if she'd earned the right to be a MacEgan.

He forced his mind away from the significance, snapping his attention back to Donal Ó Phelan.

'She is my wife,' he interrupted. 'And unless you want her to release the next arrow, you should go.' He kept his voice even, as though he were fully aware of Isabel's intentions. In truth, he didn't know what she planned to do.

Donal Ó Phelan stared at her and grunted. Without taking his eyes from her, he tore the arrow shaft from his shoulder and snapped it. Though the wound bled badly, he mounted his horse and commanded his men to follow. Not until they were gone did Patrick breathe easier.

'Go inside the *rath*, and see if everyone is all right,' Patrick ordered Ruarc. 'We'll follow in a moment.'

Fear and anger snarled knots of tension inside him. He didn't know whether to punish Isabel or thank her. Instead, he beckoned for her to come forward. He sheathed his sword, his fist curling around the hilt.

Her recklessness might have cost them everything. She could have been hurt or killed. If she died, the tribe would suffer for it. His anger swelled up, threatening to spill over.

When she reached him, she lowered the bow. 'Was anyone hurt? Did you lose any of the sheep or cattle?'

He reached out and took the weapon. 'This does not belong to you.'

She covered his palm, gripping the weapon. 'It was on the island. And so it does belong to me.'

'I ordered you not to come. It wasn't safe.'

'I stayed out of the way,' she argued. The firm set of her

mouth and the stubborn glint in her eyes warned him that she saw nothing wrong with what she'd done. His hand slid around her waist, holding her in place.

Chains and manacles definitely had their appeal.

'You shouldn't have come.'

'But I stopped them. They didn't take any of our livestock.'

'You embarrassed the chieftain of the Ó Phelan tribe. He won't soon forget what you did.'

'Then he shouldn't have been out trying to steal cattle, now, should he?'

She grasped his hand to pull away, but he held her fast. 'You aren't going anywhere.' For this night she would stay at Laochre.

At least then he could keep a closer eye upon her.

It was the first time she'd been inside Patrick's bedchamber. Deep blue curtains hung down from the canopy bed, and a simple wooden table and chair stood by a window. When she neared the table, she noticed elaborate carvings upon the wood. It must have taken years to create such a work of art.

'Did you make that?' she asked, pointing to the chair and table.

'My grandfather did.' A slight hint of pride brimmed in his voice.

Isabel sat down upon the chair, studying the carvings to avoid looking at Patrick. She didn't know why he'd brought her into his private chamber, but the tightness of his jaw and the caged tautness of his body made her uncomfortable. It was as though he wanted to berate her for her interference, but didn't know how to begin.

In the corner, a large grey-and-white cat slept. It made her smile. 'At least I won't have to worry about the rats this night.'

Patrick did not return her smile. 'You have much more to

worry about, *a chara*.' He stood near her, his stance intimidating.

But Isabel squared her shoulders and let him see that she wasn't afraid. She'd made her decision to help them without taking anyone's life. It had felt good to offer her skill, though it wasn't wanted.

'Go on. I know you're angry. Tell me that it wasn't my place to intervene, and that I don't belong here.'

'You seem to believe my orders are unnecessary.' A hard rim of iron coated his conversational tone.

She rose from the chair. 'I'm not a child, Patrick. I make my own decisions. And from where I stood, you needed my help.'

He did not soften. Instead, he moved forward. His black hair framed a grim, resigned face. In the firelight, the golden bands around his upper arms gleamed. 'You could have been hurt. I won't allow that.'

She shot him a doubtful look. 'You're only angry because a woman saved your men.' She knew better than to think he cared whether anything happened to her.

'What if you'd missed?'

'I never miss my aim.'

'It was far too dangerous. And since you have such difficulty with obedience, you will remain in this chamber for a night and a day. You will stay confined until I give the order for your release.'

Isabel didn't like that idea at all. She bargained for time. 'You're injured. Let me tend your cut.'

'It's nothing. And I need to speak with my men.'

'Are you afraid I might hurt you?' She feigned a motherly croon. Taking his hand, she led him to the bed. 'Sit down. I promise to be gentle.'

He cast a disbelieving look, as if he didn't think it were

possible. With a soft push, she forced him to be seated. Even in such a position, his height nearly reached hers. 'What are you doing, Isabel?'

'Stalling,' she answered honestly. 'You can continue ordering me around when I've finished binding your injury.'

His mouth twitched, but he held out his wounded arm. Isabel removed his leather bracer and saw that the blade had only sliced the surface. His arm would not need stitching.

'It isn't as bad as it looks.' She lowered his hand, planning to get water, but he pulled her forward until she stood between his thighs. His powerful muscles pressed against her legs. The touch of his body seemed to melt away the clothing she wore, burning her own skin.

'When did you learn Irish?' he asked. The deep tone of his voice washed over her like honey.

'Annle is teaching me. I don't know very much yet.'

He stared at her, his eyes catching the light until they turned silver. The roughened stubble of beard, the fullness of his mouth, seemed to beckon.

He was one of the most powerful men in Erin. A handsome king whose kiss ripped apart her imaginings of what a husband was like. The raw masculinity of him made her crave his forbidden touch.

She forced herself to step backward. 'I'll get water and linen.' Her voice was not strong, revealing the uneasiness she felt.

Why was he looking at her this way, as if he wanted to share her bed? This marriage was not going to last much longer. She crossed the room, grasping a pitcher of water.

Gather yourself together, Isabel, she warned herself. *Don't fall prey to him.* With steady hands, she poured the water into a basin. She knew better than to let this intimacy deceive her. Patrick MacEgan did not see her as his wife, only an inconvenience.

When she turned back, he removed the other bracer and then lifted away his tunic. Bare-chested, he sat upon the bed watching her. His dark hair covered the back of his neck, and sweet saints, he made her nervous. Her plan to delay her imprisonment now seemed foolhardy.

She cradled the basin against her stomach, almost like a shield. Dipping the edge of her *brat* into the water, she wiped the blood away.

'Aren't you afraid of ruining your wrap?' he asked.

'I would be happy to see both of these garments set on fire,' she answered. 'Sadly, I have nothing else to wear.' She finished wiping the cut and set the *brat* upon the bed.

'Haven't you?' His voice grew deeper, seductive. He rose, standing so close, she felt the hard evidence of his desire.

His expression transformed into a man bent upon conquest. He pulled her into his embrace, until she could feel the heat of his skin against hers.

'Don't,' she whispered. His mouth was a bare shadow away, and saints, she wanted him to kiss her.

'You should know that your Norman blood is the only thing that keeps me from joining with you. If you were Irish, you would lie naked upon that bed with me inside you.'

His words shocked her. Before her feet could move, his mouth lowered to hers. Like an uncivilised savage, she expected him to bruise her mouth. But instead, he took his time. Slowly, with infinite tenderness, he explored her mouth.

'If you were Irish, I would remove this gown.' His hands moved up to cup her breasts. With his thumb, he teased the nipples until desire made her insides ache. 'I'd take you into my mouth and make you forget everything else.'

The taste of him shook her senses. Never had a man kissed her like this. He didn't conquer, but silently asked her to yield. Teasing, arousing in the way he probed with his tongue, until she allowed him entrance.

Against the softness of her shift, her nipples tightened. Without warning, she found her arms about his waist, clinging for balance. Her sensitive breasts grazed against the heavy wool of the *léine*.

His tongue moved over her lips in a caress, and she opened to him. At once, the kiss changed into everything she'd feared. Ruthless and demanding, he cupped her bottom, letting her feel the fierceness of his desire against her womanhood.

She ached to feel him, her body growing wet with need. She hungered in a way she couldn't understand. And she wanted to curse him, for somehow she understood that this was her punishment. To desire him and to be left unfulfilled.

'I'm not Irish,' she managed, pushing him away. Her knees wanted to give way, and she sat down upon the bed.

'Be glad you aren't,' he said.

Without another word, he left. Isabel heard the door lock, imprisoning her. And she sank down upon the bed, not knowing what he planned to do next.

Or how she could convince him to release her from his bedchamber.

Chapter Twelve

Patrick returned to his chamber late at night when he knew she was sleeping. The sight of her curled up on his bed made him ache with wanting her. Her soft, golden hair was braided, and she still wore the loathsome brown *léine*. Her body was half-tangled in the coverlet, while a long bare leg lay exposed to him. He wanted to touch her skin, to feel those long legs wrapping around his waist.

Lug, he didn't need this. He'd thought it would be so easy to keep her confined upon Ennisleigh. She would lead her life and he, his own.

Instead, she had fought for them. He'd ordered her to remain behind, but she had taken up a bow and shot the Ó Phelan chieftain like a female warrior of old. He hadn't guessed she possessed such skill. But now, as he studied her upper arms, he saw the moulded strength from practice. She had clearly aimed to wound the chieftain, not to kill him. And she had enough confidence to shoot in the midst of a fight, knowing she would not hit one of them.

Rarely had anyone surprised him. Not only had she given

them the victory, she had spoken Irish. He'd never thought to hear his own language coming from her lips.

He moved to sit upon the bed. Her body heat allured him, making him want to remove his clothes and pull her close. He didn't dare sleep beside her. Already she was stealing away his logic, making him consider bedding her.

He wouldn't break the vow. No matter how much he desired her, he couldn't risk a child.

Patrick sank down upon a chair. His arm stung from the earlier cut, and he'd wrapped linen around it. Moonlight pooled over his wife's face. In sleep, she appeared pensive, trusting. But by God, she was beautiful. He supposed he deserved this penance, to be driven mad with wanting and to be unable to possess her. If Liam had lived, he'd never have set eyes upon Isabel de Godred.

He closed his eyes, leaning back against the chair. Even now he could not dwell here without remembering his older brother's presence. As he unbuckled the sword from his waist, he wondered if he would ever be a true king.

He bowed his head, praying for strength and the wisdom he lacked. Then he lifted his gaze to Isabel, and prayed for the steadfast resolve to leave her untouched.

For one day soon, he'd have to let her go.

If anyone discovered what he'd planned, it would mean his execution. Ruarc rode quickly, urging the mare faster. Wind whipped past his face, whispering warnings. He'd have to be back soon, before anyone discovered both he and the horse were gone.

Raw energy and fear pulsed through him, tightening his nerves. This was the last thing he wanted to do, but it was necessary. No longer could he trust his own king. Patrick had failed to keep the Normans out, and because of it, one of them had dishonoured his sister.

As he crossed into the boundaries of the Ó Phelan land, he slowed his pace. He'd been raised to view them as an enemy tribe, not to be trusted. Many a time, he'd fought alongside the MacEgans during a raid. He had a few scars to show for it, along with fresh cuts from earlier.

But now he needed their help.

Guilt sank deeply into his heart. Sosanna had tried to take her own life, and he blamed himself. He should have been there for her, should have protected her better. She was his little sister, and he was responsible for her.

But more than sister and brother, they had been close friends ever since she'd returned from fostering. Years ago, they'd made a bargain. She'd chosen a potential wife for him, and he'd set his sights upon Liam MacEgan for her own husband. Neither of them had wed, in the end. After the battle, he couldn't consider taking a wife until he'd found someone to look after Sosanna.

She hadn't conceived her child during the Norman invasion. No, this babe was from last winter, long after they'd suffered defeat. From her refusal to speak, he could only imagine that it must be one of the Normans living among them. And for the past few moons, she'd had to look upon the bastard's face every day.

But who was it?

She wouldn't answer. And so, he was left with no choice but to get rid of every Norman. It wouldn't be easy. King Patrick had wed one of them. And *Críost*, but the chieftain of the Ó Phelans would be wanting vengeance after what the lady Isabel had done to him.

He drew his horse up to the gates of the ringfort and waited.

He scented the acrid smoke of cooking fires, mingled with the animals. It took moments for the Ó Phelan men to sight him, and one loosed an arrow. Ruarc raised his shield, catching the shaft in the wood. Though he suspected the shot was a warning, he wouldn't put it past them to kill him where he stood. He prayed that this visit would work to his advantage and not become his death.

Raising his palm and shield, he rode in the midst of his enemy. A few of the men drew their weapons, but Ruarc kept his gaze fixed upon the chieftain's dwelling. He kept his purpose firmly in his mind, ignoring the insults.

A man's fist swung towards him, but Ruarc caught the wrist. He tightened his grip and stared at the man. 'I could break your wrist and then you'd not be able to hold a weapon again.' The man paled and withdrew his hand. Ruarc raised his voice. 'I've come to speak with your chieftain, Donal Ó Phelan.'

Moments later, the door to a large thatched stone hut opened. The chieftain wore a blue cloak to conceal his injury. Black eyes bore into him with distaste. 'What do you want?'

'I have a proposition for you. I'll discuss it with you in private.'

'You'll present it here or not at all. I'm sure your offer holds interest for many of my people.'

So be it. Ruarc regarded the chieftain. 'I want my cousin removed from power. The Normans have infiltrated our *rath*, and we haven't the forces to drive them out. I've come to ask for your help.'

'And make you the new king, is that it?'

Ruarc said nothing. He did want the kingship. It could have been his, but for Patrick's greater skill with a sword. Ever since his cousin's crowning, he had increased his own training. He didn't like being second best.

But at least he understood loyalty to the tribe. He'd never have accepted such a coward's bargain, wedding a Norman. 'If I become king of Laochre, I can grant you lands to the west.'

The chieftain's eyes grew cunning as he considered the offer. 'Come inside, then. I may be able to help you.'

Isabel awoke, not knowing where she was. She squinted at the morning sunlight and something soft tickled her nose.

The grey-and-white cat padded across her torso, eyeing her as if wondering how a human had come to occupy her bed. Isabel ruffled the cat's head, and the feline pushed into Isabel's palm, purring lightly. A moment later, the cat deposited herself on Isabel's lap, cleaning herself with her tongue.

Isabel eased the cat off and rose from the bed, stretching. She didn't remember Patrick coming back inside the room. It had been a long time since she'd lain in a proper bed, and for the first time in many nights, she'd slept well.

A blue length of cloth rested atop a chair. Isabel walked closer and saw that it was a new gown, the colour of a midnight sky. When she touched it, the softness of the finely woven linen was a stark contrast to the coarse brown wool she now wore. With long voluminous sleeves and a skirt that hung to her calves, the *léine* was similar to her former kirtles. An emerald overdress lay beneath it.

She couldn't stop the smile of thankfulness. Though she expected her dowry and her clothing to arrive at any moment now, no longer did she have to dress like a slave.

Turning to the cat, she inquired, 'What do you think? Should I burn the old gown?'

The feline flicked her tail in the air and sniffed before curling up on the pillow for a nap.

'You're right. I should wait until I know if the new gown

is truly mine.' But the desire to be rid of the coarse brown *léine* overcame any hesitation she might have felt. She stripped off the garment and then her ragged shift. Naked, she pulled the midnight-blue gown over her body. The linen clung to her skin, and she closed her eyes, revelling in the luxury. The over-dress took some arranging without a girdle to hold it in place.

Before she had finished, a knock sounded upon the door. 'Enter,' she said.

Her husband walked inside, dressed in more common attire this day. It did not diminish the strength and power of his presence. He'd tied his black hair back with a leather thong, and it emphasised the deep planes of his face. Her attention was drawn to his mouth, remembering the way he'd once kissed her.

Right now he was looking at her as though he'd never seen her before. Had she put the gown on wrong? She fumbled with the overdress, wondering how it was supposed to drape.

'The *léine* looks well on you,' Patrick said. He closed the door and bolted it.

'I'm grateful for it.' Isabel ventured a smile, but he did not return it. After last night, she didn't know what else to say. He'd touched her the way a husband would and had left her wanting. But now he behaved as if nothing had happened.

'Why did you bring me to your chamber last night?' she asked.

He crossed the room to stand before her. 'I didn't want you causing any more trouble. And, as I've said, I intend to keep you here for the next day. You won't leave this room.'

She glared at him. 'Why not imprison me in chains, then?'

'It's not a bad idea.'

His rough voice transfixed her. She imagined her arms bound while his mouth moved over her bare flesh.

'I wasn't being serious.' She shivered at the thought.

His mouth curved upwards. 'But I was.' He captured her hands and drew them to her sides. Her skin warmed beneath the touch of his hands, and she closed her eyes to shut him out.

'Don't touch me. Not if you're going to end the marriage.'

His reply was to cup her cheek, threading his hands through her hair. It was a slow torment, one that pulled apart her will-power. She wanted to sink against him, tasting his mouth against her own. Fierce needs gripped her, and she struggled for composure.

'What will you do with me?' she managed to ask.

'I haven't decided yet.'

Her hands gripped the edge of her gown while she tamped down her frustration. Did he really intend to keep her here for the remainder of the day? She would go mad, were she forced to remain within the walls with nothing to do.

'Let me go,' she urged him. 'Take me back to Ennisleigh if you must, but don't make me stay here.'

'I wanted you to stay on Ennisleigh to begin with. It was for your safety, and you still disobeyed.'

'I only disobey orders I don't agree with.'

He muttered a curse beneath his breath. 'This isn't about choices, Isabel. It's about keeping you safe.'

'You cannot keep someone safe by locking them away,' she said softly.

She was helpless to understand the king she'd wed. A wall of responsibility hid the man. Only now and again did she catch a glimpse of him. A man who devoted himself to family and his tribe. A man who possessed a dark passion, barely concealed from her.

'It is my duty to protect you. Your father would slaughter us all if you were to come to harm.'

'He might. But only because it would be an excuse for war. Not because he cares anything for me.' A time or two, she'd run away from her father's castle. The soldiers had brought her back, but Edwin de Godred hadn't noticed she was gone.

Patrick didn't answer. His face remained emotionless, a warrior's cold demeanour. Isabel's skin chilled with his silence. 'The war between you and my father isn't over, is it?'

He shook his head slowly. 'Our marriage delayed it. But our people haven't surrendered. We won't give up our freedom to the Normans.'

'Don't do this,' she pleaded. 'Your men will die, and my father will want your life as forfeit.'

'My life is already forfeit to the tribe.'

Anger surged within her, that he would consider sacrificing himself. 'Then you might as well be dead. You don't care about anything else.'

Hurt welled up in her eyes, and she closed them to hide the unshed tears. Why was she letting herself think of him as a true husband? He'd done nothing except push her away.

'They are my family. My blood.'

Isabel rested her cheek upon her hand, leaning upon the table. She traced a finger across the deep scars of the wood, wishing she could understand him. Outside, clouds suffocated the sunlight.

When she raised her gaze to him again, she saw the resolution in his eyes. And she wondered what it would be like to have a man love her, the way he cared for his brothers and his tribe.

'Tell me something,' she said. 'Why do you live your life for your tribe and not for yourself?'

She wanted to provoke him, to see an ounce of feeling. But there was only emptiness in his gaze. 'You know nothing of my responsibilities.'

'You're right.' Her voice was hollow with the aching inside of her. 'Because you won't let me know you. I don't know anything about the man I married. All I know is that you won't let me be a part of your tribe.'

He still saw her as the enemy, no matter what she did. And she was so very tired of trying to help, when he would not change his opinion of her.

She stood and opened the shutters, though there was little sun to illuminate the space. 'Do you think I don't see their suffering? And I'm to stand about and pretend it isn't happening.'

'You cannot help.'

'Aye, I can. And so can my father's men. Give them a reason to help you, and they will. Put aside your differences and join together.'

'It isn't that simple.'

'Yes, it is. Let them be a part of this fortress. They cannot fight for something they have no connection to.'

His face hardened. 'I already know the Normans, Isabel. They are the ones who made me a king when they sank their sword into my brother's heart. I watched Liam die in battle, and I couldn't do anything to stop them.' Rage and pain lined his voice.

'The battle is over.' She reached out to touch his hand. 'But you have another chance to save your tribe. Bring the men together as one. You'll double your forces and have the men you need to defend Laochre against your enemies.'

'The Normans did nothing when the Ó Phelans attacked.' He shook his head, denying her proposition.

Isabel lowered her hand. 'And have you seen the way your men treat them? They don't speak to the Normans, nor offer any hospitality.'

'My men do not speak the Norman tongue,' he pointed out.

'Your men also provoke them at every turn. That day when I came to Laochre for the first time, I saw their bruises and injuries. I can well understand why they wouldn't fight for you. They're too busy fighting against you.'

She drew closer to him, her heart racing. 'But we could change it.' Isabel placed her palms upon his tunic, half-wondering if he would pull her hands away. 'Yesterday, I was prepared to kill the Ó Phelan men if I had to.'

His eyes grew hooded with intensity. Beneath the linen tunic, his hardened muscles flexed. 'You've never killed a man before.'

'No. But I could.'

'Would you slay one of your own kinsmen, for our tribe?'

'Would you slay one of yours?' She didn't wait for a reply, but before she could move her hands away, he trapped them around his waist. 'I don't want to be your enemy,' she whispered, 'and yet you treat me the same way you do the others.'

'Not last night, I didn't.' He drew her against his length, while his hands moved over her spine in a soft caress.

Deep longings rose within her, and she lowered her chin. 'I am your wife, Patrick. And I am trying, the best way I know how, to become one of your tribe.'

He cupped her jaw, his hand warming her cheek. 'You're the most frustrating woman I've ever met.'

'I could say the same for you.'

A glint of amusement rose up in his eyes. 'I'm not a woman, *a stór*.'

Isabel bit her lip. And wasn't she well aware of that? 'You know what I meant. A frustrating *man*.' He expelled a low laugh, and she was caught up by the rumbling sound. 'I didn't think you knew how to laugh.'

His palm lowered to the back of her neck. Gently, he

massaged the knots at her nape, and she grew still. The sensation of his hands upon her skin, the feeling of surrender, made her long to embrace him. 'I know many things, Isabel.'

'What do you want from me?' she asked softly. His body was so close, she fought her own feelings. He made her desire more, though she could not understand what it was she needed.

'I know well enough what I want,' he said huskily. 'But it isn't what either of us needs.'

Abruptly, he released her. 'I won't see you for a few days. I'm going to meet with Donal Ó Phelan on the morrow.'

'He tried to kill you,' Isabel protested. Why would he want to risk his life meeting with the chieftain? A sudden coldness swept over her conscience. He wouldn't be going to see the chieftain, were it not for what she'd done.

'I owe him *corp-dire*, a body price for his injuries. I'll pay the fines and restore peace.'

She couldn't believe what he'd said. The king of Laochre intended to lower himself to that thief? 'He was trying to steal your cattle! He doesn't deserve peace.'

'I don't need a war with the Ó Phelans as well as with the Normans.'

'You would seek peace with their chieftain and not with my father's men?' Why were her people any different?

'The Normans killed our men. A far greater crime than stealing cattle.'

She had believed there was hope of moving beyond the conquest. But it seemed impossible. 'You won't ever let the past lie buried, will you?'

'No. I can't.' He folded his arms across his chest. 'I've received word that more invasions are happening in the east, at Ath-cliath.'

Isabel didn't look at him, afraid to hear what he was about to say.

'Over three thousand men were driven from their homes. The Normans are capturing the chieftains.'

'For what purpose?' A numbing chill passed through her at the thought of someone taking Patrick captive.

'Execution.'

'And they're coming here?' Her voice trembled. She knew without having to ask from his austere manner.

Patrick nodded. 'I've received word that they are not far from Port-lairgi. If we are to survive, we need the help of the Ó Phelan tribe.'

'And my father's men.' Trepidation iced through her body. She had never seen the face of war, not in her nineteen years of life. But she knew without any doubt that their survival depended on bringing the men together as one.

'They'll never fight for us.' The grave tone in his voice sounded distant and hollow.

She feared he was right, not if his men continued to treat the Normans as enemies. 'When do you expect the invasion forces here?'

'At any moment. And my men aren't ready.' He studied her, concern lining his face. 'This is why I wanted you to remain on Ennisleigh, away from our battles. But now they may invade our lands.'

He softened his tone, reaching out for her hand. 'I could send you away, far from the bloodshed.'

Though he'd given her the chance for a reprieve, to take it would mean turning her back on everyone. Their fate should be her own. Isabel laced her fingers with his. 'I won't deny that I'm afraid. But my place is here.'

He watched her, his expression discerning. 'Perhaps one

day you'll have a castle of your own, with many sons and daughters. And you'll forget about all of this.'

Though his words were meant to reassure her, instead they pierced her with the knowledge that he would never view her as his wife. Only an outsider.

Chapter Thirteen

At sunset, Patrick returned to release her from the chamber. She was barely aware of how much time had passed, so troubled had been her thoughts. All her life, she was accustomed to looking after people. Her father's castle, the servants, and the common folk all knew her. She felt responsible for their care and well being.

But here, she was only a burden. And no matter how hard she tried to forge a place for herself, her husband fought her at every step. Part of her wondered whether she should give up.

While Patrick went to collect more supplies for Ennisleigh, Isabel walked across the ringfort towards the Norman soldiers. She studied the faces of the Irish as she passed, and most turned away, pretending as though they didn't see her. She squared her shoulders, hiding the disappointment.

Sir Anselm stood near a group of Normans sparring. He was correcting one of his men, but when he saw her, he bowed. 'Queen Isabel.'

The title almost felt like a mockery, but she did not say so. 'May I speak with you for a moment?'

'Of course.'

She stood at the gatehouse, leaning up against the wood. Ewan MacEgan sat above them upon a wooden platform. Listening to their conversation, no doubt.

'Why didn't you help the Irish during the raid?'

He crossed his arms and flicked a glance towards the tribesmen. His gaze was set in stone, merciless. 'The MacEgans follow their own path, my queen. They want no part of us, and we would rather not help them.

'They seek to provoke us at every moment,' he continued. 'My men must constantly be on guard for a knife in their backs. It is better to remain separate.'

So nothing had changed. And she didn't know if there could ever be a difference in their thinking towards one another. 'Do you want to return to England?' she asked.

'My men would leave within the hour, if the order were given.'

'And what of yourself? Do you want to leave?'

'It matters not whether I go or stay,' he admitted. 'My sword belongs to Lord Thornwyck. But there are those among my men who long for their wives and children.'

'If I sent for them, would your men make their homes here?'

Sir Anselm shook his head with a sad smile. 'They would only fear for their wives' safety among the Irish. The division is too deep between us.'

'Is there any way to end the animosity?' she asked.

'No.'

Though she suspected he was right, she hated the thought of abandoning hope. Within the ringfort, the Irish resentment was palpable. The men could not see past their previous battle.

But it would be much harder for children to stay away from each other. Their natural curiosity might help bring the sides together, however grudgingly.

Her earlier thought of bringing the wives and children gathered strength. If the men would not come together, the women might. The more she considered it, the better it sounded.

She studied each of the people, and when she saw Ewan still eavesdropping, she relaxed. She would bribe the boy to send a message to her father. With any luck, before summer's end, her father's men would find a reason to shift their loyalties.

Spring blossomed into summer, and with each passing month, Isabel understood more and more of the people around her. Her grasp of the language had moved beyond pitiful, and she now could speak enough Irish to hold a minimal conversation with Annle. Though the people upon Ennisleigh had not yet befriended her, at least they seemed to tolerate her presence.

Today the rain poured down, and she huddled near the fire inside the fortress. A fortnight ago, she'd convinced the islanders to help her patch up the roof of the donjon. It had allowed her to move out of the cottage, and she'd spent time fixing up the interior.

Though the Great Chamber was not a large one, she had spread fresh straw rushes and Patrick had granted her some furniture from Laochre. Trahern had made her a new chair, and Isabel had coaxed Annle to bring in one of the weaving looms.

The rhythm of weaving and the familiar wool set her mind at peace. In the past moon, she hadn't seen Patrick but once or twice.

Ever since the night he'd almost shared her bed, he had avoided her. She tried not to think of it. They had agreed to go their separate paths after her father's visit.

And yet, somehow, she missed him. Even on the fleeting

moments they had seen one another, he'd watched her as if drinking in the sight. As though she were forbidden to him.

The door burst open, and Ewan rushed inside. 'We need to use the Great Chamber.'

Isabel stood and set her wool aside. 'Why?'

He shifted his weight from one foot to the other, half-dancing with excitement. 'Trahern has come for the storytelling. But he can't use the gathering space because of the rain, so they're coming here.'

'Who is coming?'

'The islanders. Trahern is one of the best bards, and he has some new tales to share.' Ewan's crooked grin showed brotherly pride.

Isabel winced. 'But I don't have any food or drink for them.' It was the first time she'd had to host a gathering since coming to Erin, and no doubt they would judge her hospitality. Or lack of it.

'You have to help me,' she urged Ewan 'Go back to Laochre and bring food and a barrel of the finest wine we have. Get the Normans to help you. Send for Sir Anselm and his men.'

Ewan shook his head. 'I can get the food, but the tribesmen won't want the Normans here.'

'I am not concerned about what they want. This is a chance for both of them to have a night of entertainment without any fighting. I want them here, mingled with the Irish.'

It might take a barrel of wine to make both sides drunk enough to endure each other's company, but it would be worth it if the men would put aside their differences.

'We might need two barrels of wine,' she corrected. And she prayed to the saints that the men would not fight amongst themselves.

Isabel pushed the loom to the side and began straightening

up the space. 'We haven't enough room for them to sit. Oh, by the Blessed Mother, what's to be done?' She muttered to herself, thinking fast. Then she whirled upon Ewan. 'Why are you still standing there? Run! They will be here before long.'

The boy scurried outside, and Isabel stoked the fire, adding more peat to warm the space. Lighting torches, she set them inside the iron sconces upon the walls. Before long, the Chamber glowed with a warm light.

She lifted her *brat* over her head, dashing outside into the rain. She needed Annle's help to bring in more seating.

Outside the rain poured, and Isabel pounded on Annle's hut. Her husband Brendan let her in, and Isabel stumbled past the tall, thin Irishman. Quiet and softspoken, he was one of the few men to show her kindness.

'What is it?' Annle asked. 'Is something wrong?'

'Yes, something is wrong.' Isabel glanced around the small hut, counting benches and stools. 'I need your help getting enough benches and stools. Trahern is coming to the island for storytelling.'

Annle shrugged. 'I know it. We'll have the gathering inside the fortress as we usually do.' She frowned. 'That is, if you do not mind.'

'Of course not. But there is nowhere for anyone to sit,' Isabel moaned. From the shadows, Sosanna moved forward. Her fair hair was braided across her forehead, the rest spilling down her shoulders. She wore a simple green *léine* with a cream overdress. Her stomach swelled out in late pregnancy, and she supported her back with a hand.

'Will you help me?' Isabel pleaded, her gaze upon both women. Sosanna offered a tentative smile, glancing at Annle.

'This is important to you, isn't it?' the healer asked.

She nodded. 'I need to find enough benches. And then I

haven't enough food or drink for the people. There aren't any decorations either.'

Isabel wanted to bury her head. This was her first, and perhaps only, opportunity to be a hostess to the MacEgan tribe. Though the people did not seem to despise her any more, neither did they welcome her.

'We'll make do,' Annle said. She remained calm and sincere. 'You should go and ask the others to bring their benches and stools. And food.'

Isabel hesitated. 'I thought I should be the one to feed them.'

'There is not time for you to cook enough, and it is not expected. Each will bring a dish to share, you'll see. Go and speak to them.'

Isabel would rather have faced a den of lions, but she knew Annle was right. She had to ask for their help. Hard memories intervened, of when she'd first asked the islanders for a torch and they'd kept silent. Would they turn her away now?

She swallowed hard. 'All right.'

She didn't mention anything about the Norman soldiers. It would only make them angry. Her nerves stretched even more, worrying that she hadn't made a good choice in asking Ewan to send the men.

Annle embraced her, pressing her cheek to Isabel's. 'It will be fine.'

Isabel paced the length of the dwelling, nervously awaiting her guests. The past hour had frayed her nerves down to a single thread. Though each of the islanders listened to her request, their expressions showed no welcome. It was as though she were still a stranger. But she'd mustered her courage and managed to visit each of the huts.

Now she stood at the entrance and saw Ewan and the islanders struggling with the barrels of wine. There was no sign of the Norman soldiers, nor her husband. Her spirits fell, for she'd hoped they would join in the celebration.

She wanted Patrick to come, to see him once again. Though he had stayed apart from her, each sennight he'd sent more supplies, and always a gift. Once, he'd sent a mirror of polished silver. Another time, he'd sent silk fabric in the same colour as her ruined wedding kirtle.

They were almost gifts a man might send to court a woman. But the gift that moved her the most was when he'd sent the grey-and-white cat. She'd named the feline Duchess, and on many days the cat would curl up on her lap, purring softly.

'Drink some wine,' Annle urged, after the men had set up the barrels. 'There is no need to be anxious.'

Isabel accepted the cup and took a deep sip of wine. The spicy aroma of fermented grapes mingled with the flavour of the barrel, and she forced herself to calm down.

Annle's husband and the others had joined together to bring several low tables into the hall. The scent of roasting venison mingled amid the peat smoke, and as each guest arrived, more platters of food were set upon the tables. Boiled turnips, carrots, platters of salmon, loaves of bread, and even a dish of boiled goose eggs were part of the feast.

Isabel breathed a little easier when she realised there would be more than enough food. As the folk drank wine and enjoyed the meal, she sat down near the entrance where the night air blew inside. The wetness of rain mingled with the warm interior, and Isabel moved away from the downpour.

Conversations rose in a din of merrymaking, and though Isabel could now understand most of their talk, she leaned back against the wall. She didn't feel comfortable joining them, not even after spending almost a season upon the island. Shyness prevented her from speaking to them.

'Why are you hiding in the shadows?' a voice asked. Isabel turned and saw Patrick. Her heart gave a leap, and she mentally berated herself for feeling like a lovesick maid. But it had been so long since she'd seen him last.

'I'm not hiding.' She did not move from her place, not knowing what he expected from her.

His black hair was pulled back, emphasising his handsome face. He wore a tunic of deep red with dark trews, and his sapphire cloak was fastened with an emerald brooch. Upon his head, he wore a circlet of gold that was slightly tilted. Gold gleamed about his muscled arms.

'You look like a king this night,' she offered.

'It's expected of me.'

Isabel set her wine goblet aside and studied him a moment. She reached out and straightened the circlet on his temple. 'This looks better.'

'I know of no one else who would dare to do such a thing.'

'A king should not wear a crooked crown.'

'It is called a *minn óir*.' He took her hands from his temples and held them at his side. The touch of his rough palms took her by surprise.

She closed her eyes, afraid to look at him. Something cold and heavy fastened around her throat, and she opened her eyes. 'What is this?'

'A gift.'

She reached out and touched a silver torque set with amethyst. 'This is too fine. Why would you give me this?'

His look grew distant. 'I hadn't intended to give it to you at all. But it is your right, as my bride.'

She shook her head. 'I've no need for jewels.'

He shrugged. 'Your dowry arrived this morn at Laochre. It will greatly help our people. This is my token of thanks.'

'You could sell it and gain more supplies.'

'It belonged to my mother,' was all he said, and she understood why he would not part with it.

The weight of the silver was uncomfortable, for she did not feel worthy to wear it. 'I am not their queen, Patrick.'

'No,' he admitted, 'But this is my repayment to you. On the morrow, I will send the remainder of your dowry and household possessions for you to use here.'

She would rather have brought them to Laochre, her husband's home. It seemed strange using the goods in a home that wasn't truly her own. After spending all spring here in Erin, she still felt like an outsider.

Patrick gestured towards the islanders. 'Annle tells me this celebration was your idea.'

'Ewan said Trahern was coming to tell stories.' She touched the torque, fingering the beautiful amethysts. 'I did not want the people to feel unwelcome.'

'You've done a great deal with the *rath*. It looks almost as it did long ago.'

Isabel tried to smile, but she couldn't seem to muster it. When he reached out to touch her hair, she flinched. 'What are you doing?'

'This belongs to you also, as part of your bride price.' He removed her veil and placed a silver circlet around her head, winding her hair around it to hold it in place. 'Take my hand, and we'll go.'

Isabel didn't move. She felt exposed without the veil. Almost like a little girl playing with her sister's jewels, pretending to be grown up. It seemed a mockery, for the circlet was far too similar to a crown. Only a queen could wear it. 'I can't wear this.'

He shrugged as if dismissing the matter. 'The islanders will expect it of you.'

He didn't understand. To him, it was a piece of silver. To her, it was a reminder of what she could never be—the lady of this tribe. She reached up and pulled it free of her hair, handing it to him. 'Take it. I won't pretend to be something I'm not.'

Consternation spread over his face, but he accepted the silver circlet. 'If that is your wish. But it still belongs to you.' He set it aside, placing it within a fold of his cloak. Then he stretched out his hand to her. 'We must greet our guests.'

Isabel forced herself to take Patrick's hand. His fingers closed over her palm and he added, 'You invited Sir Anselm and a few of his men here tonight.' There was an edge of warning beneath his voice. 'Ewan told me of your request.'

Of course the boy would. Asking Ewan to keep a secret would be like asking the sun not to shine.

'Yes, I asked them to join us.' The Normans needed a night where they could see the Irish as friends instead of enemies. 'I thought they would enjoy a night of feasting and celebration.' She narrowed her gaze. 'Will you deny them that chance?'

He held back his answer, studying the islanders who were devouring the feast. His fingers imbued warmth into her hands, and Isabel tried to mask her reaction to his touch. Her feelings hadn't diminished at all since the last time he'd touched her. If anything, she was even more drawn to him.

'I'll allow it,' he said at last. 'But only because there are so few of them.'

Trahern entered the dwelling at that moment, greeting each of the islanders with a warm smile. He winked at Isabel, and Patrick led her up to the small dais. The eyes of the people watched her, and a few whispered at the sight of the silver torque around her throat. Though all of them knew she was

Patrick's wife, it was the first time he had publicly acknowledged her as such.

'My brother Trahern has come this night to bring stories,' Patrick began. 'He talks too often, as we all know. But perhaps with good wine and food, we can listen to his tales.'

The crowd smiled their approval, and Isabel stepped back a little. Patrick took her wrist, forbidding her to shrink away. 'I understand the Lady Isabel arranged for this celebration. Will you not honour her for her hospitality?'

Silence met his question. Behind the islanders, Annle raised her wooden cup in salute. Yet the others did not follow her gesture. Isabel's skin coloured with embarrassment. She wished he hadn't drawn attention to her.

Patrick's gaze transformed into anger. 'When you dishonour Isabel MacEgan, you show dishonour to your king.' At that, a few tribesmen muttered words of thanks for the hospitality. Isabel wanted to sink into the floor and hide beneath the rushes. Her face burned with mortification.

Patrick gestured for Trahern to begin the stories. One of the men took up a round drum with a goatskin stretched across the frame, using it to accentuate the tale.

Isabel nodded politely, then moved behind the crowd of her guests. With any luck, she could flee and escape anyone's notice.

But Patrick caught her first. 'You cannot leave,' he said softly in her ear. 'It is your duty to stay.'

'I have done my duty,' she whispered. 'Did it please you to see them spurn me?'

'No,' he answered honestly. He saw the stricken expression on her face. Irish or Norman, she was a woman who had tried her best to offer them a night of feasting. She deserved thanks for her attempt. 'But your efforts did not go unnoticed. And it pleases me to hear you speaking Irish. I cannot believe you learned it so quickly.'

'I had no choice. I'd be talking to grass, otherwise.'

She drained her cup, and he refilled it. 'I am sorry.'

As she drank, he studied her features. Her golden hair shone in the flicker of the torch, the silver gleaming around her throat. Deep, copper eyes seemed to have lost their hope. He didn't like the way they had treated her, though he had predicted it.

And as for himself, he'd tried to keep her out of his thoughts. But each day he found himself watching the island, wondering about her. He had expected her to live upon Ennisleigh, spinning and weaving. Instead, she'd learned to speak their language and rebuilt his grandfather's home.

His hand moved to the dip in her spine, and her breath caught. She met his gaze, her lips parting. She was looking at him with a woman's desire, as though she felt the same for him. He moved his hand across her lower back, needing to touch her. And though it was wrong, he'd missed her.

'Would you like some wine?' she offered.

He took her cup and sipped from it. Isabel's mouth twisted. 'I didn't mean from my own cup.'

'I like yours.'

She sent him a warning look, but her wariness sounded like a challenge. They listened to Trahern's tale, and Patrick saw her face soften with humour. He reached to take a sip from her cup again, and she held fast to it.

'Do you wish to fight me for it?' she threatened, in a teasing tone.

'I might.' Right now he wanted to drag her outside in the rain and kiss her until no barrier lay between them. Instead, he released the cup and went to find his own. Apart from her, he studied his wife. She held herself back from the folk, feigning a smile. Though she pretended to enjoy herself, he noticed that she had a closer fellowship with the wall than with the people.

It bothered him more than it should, for it made her seem more distant. The green overdress and blue *leíne* accentuated her womanly curves, the fabric skimming her figure.

Patrick took a long sip of wine, forcing his attention away. The stories continued, and when Trahern stopped to enjoy food and wine, several islanders took up musical instruments. The mingled sound of harp and *bodhrán* drum joined in with the conversations of the folk.

Finally, the Normans arrived. Only six men had come, and thankfully they wore no armour. At first, the Irish didn't notice them, for the Normans slipped into the background. Isabel held out her hands in greeting to Sir Anselm.

Patrick tensed, unsure of what his people would say. He doubted that the Irish were drunk enough to welcome the Normans. He hadn't wanted them to come and would have outright refused his wife's request, but for two reasons. Sir Anselm had begun training his Irishmen, transforming them from farmers into soldiers. He'd seen the results. They would be ready to face a Norman army soon enough.

And then, too, the presence of the Normans had kept the Earl of Pembroke's men away. Dozens of chieftains had lost their lives after a Norman lord, Raymond Le Gros, had ordered their legs broken and their bodies tossed over the cliffs.

He'd been one of the few kings to escape, and he knew it was because of the enemy housed within their gates. The shadow of death had passed over them, and his people knew it not.

And so, he'd agreed to offer the men a brief moment of celebration. The reward of good wine and a night of entertainment seemed appropriate, particularly when it was only a few men.

For many of the soldiers, it was their first visit to the island. They looked uneasy, and Patrick wondered if Sir Anselm had forced them to come. Isabel excused herself to bring the men goblets of wine, and it was then that the folk finally noticed the Normans.

'What are they doing here?' one man demanded in Irish. His gaze switched to Isabel, filling with accusation. 'Ennisleigh belongs to us. They've no right to be here.'

Isabel looked to Patrick for a response. Before he could speak, she raised her voice, speaking to the islanders in their own tongue. 'They are my guests. This is my home, and all are welcome within it.'

'She says that because she's one of them,' another remarked.

Isabel turned pale, her hands clenched. 'Yes, I am one of them. But I've lived upon this island for the past season. And it is my right to invite whomever I please into my home.'

Patrick saw the impact of her proclamation. Though a few of the men and women did not seem to care, others began to leave. As each one passed beyond the threshold, they did not raise their knee to him, nor offer the expected salutations. He was their king, but he'd slipped further in their eyes.

It stung, watching his childhood friends turn their backs on him. And he saw Isabel valiantly trying to hold back tears. It was useless thinking that the men could ever be brought together. They could never be allies, only enemies.

A few of the islanders stayed, though not more than a handful. Annle stood by Isabel's side, while Sosanna remained in the shadows.

When the rest had gone, Patrick addressed the group of less than a dozen men and women. 'I thank you for not paying insult to my wife.' To Trahern he asked, 'Can you offer them another story?'

Isabel stepped through the crowd until she reached his side. With hopeful eyes, she asked, 'Will you translate for my father's men? My Irish is not yet strong enough.'

Patrick wanted to say no. He wanted to return to Laochre and abandon this disaster of a night. Why did she keep on trying? Allowing the Normans entrance to Ennisleigh had cost them the support of many islanders. Could she not see the rift?

But then she placed her hand in his. 'Please.' She did not beg or cajole, but the simple request made him feel foolish. In her eyes she looked upon him with hope.

He cursed himself for his weakness, knowing that he was going to give in.

'If that is your wish, *a chara*.'

The warm smile on her face was genuine. She touched her palm to his cheek, and though he did not speak a word, he kissed her palm.

Isabel's face flooded. 'Go and sit with your brother.' She gestured towards Trahern, as if he were not fully aware of his own brother's location. 'I'll—I'll get the men some wine.'

It took half a barrel of wine for the Normans to begin enjoying themselves. Patrick translated six stories, Isabel keeping his goblet full. He didn't know how much wine he'd drunk, but the room swayed.

He wasn't alone, for more than one islander lay against the wall, snoring from the effects of the drink. After a time, one of the soldiers asked to see the *bodhrán* drum. Annle's husband picked up the smooth drumstick, the length of a man's hand. The soldier grinned and tried to beat out a simple rhythm. It was terrible, but one of the islanders showed him how to hold it and eventually both were laughing.

When the wine barrels were empty and the food gone, more of the men and women went to sleep, curling up against one another in the Great Chamber. Isabel yawned, leaning against one of the low tables.

Patrick watched her, wanting to draw her into his arms and take her back to her chamber. Sleepy-eyed, she turned to the Norman soldier beside her and smiled in response to something the man said.

A darkness tightened in his gut. Though the man had done nothing more than speak to his wife, it reminded him of his oath to let Isabel choose another husband. His mind imagined another man touching her, giving her children. He didn't like the thought, not at all.

He was about to snarl at the Norman to get away from his wife when Sosanna stepped towards the harp. Along with the others, the man moved over to watch while she seated herself with the instrument between her knees. The round hardness of her belly touched the golden brown wood while her hands plucked a mournful tune.

He hadn't heard her play in over a year. Sosanna had often joined the other musicians during gatherings at Laochre, offering lively tunes that inspired men and women to dance. He'd almost forgotten the joy she'd brought to their celebrations. Ever since the harm that had befallen her, she'd lost her music, as well as her voice.

This song was a lament, enchanting those who were still awake. Others listened, but it was Sir Anselm who caught his attention. The knight watched with the look of a man noticing a woman.

Nothing good would come of it. But still, he said nothing.

Anselm had saved Sosanna's life, and perhaps that was all there would be between them.

When the song ended, Isabel rose and drew nearer. 'Will the king grant me an audience?' she asked, offering Patrick a stumbling curtsy. Her face was flushed, though from the drink or from embarrassment, he could not be sure.

'What is your wish?'

'Come.' She took his hand and led him behind a wooden partition, dividing her bedchamber from the rest of the gathering space. He entered and drew the hide covering over the opening, granting them privacy.

Before he could ask another question, her arms wrapped around his neck. 'I want you to kiss me.'

'That isn't a good idea, *a stór*.' Even though he wanted to touch her, to thread his hands through her silken hair and to take what she had offered. The open invitation inflamed his senses, making him want to cast everything aside but her.

Isabel leaned in, touching her nose to his. Her woollen *brat* fell to the ground, as if forgotten. By God, she was beautiful. An enemy with the face of an angel.

'Every man upon the island and the mainland believes that we are man and wife. In flesh as well as in name.'

'But we aren't.' *Step away from her*, his resolve warned.

'Is there something wrong with me?' Though she kept her tone light, he sensed the deeper fear beneath it. There was honesty in her question. He no longer knew what to say. She had somehow grown into their lives, learning their language and shifting his doubts.

Was it even possible to keep her as his bride?

No. He'd seen the way the other islanders had turned their backs upon her. They could not see the woman she was, only what she represented.

Just the way he had once thought of her.

He didn't breathe, and when she rested her cheek against his, he wanted to damn them all and take her into his bed. He embraced her, holding her curves against him.

'No. There's nothing wrong with you.' He didn't pull away when she kissed him. Instead, he took from her, welcoming the momentary respite from being a king. He tasted wine upon her lips, the heady fullness of this woman who stood between him and his tribe.

He wanted to lie with her, to damn the consequences. She was his wife, and there were ways to give one another pleasure without risking a child.

Lug, what had she done to his willpower? He no longer thought of her as the enemy. She'd tried so hard to make the celebration festive for the islanders. Instead, they'd turned on her. She deserved their respect and admiration. How many women would have worked so hard to learn their language and rebuilt a broken-down fortress?

He admitted the truth to himself. He didn't want to give her up, especially not to another man. He didn't want anyone touching this woman or giving her children. Except himself.

And that was the greatest problem of all.

His mouth brushed against her temple, burning her like a brand of possession. 'We cannot become lovers, Isabel. There might be a child.'

Beneath her hands, she could feel the heat of his skin, and her body yearned for more. 'There are ways to prevent it, are there not?'

Silence again. Then he lifted her face to look at him. The darkness in the set of his mouth, the ferocity of his enslaved needs, took her senses apart.

'Some day you'll be another man's wife,' he replied.

'Someone else will touch you.' He lowered the shoulder of her shift and kissed the bared skin. Shivers of desire raced through her at the contact.

'I don't want another man,' she answered, raising her mouth to his. 'I'd rather stay with you.'

She hadn't meant to voice the words aloud, but they were true. Here, she was needed like never before. There was a sense of purpose, the hope of bringing enemies together.

'If I were not a king, there's nothing that would take you from me.'

And she knew the truth suddenly. Given a choice between his tribe and her, he would never give up his duty.

'You are a king,' she murmured, touching her hand to his brow where the *minn oír* rested. 'And always will be.'

She stepped back, the fierce pain of letting him go filling her up inside. A thousand regrets passed between them.

When he'd gone, Isabel watched the wooden door for a long time. And wondered why in heaven's name she had been foolish enough to fall in love with a man she could never have.

Chapter Fourteen

Summer waned, and Lughnasa drew closer. The corn had grown ripe and some of the ears would be ready to harvest. Patrick stood, surveying his land when two horsemen drew near. He recognised the orange and crimson colours of the Ó Phelan tribe.

Though he didn't know what they wanted, their presence was uninvited. Weeks ago, Donal Ó Phelan had not accepted his *corp-dire* offering, as compensation for his wounds. Though Patrick knew he could have pressed further in the Brehon Courts, he suspected Donal had another payment in mind instead of silver.

He stepped away from the corn, his hand palming his sword. He didn't trust the Ó Phelan men.

The men dismounted, and each raised a knee in courtesy. Patrick nodded acknowledgement, but wondered why they had come.

Two of his tribesmen emerged from the cornfield, joining alongside him. A single magpie flew past the men, an ill omen.

'Our chieftain sends his greetings,' one of the messengers

began. 'He sent us to ask that you meet him tomorrow at sundown on the hill of Amadán.'

'And what does he wish to discuss?' Patrick knew better than to believe Donal Ó Phelan wanted a conversation. The chieftain held grudges, and he did not want the man desiring vengeance against Isabel.

'He desires a truce between our tribes and an alliance. He offers this as a token of good will.' One man dismounted from his horse, offering Patrick the reins. The grey gelding was a prime piece of horse flesh, but he had no desire to accept a bribe.

'Tell Donal I will meet with him. But I've no need of his horse.' Patrick dismissed the men, but kept a close eye upon them.

As he passed through his lands, he watched the people preparing for Lughnasa. Young girls busied themselves stringing garlands of flowers. His men practised with weapons, working to perfect their archery. Many would compete in the games over the next few days.

It made him think of Isabel and the way she had defended them with her bow. Her skill was undeniable. But though she could have defeated any of their kinsmen in the contests, he bridled at the idea of Normans joining the ceremony. Even his wife.

Their rituals were as old as Eíreann itself, and he did not want to risk angering the gods. But he didn't like leaving her behind either. She was trying the best way she knew how, to be a good wife. It humbled him.

Sunlight glimmered upon the waters. Though he had granted Isabel a boat of her own, not once had she made use of it to come to the mainland. Though she claimed it was near to Sosanna's birthing time, he suspected she was avoiding him.

She had withdrawn from him and from the islanders. Annle told him that she had stopped visiting the others, save herself and Sosanna. It was as if she meant to isolate herself in preparation for her departure.

He blamed himself for her unhappiness. She deserved a better husband, a better life than this. He mounted his horse and rode along the pathway leading to Laochre. The late summer sun warmed his face, and all around he could see the harvest ripening. In the distance lay the hill of Amadán. On the morning of Lughnasa, the entire tribe would climb to the top of the hill and bury the first ears of corn as an offering to Crom Dubh.

And tomorrow, he would meet with Donal Ó Phelan and discover exactly what the man wanted. Patrick drew Bel to a stop, murmuring words of praise to the animal. Then he gazed out upon the sea.

A glimmer of white appeared on the horizon. At first he thought it was a flock of gulls diving for fish. But when he shielded his eyes, he recognised it as three ships.

The Baron of Thornwyck had come. He was sure of it. And with the Norman's impending arrival, the day turned from promising to threatening. He predicted at least fifty men, if not more.

His men caught up to him and saw the direction of his gaze. 'Should we arm ourselves, my king?' one asked.

'You should. But no one attacks unless I give the command. We will see what Thornwyck's intentions are first.' And if the Baron intended war, they would meet their fate.

He'd known this moment would arise. His men had trained for it ever since he'd brought Isabel home as his wife. They would fight the enemy if needed, and if they seized victory, the Normans would leave, once and for all.

Including his wife. After this, he would set her free.

He should have felt a sense of relief, but instead, a part of him felt empty. He admitted to himself that he'd miss her. A more courageous woman he'd never met. But it was the right thing to do. She would gain the life she deserved, among folk who treated her with respect.

After the battle ended, if he and his men survived, he'd petition the Archbishop, Arthur of Bardsey, for an annulment. Arthur had not yet returned to his seat in Wales after his consecration in Ireland, and Patrick knew Isabel's dowry could become the bribe needed to end their marriage.

To the other man he commanded, 'I'm going to meet with the Baron. Be prepared to defend Laochre.'

He urged Bel forward, racing towards the coast. If he could divert the Baron away from Laochre, it would grant his men more time to prepare for the invasion. Edwin could meet with his daughter upon Ennisleigh, and there Patrick could learn the Baron's intentions.

He steeled himself for what was to come.

Isabel could not help but smile when she saw the ships. She rowed out to meet them, recognising the soldiers' wives and children. For a long time, she had wondered whether Edwin de Godred would send them. She had specifically asked him not to come with the women, for his own presence would impede her efforts.

He hadn't listened. Standing at the bow of the ship, her father wore his best armour, trimmed with gold and silver. His hair appeared greyer than the last time she'd seen him, the lines of age a little deeper around his eyes. When he saw her, he did not smile.

Her stomach tightened with fear, and she wanted

suddenly to turn the boat around. But it was too late for that. Instead, she rowed closer, inwardly prepared for his disapproval.

When she reached the first boat, one of the men helped her climb onto the vessel, tying her boat alongside theirs. She estimated approximately thirty people in each boat, a mixture of families, mostly women.

'Father,' she said softly. She was glad she had worn the silver torque this day, along with a white *léine* and a ruby overdress to show her rank of queen.

Edwin's gaze inspected her, and he frowned. There was no embrace of welcome, only a critical eye. 'Why would the queen of Laochre approach alone, with no escorts?'

Isabel ignored the question. 'We will speak of it later.' To the women and children she smiled. 'I am glad you have come.' The children hushed, a few of their eyes widening. 'I bid you welcome to Erin. We will go to one of the smaller fortresses first, where you may rest and refresh yourselves. I will send word to your husbands and the other men of your arrival.'

Edwin gripped her arm. 'Why are you avoiding Laochre?' he demanded. 'As queen, you—'

'As queen, it is my right to decide where it is best to bring the women and children.' She kept her tone calm, though her knees were shaking. She would not risk taking them to Laochre. Already she would have a good deal of explaining to do, and Patrick would not be pleased. But thank the saints, Edwin had only brought a dozen knights as escort instead of an army.

'You have much to explain, Daughter,' he said. 'When we reach land, I wish to have words with your husband.'

Isabel inclined her head. 'As you will.'

One of the women near to her age dropped to her knees, lowering her head. 'Thank you for sending for us, Lady Isabel. We have missed our husbands over the past year.'

'Can we not go to them now?' one of the younger mothers asked. She carried an infant in her arms, a child the father had likely never seen.

'They are training,' Isabel said, 'and you will see them after sunset.'

When they reached the shores of Ennisleigh, she led the families into the ringfort, and bid them gather in the donjon. Though several of the islanders saw them while working in the fields, they turned away as though she'd betrayed them.

Isabel hid her own dread, praying that somehow she had not brought more problems among them. When she reached the interior of her donjon, the sounds of excited conversation, crying infants, and whining children soon filled the space.

Her father sat in the high chair at the end of the Great Chamber, waiting. His knights surrounded him, and Isabel brought food and drink to all of them.

Over the next hour, she helped distribute food, sent the children off to play, and helped arrange pallets for the younger ones. When at last the needs of each person were met, Edwin stood. 'We will talk privately now.'

There was no avoiding it. She led him out of the Great Chamber and paused at the threshold of her room. Fresh rushes covered the floor and she had made small woven tapestries for the walls. In her chamber, gone was the straw pallet she had once slept upon. In its place stood a canopied bed of sturdy oak. The rich blue coverlet, dyed with woad, was part of her dowry, as well as the goose-feather mattress. Soft cream curtains hung down around the bed to keep the heat within.

She gestured towards a chair. 'You may sit down.'

Her father remained standing, displeasure tightening his features. 'Where is your husband?'

'At Laochre, I imagine.' She sat down in another chair, folding her hands. Her nerves had grown steadier, and she saw no reason to hide the truth. 'I live here.'

Edwin's expression darkened. 'I arranged this marriage to make you a queen, not an exile.'

'You arranged the marriage to gain control of Laochre. But our men and the Irish are enemies still.' She met his gaze directly. 'Nothing has changed in the time since I've come here.'

Especially her marriage. Though Patrick had softened towards her, she was still a virgin. And though he'd claimed that nothing was the matter with her, it wounded her pride to think of his denial.

'I should have known you could not manage ruling a kingdom.' Edwin crossed his arms and shook his head with exasperation. 'But it won't matter. In a matter of days, the Earl of Pembroke's army will arrive here. I will be joining them.'

Isabel's heart bled at the thought of another battle. 'What do they want?'

'Conquest,' Edwin said. 'The Earl of Pembroke has come to aid King Dermot MacMurrough in regaining his kingdom. Dermot has promised the Earl his daughter's hand in marriage.'

She shivered, sympathising with the Irishwoman's plight. But another matter concerned her more. 'Will they attack Laochre again?'

Her father narrowed his gaze. 'That all depends on how cooperative your husband is.' His anger seemed to escalate. 'But I can see already that he has not followed the terms of our agreement.'

'He wed me, as you ordered.' Needles of fear pricked at her, wondering what else he'd wanted.

'You are not carrying his babe.'

She blanched and shook her head. With a frank appraisal, her father added, 'And I would wager you're still a virgin.'

Isabel's mouth tightened, and she did not answer. Her father expelled a curse. 'I might have expected this.'

Heavy footsteps approached the chamber. Isabel rose and moved towards the door. It flew open and her husband stood glaring at her and Edwin de Godred.

Patrick had not donned the finery of a king, but even in a soldier's garb, his presence commanded her. His sun-warmed skin peeked from behind a leather corselet while the grey tunic accentuated the steel of his eyes. Isabel could hardly breathe, for he looked upon her as though he wanted to take her apart with his bare hands.

He didn't speak, but closed the door behind him. His furious stance made her wonder exactly what to say.

'Hello,' she began.

His eyes focused on her, an intense gaze that burned her confidence into ashes. 'What is *he* doing here? And the Norman women and children?'

Isabel didn't quite know how to answer, since anything she said would only fuel his anger.

But it was Edwin who replied. 'I told you I would come at the end of harvest to see to my daughter's welfare and to ensure the terms of your surrender.'

'You've brought more Normans upon my island,' Patrick accused. 'Those were never part of our terms.'

Isabel was about to confess that it was her idea, but Edwin strode forward to face Patrick.

'It was never part of the terms for my daughter to remain a virgin. And she is, isn't she?'

'No child of your blood will ever sit upon the throne of Laochre,' Patrick proclaimed.

The fury upon her father's face made Isabel long for an escape. Her cheeks burned with humiliation, and they spoke as if she weren't there. She stood, fully intending to leave. But Patrick blocked her path.

'Within days, the armies of the Earl of Pembroke will invade these lands,' Edwin answered. 'But they will leave you in peace if I ask it.'

'I am not hiding behind your men,' Patrick gritted out.

'You will do as I command, in order to save your people's lives,' Edwin countered. 'This marriage will not be annulled.'

'Won't it?' Patrick's voice dropped to a low pitch, though Isabel recognised the contempt behind it.

'Let me go,' she murmured to her husband. 'I don't wish to hear any more of this.'

'You aren't going anywhere,' Edwin said. 'This marriage will be consummated now, and there will be no divorce.'

'Father, please. This isn't your concern.'

'It is. This marriage will be binding or I will let the Earl's men do whatever they like to these lands. They can slaughter the entire tribe, for all I care.'

Hot tears gathered in her eyes. Isabel sank down in the chair, wishing both of them would leave. Caught in the middle, she sensed that Patrick could not win this argument.

Patrick opened the door and glared at Edwin. 'Get out.'

Her father held his ground. 'It is your choice, MacEgan. I want to see the evidence of my daughter's bedding. You won't be ending this union. And my grandsons *will* be among the kings of Erin.'

While her husband forced her father to leave the room, Isabel could not stop the tears from falling. She had feared Edwin's arrival, but she'd not expected him to go this far.

Patrick bolted the door and removed his cloak. He moved towards her like a predator, not a trace of mercy written on his face.

'You heard his orders.'

'Don't, please,' she whispered, lifting her face to meet his. 'Not like this.'

He unlaced his tunic, revealing the carved muscles from his training. Only a few nights ago, she had desired to touch him, to feel his skin against hers. But now he had become the warrior once more, unreachable.

She turned away, tears burning her cheeks.

His hands touched her shoulders. 'I am sorry, *a chara*.' He moved her hair aside, drying her tears. Then he raised her to stand before him.

Powerful and sleek, her husband intimidated her with his strength. Her body trembled with the knowledge of what he must do. 'Patrick,' she breathed.

His hand moved up her back, the lazy touch prickling across her skin beneath the thin layer of fabric.

'I won't hurt you,' he said brusquely. Before she could say another word, his mouth crashed down upon hers. Isabel clutched at him for balance, her mind hardly able to think. The forbidden heat of his mouth, and his hands moving over her skin made her burn for more.

He lifted away her overdress, his mouth hungry upon hers. Isabel clung to him, trying to silence her fears. But when he lowered her *léine* and bared her skin, she tried to cover herself.

Patrick trapped her hands at her sides, looking upon her with intensity. Though she had wanted him to share her bed at the gathering, now she was afraid. This was a man trapped by duty, infuriated by her father's will. Not a husband who wanted to touch her.

With a kiss, he conquered her, battling for control. He placed her hands upon his chest, and Isabel felt the violence of his heart beating. She moved her hands over the firm muscles, and then drew her hands lower to his hips.

His hard arousal rubbed against her, and her breath splintered, her womanhood responding by growing moist.

In a single motion, Patrick picked her up and lowered her on to the bed.

Inside, this was killing him. He wanted her; there was no question of that. But he resented being forced into this.

He caressed her hips, moving down her thighs, and she jerked. 'Shh,' he whispered, opening her legs. With his hands, he teased her womanhood, stroking her until she trembled. He inserted a finger and felt from the wetness that she was ready for him.

He removed his trews and covered her body with his own. Guilt and resentment flayed him, for he wanted to join with his wife. The Baron's command infuriated him, but, worse, he craved touching Isabel. He didn't deserve taking pleasure from this moment.

Patrick closed his eyes, steadying his willpower. He shouldn't do this, for it would make it even more difficult to end the marriage. But instead, the softness of her silken skin, the sweetness of her, invaded his mind and drove out all reason.

He poised at the entrance and slid himself inside, inch by inch until he felt the barrier of her maidenhead. Then he plunged inside her and broke the fragile membrane.

Her cry of shock caught him like a fist in the gut. Had he hurt her? Shame invaded, and he watched her face for signs of pain.

He moved inside her a few times, but then stopped. At the moment, he despised himself for what he'd done. He could have shed a few drops of blood on the sheets without even touching her. Edwin de Godred wouldn't have known the difference.

But selfishly, he'd seized this moment, wanting to be with her. And she hadn't known any pleasure at all.

He withdrew without letting himself come to fulfilment. Upon the sheets he saw the evidence of her lost virginity.

'Are you all right?' he managed to ask.

Her face was pale and stricken. Isabel turned away, sitting with her back to him as she pulled the *léine* over her bare skin. The silence cut him like a blade, and he dressed quickly, stripping off the sheets.

'I am sorry, *a stór*,' he murmured. As he left her chamber, he damned himself for what he'd done.

Chapter Fifteen

Isabel stood beside the window, staring outside at the crowd gathered. The women mingled inside the ringfort, smiling and anxiously awaiting their husbands.

She hugged her waist, feeling numb about what had just happened. Her body ached, and her heart was hurting. Patrick had started to treat her like a lover, arousing feelings deep within her. And then he'd stopped. Without any warning at all, he had joined their bodies and ended it.

Why? Did he loathe touching her that much?

A soft knock came at the door, but she gave no reply.

'Isabel?' The voice of her father intruded, and she heard the door creak open.

She didn't know what he wanted now, nor did she particularly care. Hadn't he done enough? 'What do you want?'

'Are you—did he—?' Her father seemed at a loss for words. Good. He deserved it, after what he'd forced.

'Aye.' She turned to face him, clenching her hands behind her back. 'It's done now, and I think you've interfered with my marriage enough. I want you to leave us. Go and join whatever armies you like, but don't return here.' Her face grew taut with anger. 'And see to it that the Earl stays far away from here.'

Her father's expression turned uncomfortable. 'I only wanted to make you a queen, Isabel. You could not have wed a more powerful man had you remained in England.'

That much was true. But Patrick's power was the last thing she wanted. She wanted only a man who could care for her, and perhaps give her children one day. A husband, not a king.

'Please go,' she whispered.

Edwin looked as though he wanted to cross the room and offer an embrace, but he didn't. His face furrowed, but at last he nodded and left her alone.

Isabel helped the women cook for most of the afternoon, and more than a few ladies waited nervously upon the shore for a sign of their husbands. Her own nerves were wound up tightly, for she knew not whether she would see Patrick this night. She had taken extra care with her appearance, both longing to see him and afraid of what he might say.

Thank the blessed saints, her father had gone. And though she understood the forthcoming threat of invasion, she wanted to pretend that all would be well.

The first boats arrived as the sun drenched the horizon in bronzed red. For the first time, she saw the Norman men smiling. A few of the women wept tears of joy while their husbands kissed them heartily. She watched one soldier's face transform with awe at the sight of a newborn babe. The babe reached out to touch his father's face, and Isabel stood transfixed at the sight.

Her smile of welcome strained when there was no sign of Patrick. Although she moved among the folk, ensuring that all had enough to eat or drink, her spirits fell. It grew worse when the folk began to pair off, after the children had gone to sleep.

She remained outside the donjon, stepping past couples who kissed in darkened shadows. With each step, her heart felt heavier.

When she reached a more isolated part of the island, she sat against a large stone, listening to the waves. She had let herself get her hopes up, wishing Patrick would return. She wanted to talk with him, to understand what had happened between them this morn.

And then, as if emerging from the dark sea, her husband climbed over the rise of the hill. The sky had grown dark with only the moon to illuminate his presence. The silver rays gleamed against the black of his hair.

'I almost did not come,' he said, his voice deep.

Isabel did not stand, but turned back to the water. 'Why did you?'

He knelt down beside her. 'To apologise.' He took her hand, and said, 'You didn't deserve what I did to you.'

She closed her eyes. 'It had to happen sooner or later.'

'Not that way.' He released her hand, contrition etching his face. 'I allowed my temper to gain the better of me.'

His cheek was smooth, his jaw tense. Isabel could see the deliberation in his eyes, the frustration. And she held the power to soothe it.

She stood and touched her palms to his shoulders. Patrick drew her closer until she could feel his body against hers. Though his grasp was easy, she sensed his desire.

'Why did you bring the women here?' he asked. 'I forbade it.'

'Because I am not convinced that our people cannot join together,' she whispered. 'The Normans need someone to fight for, someone to protect. Who better than their own loved ones?'

'My tribesmen won't allow it.'

'They could stay upon the island,' Isabel offered.

'There is not enough space. Even now, I do not know where you plan to house them.'

'The night is warm,' she reminded him. 'The men and women will need no huts for shelter. This evening the island will be filled with lovers.'

Her skin felt flushed, her body awakened to desire. She tried to calm the tempest raging within her, but she wanted nothing more than to remain here with him, to finish what they had begun this morning. Like the other men and women, she wanted to surrender to her husband's desires.

'What is it you want from me, *a stór*?' he asked. In his dark grey eyes, she saw tumult and indecision.

'I want my husband. Not a king,' she whispered. She wanted the man she sensed he could be, a passionate lover who would fulfil the desires kindling inside of her.

'I cannot give up being a king,' he said. 'It is my burden to shoulder.'

She was afraid of that. 'What will happen to us now?'

He traced the line of her jaw, touching his nose to hers. 'I don't know.' His honesty made her feel even more vulnerable, afraid to seize this moment. Afterwards, everything would go back to the way it was before. He would reign over Laochre while she remained behind on Ennisleigh. And she didn't know if she could bear it.

'Will you grant me one night?' she whispered. Though she was afraid of being hurt again, she saw past his hesitation. Without the threat of her father, with just the two of them alone, could he not set everything else aside?

'I hurt you this morn,' he argued.

'Aye, you did.' She reached up and wound her arms around his neck. 'So make me forget what happened.'

elighted in the wickedness of his mouth. Her hips moved
gainst him, cradling his length against her.

She met his touch with her own hunger, both afraid and
desperately needing him. Her womanhood ached for the
fullness of him inside of her.

'Am I still your enemy?' she whispered.

'Not tonight.' The deep baritone of his voice wrapped
around her like an embrace. He brushed his hands across her
warmed flesh. 'Tonight I intend to make you suffer the way
you've tormented me for the past months. I'm going to love
you until you can't stop shaking.'

He wrapped them in his cloak, a cocoon of warmth. When
he kissed her again, Isabel wrapped her arms around his waist,
palming his buttocks. The tightness of his muscles fascinated
her, and he groaned when she opened her legs, letting him rub
his length against her wetness.

She could hardly breathe from the pleasure of sensations
filling up inside of her. His hand reached between her legs and
he slipped a single finger inside her. With slow, easy strokes,
he kindled her arousal, rubbing her womanhood until she
arched against him.

'Patrick,' she moaned, needing him inside her. She touched
him, running her hands over his chest and shoulders. 'Please.'

Instead of answering her plea, he bent his head to her
breasts once more, tonguing her nipples until she cried out.

Her hand closed over his hardened manhood, stroking him.
Patrick's expression shadowed, and he hissed as she explored
the texture of his skin. He felt like warm satin, and she was
surprised to hear his answering groan when she cupped hir

'Enough,' he growled. He trapped her hands beneath h
spreading her legs apart with a knee. Then she felt the thic
of him at her entrance, slowly penetrating her. It was not

With that, Patrick stepped back and unfastened the br
that pinned his cloak. He spread the garment on the g
before them, like a blanket.

'One night,' he swore.

Her heart thrummed against her chest, the anticipatic
filling every part of her. His hands caressed her hair, and h
mouth skimmed over her temple.

He whispered endearments in Irish, words she had only just
come to understand. As he undressed her, Isabel shivered.
Bared before him with only the moonlight, the fears and
doubts threatened to consume her.

But then, he disrobed, standing before her like a pagan
immortal. His warrior's body captured her attention, with
carved muscles and a few white scars that stood out from his
golden skin.

He laid her down upon the woollen cloth, covering her
chilled skin with his flesh. His erection rested upon her
stomach, his hands moving over her skin.

'You're the most beautiful woman I've ever seen,' he
murmured, kissing her throat.

Her breasts tightened, aroused by the feel of his body against
hers. His skin blazed with heat, his mouth lowering to the
hardened tip of her nipple. When he tasted her, the shocking
sensation pulsed a wave of delicious agony through her body.
His hands moved over her skin, touching every part of her.

'I wanted you from the first moment I saw you,' he con-
fessed. 'Even when you tried to run from me.'

'I thought you hated me,' she whispered.

'I hated myself for weakening to an enemy.' He kissed her
houlder, turning his attention to the other breast. With soft
rcles, he teased her with his tongue. At the tip of her nipple,
sucked hard and she fisted her hands in his cloak. Her body

this morning. He moved with no haste, letting her stretch to accept him. When he was fully sheathed inside her body, he stopped moving. For a moment she wondered if it was over.

And then he lifted up and began to move inside her. Trembling waves of arousal crashed over her, as a frenzy of desire seemed to build and shift. He increased his movement, filling her and withdrawing, building up the pace until something tightened deep within her womb. The startling sensations built up higher and higher until he plunged deeply inside her and she broke apart in his arms. He covered her cry of pleasure with a kiss, still moving.

'I haven't finished with you yet, *a chroí*.' His hands moved over her breasts, lifting and teasing them. Isabel gasped for breath, unable to understand the violent need for him.

He turned her onto her stomach and moved her into a kneeling position. He penetrated her again, grasping her hips and forcing her to accept his length. His erection seemed to grow even harder, and she began to weep at the sensation of him filling her. Over and over, until she sobbed with the aching pleasure.

At last he roared and withdrew from her, spilling his seed upon the ground beside her.

She lay beside him, her bare skin warm. Her body trembled with aftershocks, and she reached out to him. He gathered her in his arms, rolling them up in the cloak.

Isabel buried her face in Patrick's chest, fighting back tears. Somehow, she had known this would exist between them. And she would have to make the most of this stolen night, for soon enough it would be over.

At dawn the next morning, the island was filled with pairs of sleeping lovers. Patrick sat beside his wife, who was curled up in his cloak. His mood had become solemn, for he hadn't ever known it could be like this with a woman. He'd lain with women before, but none had made him feel this way. He wanted to shut out the rest of the world and protect Isabel. His beautiful proud wife, who deserved more than he could give her.

Though he had not planned on waking her, she rose at the sound of his movement.

'Are you going back?'

'I am.' He wanted to kiss her again, to love her the way he had twice more last night. But if he did, he'd never leave. 'Stay with the women until I decide what's to be done with the families.'

She let the cloak fall away, sitting naked before him. Her skin glowed in the morning sun, her body tempting him in an open invitation. 'What are you doing?'

'Getting dressed.' She smiled serenely and picked up her fallen *léine*. The fabric skimmed over her flesh, and he gritted his teeth.

Only when she was fully clothed did he dare look at her again. 'We must gather the people together,' she suggested. 'Today is Lughnasa. You said that every man, woman and child of the tribe climbs up to the top of the highest hill.'

'To Amadán, yes,' he answered, pointing to the gentle rise of a hill upon the mainland. 'But it is only a ritual for my tribe.' He wanted the Normans to take no part in it. Their traditions were their own.

'And what of me?' she asked. 'Do you want me to remain behind as well?'

He didn't know what to say. He should keep her away from the tribe, but with each passing day, he admitted to himself that he wanted her by his side. He wanted her to learn their traditions, to be part of them.

He sobered, knowing that he had to disregard his own feelings and do what was best for the tribe. 'You should stay behind with the others,' he advised. 'My people have endured much over the past season. They are entitled to enjoy their festival without fighting.'

She stared hard at him. 'So this is how it will be. You still will not offer the Normans a place among you. Not even me.'

The pain in her eyes pierced him. 'It is not possible.'

'I thought things might be different now,' she whispered. Hurt surrounded her voice, needling his guilt. 'After last night…' Her voice trailed off, as though she knew not what to say.

He reached out to her, clasping her hand. Her fingers were cold within his palm. 'I am sorry, Isabel.'

Isabel bit her lip. Anger coursed through her veins, for he truly would not accept her as his wife because of her heritage. She had believed he saw past her blood and into her heart. She'd been blinded to him, wanting so much for him to accept her.

She stepped backwards, her skin feeling like ice. 'No, I am not one of you. I can't ever be Irish. And though I've tried to be part of your tribe, it's clear that it will never happen.'

Patrick looked as though he were about to protest, but she cut him off. 'Do not worry. I'll behave like the false queen that I am and not disgrace you.' She picked up her skirts and strode up the path away from him.

He ran past her and stood in front of her, blocking her way. 'You deserve better than us, Isabel. Would that I could change things.'

'You have the power,' she said softly. 'But you've chosen not to use it. You've put them in command of your life.'

'What would you have me do? Give up my duty?'

She didn't answer. He'd already chosen his tribe over her, and nothing she could say would make any difference.

He placed a hand on her shoulder. 'I can still give you your freedom. The Archbishop can grant a divorce—'

Isabel turned her back on him, not waiting to hear the words. She began to run, needing the exercise to release her frustrations. Her mind raged at him, and she ran until her lungs ached. She sat down upon one of the rocks on the far end of the island beach, her heart burning.

This was what she deserved, for letting herself believe they had a chance. He didn't care for her, and in spite of the wonderful night they'd spent together, nothing had changed. She wanted so badly to weep, but she could not change the way Patrick thought.

Ruarc stared at the lights upon the island. This afternoon he had watched the Norman lord depart the island, accompanied by his escort. And yet the enemy women and children remained behind. Patrick had done nothing to stop them.

With each passing month, his desire for vengeance grew stronger. Though Sosanna's time for birthing drew near, not once had she spoken of the man who had harmed her. Ruarc grasped his knife, wishing he could strike the Norman bastard down. He had studied each man over the past few moons, looking for the likely culprit. But he was no closer to finding him.

Rage seethed inside him. Now that the women had come, it meant the Norman soldiers would stay here. He couldn't allow that to happen. And he no longer trusted his king to act in the tribe's best interests.

He took a breath, sheathing the dagger once more. If all went to plan, Patrick MacEgan would no longer be king. And he could drive the Normans forth once and for all.

Chapter Sixteen

In the early afternoon, the MacEgan tribe finished their walk up the hill of Amadán, Patrick stood back while his brother Trahern buried the ceremonial ears of corn. They murmured prayers of thanksgiving and the tribesmen stood together as one. Afterwards, his people enjoyed games and competitions, while the mead flowed freely. Patrick remained upon the hillside while his people journeyed downhill for the blessing of horses within the small river cutting across their lands. From his vantage point, he watched the festivities and awaited the arrival of Donal Ó Phelan. A few kinsmen stayed with him as escorts.

At sundown, the chieftain arrived. Torches blazed along the pathway, while the sky darkened. Donal Ó Phelan raised his hands for silence and regarded Patrick. He raised a knee in deference, then spoke. 'Our tribes have raided one another for many seasons,' he began in a booming voice. 'On the last raid, Isabel MacEgan wounded me with one of your arrows. She is one of the Normans, isn't she? You wed her to save your people.'

Patrick did not deny it. 'What is it you want from me?'

The chieftain did not answer the question. Instead he

remarked, 'The Normans outnumber you.' He gestured towards Laochre where the fortress stood, illuminated by torches. 'And in time they will destroy your tribe. Unless you accept my help.'

Patrick crossed his arms. 'My men are strong enough to defeat any foe.'

'What if my tribe joined with yours?' Donal asked. 'You would have double the forces to overcome the Normans.'

Patrick didn't trust the Ó Phelan chieftain. Donal would never offer to join their tribes, not without a better bargain for himself. 'And what did you want in return?'

'Set your wife aside and wed my daughter. Meara is a beautiful maiden, and she would make a better queen than the Norman you have now.'

His men would approve of the match, but Isabel's words came back to plague him. *You've put them in command of your life.* He had sacrificed his own desires once, wedding Isabel to save his tribe. And the marriage had been nothing like he'd expected. She was impulsive, disobedient…and the most fascinating woman he'd ever known.

'There are greater problems at the moment,' Patrick stated. 'Edwin de Godred informed me that Strongbow is planning another invasion. Their ships will arrive at any moment now, and we must be prepared for them.'

'And what makes you think Strongbow's men will not conquer Laochre?' Donal scoffed. 'They will take the fortress and put a Norman king in your place.'

'They would already have done so, were that true.' He dismissed the idea. 'Your men should prepare for what lies ahead.'

Donal's gaze narrowed. 'I wouldn't trust the Normans. And my offer stands. Set your wife aside and wed my daughter. Send word to us when you've made your decision.'

Patrick stared hard at the man. He refused to let anyone intimidate him, especially not a chieftain whose loyalty he questioned. 'I have made my decision. And the answer is no.'

He turned to walk down the hill. Donal Ó Phelan was not a man he trusted, and he saw no reason to ally himself with the tribe. They'd been enemies for far too long.

Across the water, he saw lights gleaming upon Ennisleigh. Though he had not lingered for long this morn, he had noticed a difference in the Norman soldiers. There was an air of contentment instead of anger. One or two had greeted him with a smile this morn, before he'd left for the mainland. Their sudden change in demeanour surprised him.

Was Isabel right to bring the wives and children? If the Norman soldiers had their women to fight for, would they join together and battle against the Earl of Pembroke with his tribesmen?

There was no question that if the breach could be mended, they would be the most powerful fortress in all of Éireann. No longer would they fear any invaders. Isabel believed it was possible, that the Normans could become part of their tribe. He was beginning to wonder.

His hand moved over the hilt of his sword. Liam's sword. Now the painful memory of his death seemed to be receding. For so long he had walked in his brother's shadow, wanting to be as fine a king as Liam.

He would never be his brother. He could only make his own decisions and hope that they were the right ones.

The wind shifted, blowing a cool breeze across his face. He wanted to go to his wife, to share the night with her once more. But likely she'd turn him away after he'd refused her the right to join in the Lughnasa celebration.

He journeyed down the hill, greeting several tribesmen.

When he came upon Ruarc, he walked alongside his cousin. 'How is your sister?'

Ruarc shrugged. 'Annle says the babe will come at any moment.'

'Have you learned anything about which man harmed her?'

Ruarc raised infuriated eyes to his. 'Would it matter to you? You seem to be more interested in bringing Normans among us instead of protecting those who remain.' He increased his stride, walking away.

Patrick would not let Ruarc away so easily. He caught up to him and gripped his shoulder. 'Do you think I like having them here, any more than you? A greater force is coming, and I mean to be prepared for it. If we war with the Normans now, they will kill every last one of us.'

'I'd rather be dead than live my life a prisoner to their whims.' His cousin's rigid glare could not be convinced otherwise. It was futile asking him to bide his time.

Patrick sat down upon one of the rocks, the wild heather blooming around the hillside. His torch cast off sparks, the light growing dimmer.

Perhaps his cousin was right, and he'd blinded himself to what his people truly needed. If he meant to continue his kingship, he would have to choose between Isabel and the tribe.

And though he knew what the answer had to be, it didn't hurt any less.

Isabel sat beside Sosanna, whose face was white with pain. Sir Anselm had come to fetch her, after he'd learned of the young woman's labour pains.

'Can I do something?' he asked, standing near the door frame while Sosanna closed her eyes at another contraction. Annle hummed lightly while preparing the pallet with clean linen.

Isabel shook her head, hiding a smile. The Norman was behaving like an expectant father, though he had nothing to do with the babe's conception. 'It will be many hours yet.'

The knight muttered something beneath his breath about how women shouldn't have to endure such pain. Though he departed, she saw him hovering, as if finding an excuse to be nearby.

The afternoon merged into evening, and later that night, Sosanna was fighting the pain, crying out with each contraction.

'The babe will be here soon,' Isabel soothed, speaking in Irish to the young woman. Though she had sent word to Ruarc, Sosanna's brother had not yet arrived.

Sosanna gripped her hand, squeezing so hard that Isabel feared she might break her fingers. She bit back her own pain, for it was nothing compared to the woman's.

When the pains only intensified, Isabel's nerves grew more ragged. She had heard of women dying in childbirth, and she prayed to God she would not see it this night. For a moment she felt faint, while the sounds in the hut seemed to come from a faraway place.

Was this what she would endure if she bore Patrick's child? She touched a hand to her midsection, remembering the way he had touched her, making love to her outside.

'Isabel, go outside,' Annle ordered. 'Take some fresh air.'

She obeyed, stumbling out into the night air. Sir Anselm waited outside the hut. In his hands, he held a few springs of heather.

'How is she?'

Isabel shook her head. 'She's in so much pain.'

Anselm pressed the sprigs of heather into her palm. 'I doubt if she would want these, but you might give them to her.'

Isabel's face turned with surprise. 'You care for her.'

The knight nodded, his cheeks brightening. 'She's still afraid of me, I know. I won't bother her.'

'Have you learned any Irish in all this time?' Isabel asked, holding the soft purple flowers.

'A little.' The knight stared down at the ground.

'You could go and speak to her after the babe is born.' Isabel did not mention her worst fear, that Sosanna would not survive the birth.

He gave a sad smile. 'No, I do not think so.'

Isabel fingered the flowers. 'I will give these to her and tell her they were from you.'

He shrugged and nodded, walking towards the edge of the ringfort. Unlike the others, he had no family who had come. He was a lonely soldier, and her heart went out to him.

With reluctance, she turned back to the hut where Sosanna laboured. Her face red, her hair dampened with sweat, the young woman had begun to push.

Isabel came to the opposite side to support her. She took Sosanna's hand and gave her the heather sprigs. 'These are from Sir Anselm,' she said. 'He sends his prayers.'

Sosanna crushed the flowers in her palm as she pushed again. The heather crumbled to the earthen floor, seemingly forgotten. Over the next hour, she fought back until at last a newborn cry emerged. All three women wept, and Annle laid the young child upon Sosanna's stomach.

'You have a son.'

Sosanna caressed her child's head, her tears openly spilling over her cheeks.

Both women fell silent as Sosanna held her babe. Her hands ran over the babe's head, touching the tiny fingers.

'He is beautiful, Sosanna.'

But still the woman did not speak. While Annle helped her

deliver the afterbirth, Isabel walked down to the water's edge of the island, dipping her hands into the cool water.

Though they had triumphed in the face of death, Isabel stared up at the dark sky. No stars glimmered, nor was there a moon. Only when she put her hands to her cheeks did she notice her own tears.

The loneliness and longing for her husband gathered around her. She wished he were here, but more than anything else she wished he were not a king. She wanted an ordinary man, someone to take care of. Someone to love her.

After allowing herself a few more moments of self-pity, she rose and walked back to the donjon. Her shoulders ached from the long night, and her limbs were stiff.

To her surprise, when she entered the dwelling, a bright fire crackled on the hearth. Upon a low table, a cup of wine was poured, and a meal of salted fish, bread and crisp spring peas awaited her. Another platter held cakes drenched in honey, sprinkled with chopped hazelnuts.

A furry motion caught her attention, and she saw her cat Duchess striding across the threshold. The feline appeared confident, as though she owned the dwelling.

When the cat reached Isabel, she stopped and sat. Meowing loudly, she licked her lips.

Isabel couldn't help but smile. 'Would you like some fish?' More meowing.

She ruffled the cat's ears and broke off several pieces of the fish, holding it out. The cat nibbled the fish, purring and rubbing herself against Isabel's legs.

Footsteps caught her attention, and Isabel turned to the door. Her husband walked inside, dropping a sack upon the floor. When he drew nearer, her pulse gave a leap. He moved with silent authority, his body prowling like a wolf towards her.

Isabel remained standing, but her hand curled around the goblet of wine. She took a deep drink as if to gather her courage. Patrick stood before her, not touching her but near enough to make her feel the heat of his body. A muscle in his cheek tightened.

'They told me Sosanna bore a son.'

'She did. It was a difficult birth.' Isabel sat down upon a large pillow beside the low table and took one of the honeyed cakes.

'But she is all right now?' He sat across from her and Isabel nodded.

Her husband watched her across the table, his eyes upon her as though she were one of the honey cakes. But he didn't move to touch her.

She leaned her head upon her hand, resting her elbow upon the table. 'What did you want to speak to me about?'

'Us. Our marriage.' He reached out as if to touch her, but Isabel drew back. Her senses were already in disarray with him sitting so near to her. She could smell the scent of pine about him, from walking out of doors.

'What about it?'

'Donal Ó Phelan asked me to set you aside and wed his daughter.'

She should have expected this. The chieftain of their rival tribe would certainly prefer an alliance with Laochre.

'And you told him yes?' Although she kept her voice calm, inside she felt as though a thousand knives were carving up her heart. Of course he would agree. Though she didn't know when he would petition the Archbishop for a divorce, enough money would buy anything.

'I refused his offer.' He stood from the low table and offered her a hand to help her up.

She sensed an underlying threat and crossed her arms. 'Why? Isn't that what you do? Wed women in order to keep the peace?'

A blackness descended over his calm, and he took hold of her waist. 'No. That isn't what I do at all. I came to tell you of his offer because you would know it soon enough. You deserved to hear of it from me, not them. And I came to ask your counsel.'

She expelled an angry laugh. 'What counsel? On whether to marry her in a fortnight or next season?' Her anger was so great, she wanted to lash out at something. She kicked the low table, satisfied when some food splattered to the floor. 'On whether to wear your blue tunic or your brown one to the wedding?'

He captured her, gripping her arms beneath his strength. Isabel fought him, but it was like trying to free herself from stone.

Lowering his voice to her ear, he murmured, 'I wanted to know your desires. Do you still want your freedom?'

The husky tone of his voice, coupled with the nearness of his mouth, made her cheeks flush. His body was pressed up against hers, and she felt every inch of his lean, muscled frame.

'Why are you even asking me this? You will choose whatever is best for your tribe. And we both know that I am not what they want.'

He didn't speak, but reached up to stroke her hair. Isabel stepped back, lowering her head. 'You know the truth, Patrick. I cannot stay here.'

'You want a divorce, then?'

She wanted to cry out *no*, to deny it. More than anything she wanted to stay with him, to be a beloved wife. But even if he did not wed Ó Phelan's daughter, another offer might come. She did not fool herself into believing that their marriage would ever be permanent.

His hands moved over her spine, caressing her. The length

of his manhood showed the evidence of his need. And saints, she could not ignore her own wild desires. She wanted him to kiss her, to push away all the loneliness welling up inside. To love her.

'Just leave me alone, Patrick,' she whispered. A tear rolled down her cheek, for she could no longer hide the heartbreak she felt. 'I want you to go.'

And perhaps then it wouldn't hurt so much.

Chapter Seventeen

Before the sun rose from the horizon, Patrick reached Ennisleigh. Trahern and Ewan joined him, each in their own boat. It would take many trips to bring all of the islanders and Normans to Laochre.

With each passing day, his nerves strung tighter. Though he was certain the two peoples would resent living together, he did not want his forces divided when the Normans arrived.

He wore the *minn óir* upon his head, the symbol of his kingship. Dressed in his finest clothing, he could only hope that the people would hold their peace this day.

They dragged the boats upon the shore and Trahern and Ewan accompanied him inside the ringfort. Whorls of smoke rose from the chimneys, and he could smell the faint aroma of morning pottage. His stomach rumbled, for he had not broken his fast.

'I will get Isabel. You summon the others,' he ordered. When he entered the donjon, men and women lay sleeping inside, their bodies twined together. He stepped carefully, moving towards his wife's chamber.

Opening the door softly, he found her sleeping on the

bed, the coverlet tangled beneath her long slim legs. Her hair hung in disarray about her shoulders while she slept. Lug, she was beautiful.

He moved with stealth towards the bed and sank down beside her. She didn't stir, and he reached down to kiss her awake. At the first taste of her warm mouth, he lost himself. When it came to Isabel, he had no discipline any more.

He wasn't sure if she was awake or dreaming, but he kissed her with all the pent-up need inside of him. His hands moved over her skin, down to cup the heavy breasts beneath her shift. His thumbs caressed the nipples, and she shuddered.

Then her eyes snapped open and she shoved him away. 'What do you think you're doing?'

'Waking you up.' And the thought of seducing her had crossed his mind as well.

'Why are you here?'

'Because I am bringing everyone to Laochre. If what your father says is true about the invasion, we'll need all the men fighting together.'

She paled, but nodded. 'Leave me, and I'll dress.'

'I've seen you unclothed before,' he remarked. He drew closer, sitting beside her on the bed. 'Unless you require my assistance.'

She drew back the bedcovers. 'I don't need you at all.'

'Don't you?' he whispered. The warm, tempting female skin sent need roaring through him.

He pulled her on to his lap, trapping her in place. He let her feel how much he wanted her, giving her a chance to leave if she would. When she didn't move, he kissed her again, giving rein to the tide of desire rising within him.

His mind cursed the fact that she could not take her place

as queen. They had only stolen moments together, and by God, he meant to make the most of them.

Her bottom twisted against him, and it only made him grow harder. With one hand, he held her waist while his palm slid beneath her shift to her bare breast. He stroked the nipple, heard her gasp when he lifted the shift away. She sat naked in his lap, and he kissed her shoulder, palming both breasts as she stood between his legs.

'Patrick,' she breathed. 'You shouldn't—'

'I know it. There are many things I shouldn't do.' He fought against the vicious desire gripping him. 'Do you want me to stop?'

Silently she shook her head. Her full lips tempted him, her hair falling around her bare shoulders like a Saracen veil. Her breath hitched as he kissed every inch he could reach. He kneaded her breasts, turning her to face him before he captured her mouth again.

Like an invader, he seized his plunder, barely aware of why he had come. All he could think of was his beautiful wife standing naked before him. And gods, he wanted her.

Her hands moved down to his trews, unfastening the ties. He tore at his own clothing, needing her skin against his. She touched him everywhere, her palms against his heart, moving down to the hot length of him. He closed his eyes with the dark pleasure.

Before he lost control, he picked her up and laid her upon the bed. Joining her, he leaned down to kiss her breasts. With his tongue he swirled circles over her skin, until he sucked the nipple deep into his mouth. She let out a low moan, and then he reached down to the centre of her womanhood. He rubbed it with his thumb, watching her strain to meet the pleasure.

Abruptly, he plunged his fingers inside and she cried out, shaking in his arms as the waves overtook her.

He rolled over and lifted her above him to sit upon his manhood. She slid down, wet and hot with desire. For a moment she sat with him inside her, and the intense agony made him want to beg her to move.

He pulled her mouth down to his, lifting her hips to move her. Her nails dug into his shoulders, but she met his rhythm, taking him deep within her womb.

As he made love to her, his sense of possession grew stronger. He didn't want any man to ever touch her, save himself. She belonged to him, and for a moment, he allowed himself to imagine a life with her. Even though it was forbidden to him.

He changed their position, standing up beside the bed. He pulled her hips to the edge of the bed and lifted her, driving deep inside. Her breath shattered and he growled as the fierce pleasure took hold. Before he could spill himself in her depths, he pulled out, his seed spurting beside her.

He had done it without thinking. Crestfallen, she turned away from him.

'Isabel, I didn't mean—'

'Yes, you did. I know you don't want a child. Not by me.'

He stood and got a cloth. While Isabel cleaned herself, he put on his clothing. 'I am sorry.' He tossed her the *léine* and overdress. 'I did not mean to hurt your feelings. You caught me by surprise.'

Isabel moved to a table and picked up her comb. Running it through her hair, she covered it with a veil.

She counted herself a fool for allowing Patrick back into her bed. She'd let herself be ruled by the needs of her body, instead of thinking clearly. And now he wanted her to join him at Laochre with the rest of the islanders and her people. She dreaded it.

Outside the donjon, the folk gathered. Trahern and Ewan had loaded their boats, and a few of the islanders took their vessels, filling them with people. The grey sky released soft drops of rain, coating her skin with a fine mist. Isabel raised her *brat* over her head to shield it from the rain.

She caught a glimpse of her husband watching her, and his gaze seared her with the memory of this morning. Though she understood the reason for bringing all of the people to Laochre, she sensed the disorder it would bring. The lack of space, coupled with the resentment of the Irish, would only increase the tension between the two peoples.

But if they remained separate, the invaders would conquer them all. The women and children remained blissfully ignorant of the circumstances, and Isabel intended to do whatever she could to soothe the animosity between both sides.

The boat rocked gently upon the journey to the mainland. Annle and Sosanna joined Isabel, along with the Norman women and children. The Normans fawned over Sosanna's baby, exclaiming at the sight of the delicate hands and ears. Sosanna glowed with happiness.

At the bow of the boat, Sir Anselm's face softened at the sight of the newborn boy. He offered Sosanna a gruff smile, and her face coloured in response.

Isabel wondered if the pair might not become more than friends. It seemed possible. She tucked her knees in, watching the green coastline. Patrick rowed along with the other men, his muscles flexing. He continued watching her, and her skin warmed under his gaze. Yet the only thread holding her marriage together was the threat of invasion. Though Patrick desired her, his feelings did not run any deeper.

She wanted so badly to believe that he might claim her as his true wife and make her queen of Laochre. More than ever, she wanted to be at his side. But she could not forget Donal Ó Phelan's offer—for Patrick to divorce her and wed his daughter instead.

When they reached the shoreline, the Norman women walked with eagerness, as if anticipating a new home. Children raced ahead, a mixture of both Norman and Irish, laughing when they tripped and collapsed into a grassy heap. Sir Anselm walked beside Sosanna, offering her his arm and letting her take a slower pace.

Patrick brought forth a horse from the small shelter near the coast, a creamy mare. Isabel recognised his own horse Bel, a sleek black stallion. Patrick lifted her atop her saddle, then mounted his own horse.

They rode side by side, not speaking, towards the massive ringfort. She was intensely aware of him, from the fine clothing he wore, to the crown upon his brow. 'How long will we stay at Laochre?' she asked quietly.

'Until the invasion is over. It's safer if we stay together.'

'What if our people fight one another?' she asked. She didn't trust Ruarc not to start another disagreement.

He looked over at her, his own doubts mirroring hers. 'I'll need your help. The women may be of use in keeping the peace.'

It was the first time he'd openly asked for her assistance. Isabel tried not to behave as startled as she felt. 'I will do what I can.'

He said nothing, but stared back at the surrounding landscape. Isabel was surprised to see the expansion efforts at Laochre. In the past few weeks, Patrick had begun plastering the exterior a pure white, to give it the appearance of stone. Just as she'd suggested.

'It looks almost like you're building a castle,' she said, marvelling at the changes. Although it was far from complete, she could see his efforts to transform the fortress into a Norman motte and bailey. Long rectangular wattle-and-daub houses formed barracks for the Norman soldiers.

'You approve of the changes, then.'

'Yes.' She couldn't hide the awe in her voice. Wooden scaffolding stood high above the donjon, while men worked to build battlements.

'Sir Anselm sent one of his men, Roger, to help with the designs. He worked on the plans for Thornwyck's castle, as I understand.'

'It isn't quite the same as my father's.' She noted differences in the structure. 'How long will it take you to finish it?'

'Years, most likely. That is, if no one attacks us again.'

When at last they reached the inner bailey, she handed the horse to a stable lad and followed Patrick inside his dwelling. She lowered the *brat* from her hair, drawing the shawl across her shoulders. The interior of the donjon, though still needing decoration, had been cleaned and fresh rushes were scattered. The trestle tables had been pushed to the side, providing a large gathering space. Baskets filled with bilberries stood waiting.

'We will speak with the people here,' he said. 'I want them to know what lies ahead.'

Isabel drew the ends of her shawl closer. 'What do you mean, "we"?' He didn't expect her to address the people, did he? Her nerves tensed at the thought.

'You will address the Normans while I speak to the Irish.' He reached into the basket and lifted out a ripe bilberry. As if to bribe her, he brought it to her lips. She tasted the blue berry, its sweetness spreading over her tongue.

Her heart quickened with fear. 'They would never listen to me, Patrick.'

'Can you not pretend to be a queen? They will heed your command.' She doubted it, but let him lead her up to the dais.

Through the door opening, she could see the people approaching. Her hands felt like they'd been frozen in ice, her pulse racing. She hated speaking in front of large groups. Saints, even her knees were shaking.

As the Normans and islanders filled the Great Chamber, they were forced to stand shoulder to shoulder. Once all had arrived, almost a hundred men, women, and children filled the space. Isabel noticed that hardly any of the people of Laochre had come; only the folk from Ennisleigh. Most of the Irish stood on Patrick's side while the Normans stood on her own side.

Isabel wanted nothing more than to flee, to hide beneath a table. But her feet remained rooted, even as she fought to keep her composure.

'I will speak in Irish,' he said in a low voice. 'Translate for me into your own language.'

'But my Irish is not good enough yet,' she protested. 'I do not know all of your words.'

'You know enough,' he said, squeezing her hand. Addressing them he began, 'People of Laochre, we are about to face another invasion.'

And so, as he spoke, Isabel translated for her own folk. They listened without interrupting, nodding their heads when she spoke of the difficulties they would encounter. As time drew on, she relaxed, realising the enormous trust Patrick had placed in her.

He had granted her the chance to be queen, even if only for a short time. It humbled her, and she suddenly understood the immense responsibility of caring for her tribe and her folk. He'd given her that gift. She straightened, finding the strength inside to be the queen he needed her to be.

'If we are to survive what is ahead,' Patrick continued, 'we must not divide our forces.'

A few of the people looked uncomfortable, but did not voice their opinions. When Patrick had finished speaking, somehow Isabel found the courage to speak on her own.

'We will face many enemies in the coming weeks,' she said, 'and the tribes do not want us to join together. Look around you,' she said, gesturing towards the immense crowd. 'They wish to keep us apart because they know that no tribe in all of Erin can defeat us if we stand beside one another. If we falter from this path, they will destroy us.'

Patrick translated her words into Irish for the islanders. But there were no sounds of approval, only a sullen silence. Isabel's face flushed. Had she overstepped her bounds?

Her husband dismissed the people, ordering the soldiers to bring their wives and children to the barracks.

'Where were your people?' Isabel asked Patrick in a low voice. 'The only Irish folk I saw were the islanders.'

'Likely hiding in their homes,' Patrick replied. 'They will answer for it later.' He followed the others, and Isabel hung back in the Great Chamber.

She stepped down from the dais, studying the interior. The empty space on the walls made her wish for her loom to weave tapestries and other decorations. For a moment she stood in the space alone, wishing she could stay. Although Ennisleigh had become a home, Laochre was a castle of dreams.

She stared at the two chairs on the far end of the room, one for Patrick, and the other for his queen. Looking at the carved wooden chair made her wonder if another woman would ever sit there.

Would he reconsider Donal Ó Phelan's offer? He'd said he would not put her aside, not until the threat of the Norman invasion was past. She blinked, wishing for all the world that she could be a part of this kingdom.

As she neared the door frame, she saw Sosanna waiting with her child in her arms. A few of the Norman women milled around near the entrance, speaking quietly. One of them moved forward and curtsied. 'Queen Isabel, what may we do to help? The others won't speak to us.'

Isabel glanced outside at the stone huts, understanding that the Irish were silently rebelling against the visitors. 'I need to prepare the Great Chamber for our guests and also arrange the food for the afternoon meal.'

She turned to Sosanna. 'Will you help the women?'

Sosanna looked down, her face showing her dismay. Isabel reached out and took the young woman's hands in hers. 'I need your assistance.'

The woman looked doubtful, but then Sir Anselm entered the fortress. In halting Irish he asked about the young mother's health. *'Conas tá tú?'*

Sosanna nodded and managed a faint smile. She lifted the infant to her shoulder, patting him lightly.

'You...sit.' Anselm's Irish was barely understandable, but he gestured for her to rest.

'Anselm, will you help Sosanna find a place where she may sit and help the Norman women work among the others?' Isabel asked.

The knight agreed. He drew close to Sosanna and waited a moment before lifting her into his arms. The young mother did not protest, but looped an arm around his neck, to Isabel's surprise.

One of the Norman women drew closer to Isabel. 'I've

never seen him in such good temper,' she remarked. 'Sir Anselm was one of Lord Thornwyck's best fighters, but I've never seen him smile before.'

'Much has changed,' Isabel replied. 'And I hope you will find a new home here.'

More than that, she hoped the Irish would eventually welcome them. The stony reception did not bode well for the future.

Throughout the morning, the Norman women worked while their children gathered peat for the fires and played games together. Despite their efforts, the tribesmen and women of Laochre kept an awkward silence, behaving as if none of the Normans were there.

Isabel never stopped moving throughout the morning, instructing the Normans, and trying to engage the folk of Laochre and the islanders in the preparations. Whenever she approached one of the people, they stiffened and turned their gaze away as if they didn't see her.

By the noon meal, Isabel was near tears. She gave final instructions to the women and walked up a winding stone staircase to Patrick's chamber, hoping for a moment alone. If she could just have a good cry, she could gather herself together again.

But when she pushed the door open, she saw Patrick standing inside. His earlier finery lay upon the bed while he stood wearing only his trews. It appeared that he was about to change into sparring attire, to train with his men.

'I'm sorry,' she murmured, and turned to leave.

'Don't go.' He approached her, closing the door so she was forced to stay inside. With his bare skin so near, she tried to keep her eyes away from him. But saints, he was a handsome man. She wanted to wrap her arms around his waist, bury her face in his neck, and forget all about the problems with the Irish.

'What is it?' he asked.

'It's been a difficult morning,' she admitted. 'Your tribe won't speak to me or any of the others. They refuse to leave their huts.'

He shrugged. 'It doesn't surprise me. They aren't likely to welcome your people here.'

'I don't know what else to do.' She sat down upon the bed. 'I thought we could bring them together as one. But they won't even try.'

He sat beside her, his expression serious. 'I'm not sure it could ever be done, Isabel. They will always be enemies.'

And with those words, he severed any hope she might have held. Her idea of unifying them was naught but a foolish dream. If Patrick did not believe it could happen among his own people, then it would never happen. Though he sat only a small distance away from her, she sensed the gap widening between them. Not once had he touched her or made any move towards her.

'I should go,' he said, pulling the training tunic over his head.

She veiled her emotions, steadying herself. 'Will you join us for the meal?'

He shook his head. 'Enjoy yourselves. I must speak with my men about our defences for the invasion.'

When he'd left, Isabel touched the ceremonial tunic he'd worn, feeling the heat of his body. And though she longed to release the tears, she held herself back.

Though he had offered her a place at Laochre for the first time, even granting her the status as a queen, it felt impossibly lonely.

Chapter Eighteen

Two nights passed and Patrick stayed away from his wife. Though he shared their chamber, he had slept upon a pallet on the floor. He told himself it was because he needed to dedicate himself to the ringfort's defences. Sleeping with Isabel would only tear his mind apart, leaving him a slave to his body's needs.

But each night, he would watch her sleep for a time, memorising her face. He remembered what it was like to join with her and fall asleep with her body entwined with his.

Though he liked having her with him, he saw the effect upon his people. Isabel worked tirelessly from dawn until dusk, trying to care for everyone, but her efforts only seemed to drive a larger wedge between his tribe and the Normans. The Normans championed her, standing by their lady, while his people stayed far away.

But this morning, a small group of Ó Phelans arrived, joined by their chieftain Donal. Though he didn't like granting them entrance to Laochre, they were joined by two brehon judges. He winced, realising that they had yet to settle the fine for the chieftain's injury.

At his command, the men were permitted entrance.

Strangely, their arrival seemed to provoke a signal. His cousin Ruarc came forward, along with the other members of his tribe. One by one, they joined together inside the inner bailey. A sense of warning pricked inside him, for the folk had not spoken to him in the past three days.

The chieftain of the Ó Phelan tribe came forward. 'King Patrick of Laochre. I offered you marriage to my daughter in an effort to unite our tribes. You refused the agreement.'

Patrick stepped forth and crossed his arms. 'Why are you here, Donal? If it is the matter of *corp-dire*, let us settle the fine for your injury now. We are not here to discuss a marriage.' He ventured a glance at the Normans, grateful that they could not understand the Irish tongue, nor what was happening.

Donal glanced at the tribesmen. 'I made an offer, one that would let you rid yourselves of the Normans once and for all. Do you not think your people would desire it? Instead, you brought more of the enemy among them.'

'You still haven't answered my question.' Patrick crossed his arms, infuriated at the chieftain's arrogance. If the man didn't come to the point soon enough, he'd dismiss them.

The tribesmen stepped aside, and it was then that he saw what they had brought forth—the large stone chair. The chair meant for crowning a new king.

And he suddenly understood why Donal had come. With a grim expression, he said, 'I refuse to bring war among my people. And what you ask me to do is for your benefit, not the benefit of Laochre. My answer is still no.'

'I thought you might say that.' Ruarc spoke, moving towards the brehons. 'And since you have broken your oath to protect our tribe, I am calling for your displacement.'

Rage and betrayal streamed through him. Ruarc's ambitions had brought this, not any desire to keep the tribe safe.

If he persisted in this action, their people would die at the hands of the Normans.

Ruarc addressed their tribesmen. 'I have agreed to wed Meara Ó Phelan and join their tribe with ours. If you will have me as your new king.'

Patrick faced his cousin, the dark anger tightening inside him. He held his temper by the thinnest control. 'You don't know what you are doing, cousin.'

'I will fight you for the kingship,' Ruarc said, raising his fists. 'If needed, I'll prove myself before the people.'

'There is no need for fighting,' Donal said. 'The brehons will allow the people to elect the king they prefer. Unless another man wishes to compete for the right?'

No one stepped forward. Patrick searched the crowd for a sign of his brothers, but none were present. He hadn't seen Trahern or Bevan since last evening, and his suspicions tightened.

Even his youngest brother Ewan was missing. Tension knotted up inside him, and he saw Isabel at the far end of the fortress. Her hands were pressed to her pale cheeks, and she shook her head at him as if trying to prevent what was about to happen.

He knew he could provoke a fight with Ruarc. But the frigid hatred upon the faces of his tribesmen stilled his sword. Even if he defeated his cousin, he could see the truth of what was happening.

As each man and woman approached the judges, giving their answer, he remained standing. And he knew, before the brehons spoke, what the answer would be.

'It is done.' One of the brehons stood and addressed the gathering. 'You have chosen to depose King Patrick and set Ruarc MacEgan in his stead.'

Patrick said nothing. It was like seeing his surroundings through a blurred haze. When the decision was announced, there were no cries of celebration. Patrick took a small measure of comfort in that. But his instincts warned him that the Ó Phelan chieftain was using Ruarc. He didn't for a moment believe that the two tribes would unite.

And *Críost*, the bloodshed. Soon enough, the invading forces would arrive. He feared what would happen when Edwin de Godred learned of this. It would mean war and death to his people.

Ruarc was addressing the crowd now, but Patrick paid little heed to his words. He walked away from them, trying to think of what he could do.

One of the Normans stepped forward. 'My lord, what is happening? None will tell us.'

Patrick forced his attention to the man. If Ruarc intended to wage war against the Normans, it would happen almost immediately. Though he could order the Normans to fight back, he couldn't risk harming his own tribesmen. It was better to pull the men back to Ennisleigh and to find another way of protecting everyone.

'Take your wives and your children, along with all the men, to Ennisleigh. Do it now, and do not protest. I will explain there. Your lives are in danger.'

The soldier nodded and gathered the others. When he began leaving with the large group, Ruarc ordered them to stop. The soldiers continued walking, for they did not understand his words. Several of the islanders joined them, which infuriated Ruarc even more.

'What did you tell them?' he demanded, striding in front of Patrick. 'I am the king now, not you.'

Patrick stared at his cousin. 'You may wear the title. But

you know not what it means to lead the people. You are bringing them to their deaths. What do you intend to do when the Baron of Thornwyck arrives?'

'With our united tribes, we will fight. There will be no more Norman invaders to bother our people.'

'You are a fool if you believe that,' Patrick said. 'If you allow the Ó Phelans to join you, you open yourself to their invasion.'

'You are wrong. And now that I hold the kingship, I'll not allow the Normans to set foot upon Laochre. It will be death to any man who does.' Ruarc set his jaw.

'I have given them sanctuary upon Ennisleigh,' Patrick said. 'They will go there now.'

'You cannot.'

'I can. Ennisleigh belongs to my family. You have no claim upon the land.'

He took satisfaction in Ruarc's fury. Then he turned his back on him in a deliberate insult. Isabel was speaking to some of the soldiers, and she moved to his side.

'We cannot find Trahern, Bevan or Ewan. I don't know what he's done with them.' She glanced behind her, as if Ruarc were listening.

Patrick stilled. If Ruarc had laid a hand on his brothers, he wouldn't hesitate to kill him, new king or not.

He strode back and grabbed Ruarc's tunic, snapping a punch directly into the man's nose. Blood trickled down into Ruarc's mouth. 'What have you done to my brothers?'

Ruarc tried to return his own blow, but Patrick blocked him with his forearm. His rage gave him a greater strength. 'Where are they?'

'They're on Ennisleigh,' Ruarc gritted.

'They had better be unharmed, or you will answer for it.' Patrick released him, shoving him down.

Ruarc stumbled, but managed to right himself. 'Stay out of Laochre,' he commanded. 'You are not welcome here again.'

'I would not set foot upon this ringfort, so long as you are leader.'

It was as though he were walking through a haze of red, he could hardly see through the anger. He blamed himself, for he should have recognised Ruarc's treachery earlier.

They rowed their boats across the channel, and Patrick noticed that Sosanna had joined them. Before they had gone too far, he cautioned, 'Ruarc will send men after you.'

Sosanna only raised her chin and looked away. He didn't know why the young woman would cast her lot with the Normans, particularly after what had happened to her. But then he caught Sir Anselm's gaze. The Norman knight seemed intent on keeping Sosanna safe.

When they reached the shore, Patrick ordered all the vessels brought out of the tide's reach, inside the cavern. With possession of the boats, they could at least avoid more problems from the Ó Phelan tribe.

He strode up the pathway, searching for a sign of his brothers. Within moments he found them, stripped from the waist up and bound to trees in the orchard. Relieved to find them alive, he cut through the ropes and freed them.

Though Trahern and Bevan appeared unharmed, Ewan's eyes were overbright as though he were fighting back tears. 'We did nothing wrong,' he said, sniffing. 'They took us here last night.'

Patrick sheathed his knife. 'Ruarc will pay for what he has done. At the moment, we need to form a council and decide how we will handle this situation.'

To Bevan he asked, 'Can I rely on you to gather the right men? I want to meet with them at the donjon in an hour.'

His brother nodded, rubbing his wrists. Blood caked his skin from where he'd tried to free himself. The sight of it heightened his fury. Ruarc would regret endangering his brothers.

Isabel moved to his side. 'Bring them to the donjon and let me tend their wounds.'

'It's nothing,' Bevan remarked. 'Leave it be.'

Patrick wasn't surprised at the refusal, along with Trahern's assent that he, too, was fine. But Ewan was young yet, and humiliated at being taken captive.

'Ewan, go with Isabel,' he ordered. To Trahern and Bevan, he added, 'Come and quench your thirst while she tends him.'

His brothers followed, and one of the islanders brought them clothing.

Isabel refused to ignore his brothers. She cleansed their raw wrists and offered particular sympathy to Ewan. The extra attention seemed to lift the young boy's spirits, along with the food she offered.

When the men dispersed, she said in a low voice to Patrick, 'May I speak with you alone?'

He nodded. Isabel led him into her private bedchamber, and though Patrick followed without argument, she sensed that he was careful to stay far away from her. At the sight of her own bed, she remembered their lovemaking a few days ago. And it hurt to think of how much had changed since then.

'I feel as though this is my fault,' she murmured. She hadn't even imagined they could take away his rank. In her country, kings were born, not made. But worse, her husband was meant to be a king. She couldn't imagine him living the life of an ordinary man.

'Ruarc was looking for a way to become king. He conspired with our enemy.' Patrick eyed the door, as if deliberating what to do.

'But you are the rightful king,' she whispered. 'You have to take your position back from him.'

'It is not a decision I can make. The people chose to take me from power. That is their right.'

Though his voice sounded calm, his eyes held the edge of pain.

'You sound as though you plan to give up.'

His mouth drew in a firm line, his grey eyes cold. 'I don't care about being king, Isabel. What I care about is my tribe. Ruarc does not see the consequences of what he has done. He cannot overpower Strongbow's men. And I have no doubt that this invasion will happen.'

'What will you do?'

He shook his head. 'I'll meet with the others, and we will decide together.'

'You'll have to attack your own people,' she said quietly. 'He's counting on you not to do that.'

He regarded her with a thoughtful expression. 'I don't think so. We'll prepare our forces and defend our people if necessary. There are other ways to infiltrate the fortress.'

'I hope you are right.' She folded her hands and drew closer. Patrick had a distant expression on his face, and she wished she could do something to help him.

Though her heart had leaped with hope when he'd refused marriage to Ó Phelan's daughter, now she understood the price he had paid. It was far too great.

She placed her hand upon his heart. He didn't move, didn't even look at her. Though he had said nothing, she sensed hidden emotions locked inside him.

'It is all right to be angry,' she whispered. 'You lost a great deal today.'

'No.' He took her hand and removed it. Isabel tried to hold a brave expression, not wanting him to see her discomfiture.

'I haven't any right to feel sorry for myself,' he said. 'What matters most is that Ruarc has brought my tribe into a crisis. I won't stand back and see them suffer for it.'

'What can I do to help you?'

He shook his head. 'There's nothing you can do.' As he left her chamber and closed the door behind him, Isabel ached inside. Their lives had grown even more tangled, and she knew that her presence was only making matters worse.

Chapter Nineteen

Ruarc stood within the inner bailey of the ringfort, surveying the land. The Normans had gone, and the entire Ó Phelan tribe entered the gates, triumphant smiles upon their faces.

A part of him curled up in wariness. He'd won the kingship as he'd hoped, but the MacEgan folk did not share in the celebrating. Although the Normans had gone, he knew they had not seen the last of them.

A few of his tribesmen quietly entered their huts while the Ó Phelans inspected the ringfort. His instincts warned him to be on guard. Though he had agreed to wed Meara, he had not given over Laochre in exchange. The Ó Phelans were behaving as though they had taken control of the land.

'Your men may stay in the soldiers' quarters this eve,' Ruarc offered. 'The wedding can take place in the morning.'

Meara Ó Phelan seemed to be a comely, soft-spoken maiden. He'd barely paid her any notice, but he supposed she would make a fair wife.

He looked to see where his sister was, but Sosanna was not among the MacEgans. He spoke with several members of the tribe, but only one had seen her.

'She went with King Patrick and the others to Ennisleigh,' the woman said.

Ruarc wanted to protest that Patrick was no longer the king, but he knew it would make him sound childish. 'Was she forced to go?'

The woman shook her head. 'She went willingly.'

He didn't want to believe it. Sosanna was terrified of the Normans. Why would she leave the safety of Laochre only to be surrounded by them on the island? He couldn't understand it. His instincts warned him that Sosanna was in danger, especially with the way Sir Anselm watched her.

And as for her child… It was hard for him to look at the infant. His sister should have been happily married by now, not a terrified woman who had lost her will to speak.

He'd wanted so badly to help her, believing that with the Normans gone, she would heal. And now with the Ó Phelan tribe bound to the MacEgans, they had the strength they had lacked before.

Donal Ó Phelan spoke quietly with his men, and Ruarc approached him at last. 'We should talk about the invasion Patrick spoke of. If Strongbow's army is coming—'

'We will discuss it inside,' Donal interrupted. 'Let us drink together and make our plans.'

When he went inside the Great Chamber, at the far end stood the king and queen's chairs. The polished carved wood appeared foreign, and he suddenly stared at the Chamber with new eyes. In his gut, reluctance caught at him.

He'd wanted the kingship so badly, believing that if he held the position, he could rid them of the Normans. He wanted the power to make the decisions. But now that he possessed it, he felt more unworthy than ever. What was he doing, usurping Patrick's place? His instincts warned him that this was wrong. Reluctantly, he led Donal to sit near him while he chose the king's seat.

Donal Ó Phelan signalled to one of his men at the furthest side, and the man lowered a heavy wooden bar across the door.

'There is no need to bar the door,' Ruarc argued. 'We are not under any danger from the Normans.'

Donal smiled. 'No. Not from the Normans.'

His skin turned cold as he regarded the chieftain. 'Are you threatening us?'

Donal laughed. 'There is no threat. You've opened the gates to us. And there are so few of you, it's an easy matter to conquer this fortress.' He raised a goblet of mead, as if in a mock toast. 'To the new king.'

Ruarc reached for his sword, but found a dagger resting against his throat. He grabbed for Donal's wrists, but three other men held him down.

He was dimly aware of blades slicing into him, as he fought to free himself. They dragged him from the chair, pressing his face against the dirt while they bound his hands behind his back.

Gods, what had he done? He had betrayed his king and his people, bringing an enemy tribe among them. Why had he trusted Donal Ó Phelan? He'd been blinded by rage, unable to see past anything but his own vengeance.

'Bind him in the Great Chamber so all can see him,' Donal commanded. 'He'll die at dawn.'

Ruarc closed his eyes, blood dripping down over his face. He deserved this.

In the shadows, a slight figure disappeared. When he turned his head, it had gone.

At night, Patrick gathered a council of both the islanders and Normans, with Trahern to translate. They had spent most of the evening arguing over what to do. Sir Anselm suggested laying siege to the fortress, while Annle's husband Brendan believed they should wait.

'Ruarc will bring about his own demise,' Brendan asserted. 'He lacks the leadership to rule the tribe. And he was never officially given the kingship.'

'They brought the stone chair,' Patrick mused, 'but they did not use it. Why?'

'Because they never intended to crown him king,' Bevan interrupted. 'The Ó Phelans want Laochre and its holdings. I don't like it. They're up to something.'

Patrick let them voice their opinions and speak freely about what to do. When the hour drew late and no decision was made, he called an end to the discussion. 'We will speak more at dawn. Go back to your dwellings.' He turned to the islanders. 'If any of you are willing to open your homes to the Normans who need shelter, it would be appreciated. Our donjon has little space.'

The men hesitated, but when Annle touched her husband's arm, Brendan relented. 'Anselm and a few of his men may come into our home.'

Once he had agreed, a few others reluctantly voiced an invitation. They left in small groups until only a half-dozen families remained in the donjon.

Patrick turned and saw Isabel standing near the door to their chamber. She extended a hand in invitation. 'It has been a long night for you.'

He wished he could close the distance and join her. But if he did, he'd spend the night making love to her instead of giving his attention to the problem of his people.

'It has.' He didn't move but instead rested his hands upon his knees. 'Go on to your chamber and sleep.'

'What about you? Are you not going to join me?'

He shook his head. 'I'm going to walk outside for a while.' After all that had happened, he needed to clear his mind, to decide what to do.

'Shall I come with you?'

'No. I would rather be alone.' He stood and walked outside the dwelling. The night air chilled his skin, so he drew his cloak around him. The familiar sounds of people talking, mixed with babies crying and couples making love, surrounded the air. Though none had spoken to him of the loss of his kingship, he suspected they had talked extensively amongst themselves.

He had never truly felt like a king while the rank had been his. But now, instead of feeling like a burden was lifted, the strain had increased.

He blamed himself for letting this happen. He should have banished Ruarc long ago, for his cousin could not conceive of the greater threat.

Patrick walked down to the water's edge, the black sea gleaming against a silvery moon. A flickering light cast a golden glow upon the water, and he saw a solitary vessel moving towards the island.

He narrowed his gaze, not understanding how anyone could have found a boat in such darkness. But as the solitary figure drew closer to shore, his face broke into a smile. It was his younger brother Connor MacEgan, back from his travels.

Connor had spent most of his childhood at Banslieve, several days' journey from here. They had expected him to return at any moment.

He raised a hand, signalling his brother. When at last Connor arrived, Patrick helped him pull the boat upon the strand before embracing him.

'It has been a long time,' Patrick said in greeting. Connor had gained the height and stature of a warrior, though his face still held traces of adolescence. With dark gold hair and grey eyes, Connor had captured more than one maiden's heart upon his rare visits to Laochre during his fostering.

'I came from Laochre just now,' Connor admitted. 'What happened there?'

Patrick explained the events while his brother listened. When he had finished, Connor added, 'Already the Ó Phelans have claimed Laochre as their own. They've taken Ruarc prisoner and mean to execute him at dawn.'

'How did you learn this?'

Connor shrugged. 'I know how to stay in the shadows.'

Patrick knew it was so. Even as a child, Connor had sneaked up upon them on more than one occasion. Like a silent wraith, he could be invisible to anyone.

The grim news sobered him. Though he disliked his cousin, Ruarc did not deserve to die. 'We'll have to get him out, then.'

Connor's attention flickered to his side, and Patrick saw Isabel standing nearby. A look of interest sparked in his brother's eye.

'She is Isabel MacEgan. My wife,' Patrick said, with warning in his voice. Connor could charm the wings off a butterfly, and he didn't trust his brother's tendency to flirt.

'This is my brother Connor,' Patrick introduced.

Isabel approached, holding out her hands in greeting. A warm smile creased her face. 'Hello, Connor.'

A wicked smile spread over Connor's face. He lifted Isabel's hand to his lips. 'A pleasure it is to meet you, and a shame that my brother has already stolen you away.'

Isabel's face coloured. Patrick took her hand back, silently warning Connor to keep his hands to himself.

'I…ah…think I'll see if there's anything to eat.' Connor grinned, stepping back towards the ringfort.

'Find Trahern and Ewan. We'll speak about Ruarc in a few moments.'

'I believe Trahern has…company this night.' Connor winked at Isabel.

'Then rouse him. We've more important concerns.'

Connor disappeared towards the circle of huts. When they were alone, Isabel said, 'You've brushed me aside all night. I want to know why.'

What could he say? His life had been ripped apart, his people's lives were in danger, and all because he'd considered keeping her as his wife. Even to his own brother, he'd acknowledged her as a MacEgan. More than anything, he wanted it to be true. He wanted her to stay, to bear his children, and to awaken at his side.

But it was as though God had cursed him. He had no right to be with her, not after all that had happened.

'I don't have an answer to give you, Isabel.'

'Do you have any feelings for me at all?'

Words could not describe the way she made him feel. Jealousy when Connor had smiled at her. Passion when she kissed him. But more than all else came regret.

He couldn't see any way to bring her into his tribe. And with each day that passed, he hurt her more. No woman deserved this. The best thing he could do was let her go.

'I shouldn't,' he said, hardly above a whisper. It was all he could give her. 'Just as you should not feel anything for me.' He glanced out at the black horizon, with only the soft shush of the tide against the sand to break the stillness.

She reached out and with the touch of her hand upon his shoulder, he moved away. 'Isabel, you were right about us.'

Her hand drew back, her eyes filling with tears. 'There is no us, Patrick. There is you and your tribe. And there is me.'

He nodded, an aching pain seizing up inside of him. In the darkness, her face remained in shadows. But he could feel her pain, as though it were a tangible thing.

'What are you going to do?' she whispered.

'My brothers and I are going to go after Ruarc in a few hours.'

He heard her sharp intake of breath. 'You're not planning to rescue him.'

'He is one of us and of my blood. We won't let him die at their hands.'

'He is a traitor to you.'

There was ice in her voice, mingled with anger. Patrick couldn't understand why she would spurn a rescue mission. 'Ruarc is family.'

'He wants you to die, Patrick,' she warned. 'I do not trust him.'

'He wanted the kingship, not my death.' He took a step closer to her, and the soft scent of honeysuckle drifted to him. It was as though he needed to be near her, even if it was wrong to touch her.

'If you are caught—' She didn't finish the rest of her sentence. Her face paled, her hands tightening. And it was then that the truth struck him. She cared. He hadn't expected it, didn't know how to respond. Even now, he could see the way she was looking at him, like he'd wounded her.

Instinct warned him not to embrace her. Instead, he held back. 'If I cannot break inside my own home and bring back a single man, then I am not much of a warrior king, am I?'

'Don't go.' Her plea rived through him. He sensed it was not a lack of faith in his abilities, but fear of what might happen to him.

'I have to. It's his life at stake.' He needed to leave now, to join his brothers and make their plans. Instead, he found it nearly impossible to tear himself away from her.

'I don't have a good feeling about this.' She wrapped her arms around herself, as if to guard against evil spirits.

'Then pray for us.' He left without saying goodbye, though it bothered him. He needed to set her free. For her own happiness, Isabel needed to leave Eíreann and take no regrets.

With only a single torch to guide their way across the small channel, Patrick rowed alongside his brothers. Connor, Bevan, Trahern and Ewan sailed with him. Though he hesitated about bringing his youngest brother, Ewan was the smallest of them and could slip past nearly anyone.

They had made their plans, intending to use the darkness to their advantage. As they traversed the mainland towards Laochre, they relied on instinct and familiarity to guide them. In the distance, he found himself looking back at Ennisleigh, his thoughts upon Isabel. She deserved so much more than he could give. And that man could never be himself.

Against the midnight darkness, pinpricks of light lay ahead, along with the fortress they would enter. They took no horses, but kept stealth as they approached.

'We could enter the *souterrain* passage,' Ewan suggested. The stone passageway led beneath the ringfort to their storage cairns and a ladder brought them inside one of the cottages.

'It will be heavily guarded,' Bevan warned. 'They would expect us to enter through it.'

'Then what should we do?' Ewan asked. 'We cannot go through the front gates.'

'Most of the men are sleeping,' Patrick said. 'There's a broken section of the palisade wall we didn't finish repairing. Connor can go inside first and find out what they've done to Ruarc.'

He turned to Ewan. 'Stay outside the gates where no one can see you. If we do not return within a few hours, bring Sir Anselm.'

Ewan grimaced. 'I want to go with you.' A hint of sulking tinged his demeanour. Nothing bothered the boy more than being left behind.

Patrick touched his younger brother's shoulder. 'There is a greater need for you here, lad. Be our eyes and our ears. If aught goes wrong, you're our only hope.'

The sense of responsibility silenced Ewan's protests. He lowered his shoulders. 'I suppose.'

'Good.' Patrick clapped him on the back. At his signal, Connor moved into his position near the broken section of the palisade. Patrick motioned for his brothers to keep silent. The Ó Phelans had posted only a few guards near the gates. His own people were strangely absent. The skin on the back of his neck rose up with warning. Though they had come here to rescue Ruarc, he sensed that there were greater dangers to his own folk.

He should have brought the Norman army, storming the defences and ridding them of the enemy tribe. But he didn't want to risk killing his own men in the fray. It was too dangerous.

Connor disappeared inside the ringfort. Though Patrick trusted his brother implicitly, he disliked sending him into harm's way. Bevan moved in beside him. 'I've an idea, Patrick,' he whispered. 'If Trahern and I go through the *souterrain* passage, we can distract the others while you and Connor take Ruarc out. They won't miss him.'

'You'd be taken captive,' Patrick argued. 'I won't allow it.'

His brother shot him a wary look. 'Do you believe Trahern

and I to be that incompetent? We can hold off the Ó Phelans long enough for you to get out.'

Although it was a sound plan, he hesitated. 'When I get him out, we will join in and help you.'

'Let us find out what Connor knows. Then we'll decide.'

They waited in the darkness for long moments until a shadowy figure emerged from the wall. Connor found them, keeping his voice at a faint whisper. 'He's being held inside the donjon. He's bound and they've stripped him of his clothes. Donal Ó Phelan and some of the others are taunting him.'

'Is he hurt?'

Connor shrugged. 'I could not tell what they've done to him.'

'How difficult will it be to get him out?' Bevan asked.

'Very. But it can be done, if we have a distraction.'

Patrick explained Bevan's idea, and Connor agreed. 'We haven't much time. Dawn will break soon.'

With silent understanding, the men dispersed into their positions. And Patrick prayed that they would escape this without harm.

Chapter Twenty

Isabel didn't know why men refused help from women, but she wasn't about to wait around for Patrick to come back.

He'd gone alone with his brothers. Only four men and a young boy against an entire enemy tribe. The Irish folk at Laochre numbered hardly more than two score. Even so, there were not enough people to win this battle.

Was he trying to die? Even now, with the kingship lost and his people under attack, he did not confide his plans. She didn't know what he meant to do, and it bothered her that he'd shut her out so completely.

The glittering blackness of the sea stretched before her, with only a small patch of moonlight to illuminate it. Isabel picked up a rock and hurled it towards the water. Though it struck the beach instead, it made her feel better to do something rather than stare out at the mainland.

'Queen Isabel.' A woman's voice broke through her reverie. She looked towards the source and saw Annle and Sosanna standing behind her.

Her heart ached, though her eyes remained dry. 'Yes?'

'Did the men go after Ruarc?' Annle asked.

Isabel nodded. 'They're going to save his life and bring him back.'

Sosanna's shoulders relaxed, and, in the faint light, Isabel saw the wetness of tears on the woman's face. She was not carrying her babe, and Isabel guessed the child was sleeping.

'Sir Anselm spoke with us about the Ó Phelan tribe,' Annle admitted. 'He told us that the Ó Phelans took control of Laochre.'

Isabel didn't know how, since Anselm's grasp of the Irish language was little better than a young child's. 'They did, yes. Connor MacEgan was there and saw it. He's gone with Patrick to free Ruarc.' She hid her frustration from Sosanna, for she didn't believe any of the men should have gone. Ruarc had brought this upon himself.

Annle's expression turned grim. 'Anselm believes that the Normans should go and support them.'

'Why would he? He and the other soldiers did nothing the day the Ó Phelans first attacked.' Though she wished it could be so, she doubted if the men would intervene.

Sosanna blushed, and Annle explained, 'Because Sosanna asked him to.'

'She spoke?' Isabel drew closer, hope rising within her.

This time it was Annle's turn to blush. 'Anselm is courting her. And there are other ways for a woman to ask.'

Though Isabel had hoped that one day the Normans might join with the Irish, she didn't believe the remainder of the Normans would help. They still held grudges against the Irish for the rebukes and teasing they'd suffered.

'The soldiers won't do it,' she argued. 'They are stubborn.'

Annle shrugged. 'Their wives side with us. They don't like living in this tiny ringfort, and they have promised to coerce their husbands. By any means possible,' she added, with a gleam in her eye.

'Do you think it will work?' Isabel asked. Her husband would never support the Normans going into battle against the Ó Phelans. But four men could never defeat another tribe, no matter how strong they were.

'We can only try.'

Patrick moved through instinct, his mind detached from the forthcoming fight. He was hardly aware of the danger, or the cold of night.

Though he knew it was the right action, to save his cousin's life, he hadn't forgotten the fear upon Isabel's face. She'd wanted him to stay behind, not to risk the danger. He'd seen the look in her eyes, the hurt.

And though it was wrong, he had wished for a moment that he could comfort her. Even though his people had turned their backs on him, found him wanting as a king, he couldn't abandon them. Not even for Isabel.

They moved past sleeping men, treading softly. A few of his tribesmen saw them, but they held their silence. Patrick only breathed easier when he reached the interior of the Great Chamber. He and Connor kept their backs pressed to the wall, while they moved into position.

Ruarc knelt upon the dirt floor, stripped bare. His hands were tied behind him, as were his ankles. With a lowered head, his cousin appeared the image of a broken man. At the far end of the Great Chamber, Donal Ó Phelan slept. He sat in the king's seat, a silver cup dangling from his palm.

Patrick let out a breath while Connor moved along the side wall, past the men. Once, an Ó Phelan yawned and raised his head, seemingly staring right at them. Then he let out a loud belch and settled back to sleep.

Patrick and Connor waited in the shadows, until the night

darkness transformed into the grey light of pre-dawn. They remained near the stairs, out of view from the others. Outside, he heard a high-pitched scream. The hairs on the back of his neck stood on end. *She wouldn't dare.*

But then, this was the woman who had swum across the channel to join them. She would dare anything.

The sounds of steel clashing and battle cries emerged from the courtyard. The drunken men roused their heads and stumbled towards the door. Donal Ó Phelan continued to snore, his head leaning against the high-backed wooden throne.

Patrick signalled to Connor to get Ruarc. His brother hissed to catch the man's attention. Their cousin jerked in surprise when Connor emerged from the shadows, a knife gleaming in his hands. Ruarc tensed, as if unsure of whether Connor meant to murder him or to free him. Connor sliced the blade against the ropes and beckoned for him to follow.

Patrick removed his cloak and tossed it. With a grateful expression, Ruarc covered himself. When they reached the back staircase of the Great Chamber, Patrick opened up a hidden doorway. It could only be unlocked from the interior, so enemies could not use it to breach their defences.

Connor stepped through first, then Ruarc, and last himself. Patrick prayed he was hearing things. He needed Isabel to stay behind, safe upon Ennisleigh.

They did not make it past the inner bailey before the Ó Phelans saw them. A small group of men charged with their swords drawn.

Patrick and Connor unsheathed their own weapons. He focused his attention on the fight, tripping one of the men and disarming him. He tossed the enemy's sword to Ruarc, who joined them. His cousin fought with a fierce intensity, a man focused upon vengeance.

His own kinsmen joined in the battle, and he noticed they had begun using their new training. No longer did they attack the Ó Phelans recklessly, charging forward. Instead, they waited for the right opportunity.

At the far end of the ringfort, he saw Trahern and Bevan fighting. They were well outnumbered, and several of the tribesmen flanked them, using whatever spears or weapons they could find against the Ó Phelans.

The Ó Phelan men refused to surrender. Within moments, several of them lay wounded or dying, along with a few of the MacEgan tribesmen. Ruarc's fighting had slowed down, as if exhaustion had crept up on him. He kept up the motions in a daze, as if completing a training exercise, rather than fighting.

Outside the ringfort, Patrick heard a thunderous noise. His attention shifted towards the entrance, and Normans poured into the ringfort. Wearing chain mail and fully armed, the Normans began to fight alongside his kinsmen.

And leading them was his wife.

Gods, he was dreaming. He couldn't believe what he was seeing. He rushed towards the men, while the Normans attacked the Ó Phelans. Isabel sat upon horseback, wielding her bow against the enemy tribe.

She loosed arrow after arrow upon the Ó Phelans, protecting both the Normans and the MacEgans as they fought for their lives. He wanted to drag her from the horse and put her some place safe. She had no right to fight among them, like a warrior queen. Patrick tried to reach her, but more and more men seemed to block his path.

Another bloodcurdling scream echoed amid the battle noise. He saw Sosanna pointing at one of the Ó Phelan men, her eyes wild with fear. Sir Anselm caught her gaze, and with a vicious swing of a battle axe, he beheaded the man.

Moments later, Sosanna buried her face in Anselm's chest, embracing him.

Patrick slashed his way past the enemy, needing to get to Isabel. Though he was barely aware that the Ó Phelans had retreated, he lost sight of his wife. Her horse was gone, and so was she.

He prayed that common sense had led her out of harm's way.

Before long, he and his brothers had encircled the remaining members of the Ó Phelan tribe. Bevan brought forward two young men, barely older than six and ten. 'Hostages,' was all he said.

'What is your name?' he asked the older boy. The adolescent's eyes glittered with hatred, and he spat upon the ground.

Patrick signalled to Bevan, who seized the younger boy, pulling his arms behind his back.

'Don't hurt him!' the elder protested.

'Your names,' Patrick commanded.

The boy looked torn, but at last answered, 'I am Fergus. He is Jarlath.' Fergus clenched his fists. 'Now let him go.'

'Bind them,' Patrick ordered. 'We may need them for negotiation.' He stared back at the younger boy, Jarlath. 'Your father will want your safe return, I am certain.'

Both boys blanched, and Patrick knew he'd guessed correctly. These were Donal Ó Phelan's sons, valuable hostages indeed. And until he knew of Isabel's safety, he would not release them.

'Go and find Donal Ó Phelan,' he ordered one of his men. An uneasy feeling tightened inside. It wasn't like Donal to avoid a fight.

He didn't wait to discover the answer, but walked into the Great Chamber. It was empty, with no sign of his enemy.

His suspicions tripled. Having both his wife and the enemy

chieftain missing was too much of a coincidence. Again, he looked around the ringfort, but Isabel wasn't there. His gut suspected the worst. He stopped to ask several tribe members if they'd seen her, but no one had.

His tribe was busy escorting the last of the enemy outside the gates. When all of them had gone, the Irish let out an enthusiastic roar.

Patrick did not join in their celebration. He stared at each person, searching for a sign of Isabel. With each passing moment, his worry increased. Was she hurt? Had Donal Ó Phelan taken her? A black fury took root inside him. If the chieftain laid a hand on Isabel, he'd lose it.

He glanced over at his hostages. His brothers had bound the boys tightly, but they were unharmed. They could be used to bargain for Isabel's release, if she were taken prisoner.

Patrick passed by the soldiers, startled to see several of the Irish welcoming the Normans, clapping them on the backs. At that moment, he suddenly understood what Isabel had wanted to accomplish. As one people, no one could defeat them. A dryness coated his throat, and he hastened towards the place where he'd seen her last. Perhaps he could track the horses.

But he was stopped by Ruarc. His cousin waited until all eyes were upon them. Then he knelt before Patrick, bowing his head. 'Forgive me, my king.'

Though Patrick wanted to continue searching, he understood what it had taken Ruarc to humble himself in this way. He touched his cousin's shoulder and raised him up to stand before him. 'I accept your apology.'

Relief flooded his cousin's face. His shoulders hung low, and he added, 'I would understand if you want me to leave Laochre.'

'No. You are part of this tribe.' The words were an absolution.

'No one here doubts who is the true king. Or the queen.'

In silence, every last man kneeled before him, including the Normans. To see the unity among the men humbled him.

'Rise,' Patrick commanded. 'I accept your allegiance.'

He moved towards the edge of the ringfort to Sir Anselm and Sosanna. 'Have you seen Isabel? She is missing.'

The Norman soldier shook his head. 'I have not.'

'I have.' Sosanna's voice was rough from lack of use. She swiped at her tears, and Patrick wondered what had driven her to speak at last. 'They took her. Connor followed them.'

His skin grew cold, his thoughts half-numb. The Ó Phelan chieftain would not show Isabel mercy, not after she'd shot him with her bow. 'We need to gather men together to bring her back.'

The commander nodded. 'I'll speak with the men.'

Patrick stopped a moment to address his cousin. 'I am glad you are speaking again.'

Sosanna stared back to the fallen body of the Ó Phelan man killed by Sir Anselm. 'He is dead, thanks be.'

'No man will harm you,' Anselm promised. Sosanna returned to his embrace, and Patrick understood suddenly that it was not a Norman who had dishonoured his cousin, but one of the enemy tribesmen.

Even Ruarc did not protest the match. He inclined his head, accepting his sister's choice. To Anselm, he said, 'Keep her safe. Or I'll cut you apart.'

Anselm only smiled.

Patrick strode towards the stables, intending to go after Isabel when a bell resounded from the round tower. With low deep tones, the warning signal was only used in times of great need.

Patrick rushed to the gatehouse and climbed up to survey the landscape. He grimaced at the sight before him. Hundreds of archers poured onto the sands, followed by even more soldiers. It looked like a thousand Norman invaders.

He crossed himself, offering a silent prayer for his people and for their safety. Strongbow, the Earl of Pembroke, had arrived on their shores. And Heaven only knew how much blood would be shed.

Patrick stared at the landscape, feeling as though imaginary chains held him in place. His wife Isabel was in the hands of his enemy while it was only a matter of time before his fortress was destroyed.

He had no right to go after Isabel. His place was here, among his people, to live or die. Even so, his fists clenched with frustration. It was as if the enemy had taken his spirit and torn it in half.

The heaviness of guilt bled through his mind, as he imagined what Donal Ó Phelan would do to Isabel. And he knew Isabel would not remain mild and obedient. She would fight back, and the chieftain would kill her.

Dimly, he saw his brothers calling out orders to stand at the ready for the impending attack. Patrick gripped the wooden limbs supporting the gatehouse. Even as he took his own position, he could not help but stare at the horizon and think of her.

He'd already lost Liam, but the loss of his brother could not compare to this. Visions tangled in his mind, of Isabel swimming across the channel, soaked to the skin. Of her wielding her bow, joining him in a fight against the enemy,

And the way she looked at him when he made love to her.

The thought of letting her go, quite simply, ripped him asunder. He was grimly aware that it might be too late, even now.

Chapter Twenty-One

When she saw her father's colours, Isabel wanted to cry out, but Donal Ó Phelan kept his hand tightly over her mouth.

'Scream and I'll break your jaw,' he warned.

Isabel had no doubt he would. She struggled to calm herself while hordes of invaders moved towards Laochre. Her heart pounded in her chest. If her father learned of her disappearance, he would kill Patrick and all the Irish.

After the army had passed them by, Donal gripped her waist and forced her on horseback. He held her captive while riding away from Laochre, further inland. Despite the warm summer air, Isabel felt cold inside.

It almost didn't matter where Donal was taking her. Patrick would not come after her. Nor would anyone else. With the Norman invasion upon their threshold, they could not abandon the fight for her sake.

She struggled to think of a way to escape, but for now her mind dwelled upon her husband. She had barely caught sight of him during the battle. Like an ancient god, he'd charged at the Ó Phelans, slashing his sword out of vengeance.

Once, he'd stared at her. The look in his eyes was of an

enraged man. He had not welcomed her interference, though it had helped their tribe.

Their tribe. She closed her eyes in frustration. The people did not consider her one of them, never would. And as for Patrick, even if he did care for her, he wouldn't seek her out.

The solitude seemed to close in around her, suffocating in its thickness. Her lungs tightened, and she blinked hard to keep herself from succumbing to self-pity.

She lifted her chin and regarded Donal. 'What do you want from me? I'm of no use to you.'

'Your life can be ransomed.'

'Not to Patrick.'

'To the Normans. I'm certain some of their men would be interested in a lady.'

'My father is among those men. And he won't allow you to hold me prisoner. You'll bring the wrath of his army upon you.'

Donal smiled. 'No, I've brought the wrath of his army upon your husband. King Patrick failed to protect you, didn't he?'

Isabel's hands itched for a bow. As it was, she studied the landscape, trying to gain her bearings. The thunderous noise of the armies behind them had ceased after an hour of riding. She closed her eyes at the thought of what must be happening at the ringfort. Were her father's men attacking, even now? Would they put Sosanna and her infant son to the sword? Or Annle?

Her throat closed up, and she tightened her fists. Donal had slowed the horse's pace, leading her to a *rath* almost the size of Ennisleigh.

The Ó Phelan tribe possessed wealth of their own, and they were far enough inland to have avoided the path of Strongbow's men. Fields appeared to sway in the wind, their stalks of corn rustling. A circle of ten stone cottages with thatched roofs stood within a wooden palisade. As they drew closer, Isabel heard the sounds of people speaking. Dozens of people crowded inside the tiny ringfort. Their voices swarmed together in her mind, and she could hardly think of how to escape the tribe. There were so many of them.

When they reached the entrance, Donal lifted her down. Isabel tried to run, but he would not relinquish his grip on her arm. Jerking her backwards, he ordered his men to bind her.

She fought them, tearing at their skin with her nails, kicking at their shins. She wasn't afraid of them. Instead, she focused the rage burning inside her upon the enemy.

Though the Ó Phelans overpowered her, lashing her wrists and ankles, she didn't feel the physical pain. Her cheek pressed against the dirt, while a man's boot stepped against the back of her neck.

She wished she had never met Patrick MacEgan. Closing her eyes, she shut out the vision of his face. The steel eyes that seemed to strip away her defences. His hands that tempted her to surrender.

Memories filled her, of Patrick guarding her on their journey to the coastline. The way he'd kissed her, as though he couldn't get enough of her. And the way he'd held her at night, as though shielding her body with his own. In those stolen moments, she'd felt loved, though she knew nothing would ever come of it.

Isabel fisted her hands, trying to work free of the leather bindings. They wouldn't budge. Donal Ó Phelan had gone with his men to speak quietly, presumably to decide her fate. The boot moved from her neck, and she took a deep breath, still feigning helplessness. She stared at the nearest hut, and men emerged carrying swords and battle axes. From the open doorway she could see more weapons lining the interior, but it was too far away to reach.

Her ankles were not as tightly bound as her hands. Isabel gritted her teeth and moved her feet again, trying to loosen the ropes. The air grew cooler, the afternoon sky swelling with rain clouds. The heavy scent of earth assailed her, and she turned her gaze towards the gatehouse. She didn't know whether to linger until nightfall or try to escape sooner.

No one will come for you, an inner voice taunted.

The sea of Normans swarmed over his lands, their chain mail armour glowing like a pool of silver. Patrick's mind moved beyond the threat of invasion, to the man who had stolen his wife.

If Donal Ó Phelan had harmed Isabel, he would flay the man's skin from his body. Patrick surveyed the troops, noting the officers and the noblemen remaining further back from the others. Thornwyck would be among them.

Would they attack once more? Or would the Normans leave them in peace? He felt as though the fate of his tribe rested in another man's hands. He resented the helplessness, needing to take command of the situation.

'We need to know Strongbow's intentions,' Patrick said quietly to Trahern. The Normans gathered in the distance, nearing the ringfort.

His brother cast him a sidelong glance. 'You know why they are here. To finish what they began a year ago.'

'Possibly.' He suspected as much. And yet, Thornwyck had sworn that the Normans would not touch Laochre, not as long as he remained wedded to Isabel. He stared out at the landscape, worried about her. The invisible ties of tribal loyalty strangled him, for he wanted nothing more than to go after his wife.

He had sworn to protect her from harm. And the longer he

stayed here, the more his chances of rescuing her diminished. If Thornwyck discovered his daughter's disappearance, likely he would invoke his wrath upon the MacEgan tribe.

Scores of men guarded the fortress of Laochre, Normans and Irish alike. An eerie silence pervaded the afternoon, like the calm before a tempest.

A year ago, he had fought like a demon against these Normans, his blade slashing through the enemy's flesh. And then he'd seen Liam, fighting with every ounce of strength against four men. Though he'd gone to aid his brother, he'd come too late.

Was it already too late for Isabel? His worry increased tenfold. He paced along the perimeter, each stride punctuating his need to leave, to find her.

If he went after her, it would likely mean death. Ó Phelan wanted Laochre at any price. Patrick stopped a moment, watching his people. Side by side, they faced the enemy. Even the Norman wives and children exchanged worried looks with his own tribeswomen.

They had come together as one group, against a common enemy. Isabel had been right. And now, seeing it with his own eyes, he could scarcely believe it. Even if Strongbow's forces attempted an attack, his people were ready. They would endure, even if something happened to him.

He caught a stable boy and gave the order for his horse. Then he neared Trahern and Ruarc who awaited the army. His cousin gripped a spear, his face set with determination.

Without waiting for him to speak, Ruarc glanced outside the gates. 'Go after her,' he said. 'We will defend Laochre to the death.'

Though Trahern looked doubtful, Ruarc continued. 'It was my fault she was taken. I would bring her back, but I suspect you would rather do so.' Regret lined his voice. 'I will help your brothers keep the enemy out.'

'I don't want Thornwyck to know she's been taken,' Patrick warned. 'He'll blame us for it.' A part of him feared that Isabel had been gone too long. Though he knew his wife had unshakeable courage, already he had failed to protect her.

'Then you must go now,' Trahern said solemnly, 'before they breach our defences. You're her only chance.'

Patrick clasped his brother in an embrace, then gripped Ruarc's hand. He said farewell to Ewan and to Connor before mounting his horse.

'If I don't return within a sennight, name a successor.' He cast one more look upon his people, fully aware it might be the last time he saw them. With a heavy heart, he rode through the gates and around the back of the fortress. The open fields stretched before him as he turned north.

When he was clear of the fortress, he let Bel free, thundering across the plains. He questioned the wisdom of leaving his tribe behind, to fend for themselves against the Normans. Another part of him recognised that the battle was out of his hands. He had prepared the men as best he could—it was now up to them to fight together and win.

As time blurred and his thoughts drifted, he recalled the way Isabel felt in his arms. The way she would lie against him after lovemaking, her fingers tracing patterns upon his shoulders. A hard lump gathered in his throat, and he increased the horse's gait.

He'd lost his temper when Isabel had come charging through the ringfort, leading the Normans. He had been too stubborn to seek help from them, but she'd been right. His true enemy was the Ó Phelan tribe, the men who had stolen Isabel from him. And if he didn't bring her back, Edwin de Godred would invoke his vengeance upon the MacEgan tribe.

When the afternoon light began to fade, Patrick reached the outskirts of the Ó Phelan lands. He halted Bel, tethering the stallion to a nearby tree. A low hissing sound caught his attention and he saw his brother Connor waiting. He was relieved to see him unharmed.

'Is she inside?'

Connor nodded. 'Too many of them are guarding her. I think you should bargain for her life, since Ó Phelan expects you. Bevan and I will help you get out.'

'Bevan?'

Connor pointed in the distance to where a lone rider approached. 'He followed you here.'

Patrick cursed. 'Is no one guarding Laochre, then?' He was relying upon his brothers to keep their tribe safe. Leaving the fortress in the hands of the Normans and Trahern seemed the greatest of risks.

Connor shrugged. 'I was busy guarding your queen. I had to stay a fair distance back so they would not see me.'

It was too late to send both of them away. Inwardly he cursed his brothers for endangering themselves.

'We'll use our arrows first,' Patrick said. 'I'll go in and you guard my back. Shoot anyone who moves towards myself or Isabel.' He handed the quiver of arrows and bow to Connor.

Moments later, Bevan arrived and Patrick explained his plan. He didn't know what Ó Phelan wanted by holding Isabel hostage. There seemed little point in it, save revenge. But at least he had hostages of his own.

'Does he think to exchange Isabel for Laochre?' Bevan asked, dismounting.

'There is no chance of that. Not with the Normans.' With the armies sweeping across the coast, they could only pray that Thornwyck's men would keep Strongbow away from Laochre.

Patrick mounted his horse, and paused a moment as if to memorise his brothers' faces.

'Is she worth it?' Bevan asked softly. The scar upon his cheek tensed. Patrick recalled the death of Bevan's wife last summer. His brother had not cast eyes upon another woman since, vowing to remain faithful to her.

Was Isabel worth dying for? A strange ache took hold inside, tensing at the thought of anything happening to her. Was it guilt? Or something more?

He stared back at his brother. 'She is worth it.' When the words fell from his mouth, he sensed the truth of them ·

He rode towards the ringfort without looking back. The early evening sun blazed hot upon his face, and he shaded his eyes to see who guarded the *rath*.

'Donal Ó Phelan!' he called out. 'I've come for my wife.'

He waited outside for several minutes, not knowing what to expect. When no one came forward, he drew nearer.

An arrow struck the ground at his feet, and seconds later, the archer dropped to the ground, an arrow protruding from his heart. Patrick's hands tightened upon his sword hilt. Thank the gods his brothers were guarding his back.

'Unless you want another tribesman to die, I'd suggest you call off your men and face me yourself,' Patrick commanded.

The chieftain revealed himself then, standing several paces inside the gate. Out of an archer's range, but close enough to be seen.

'My men stay at their positions,' Donal answered. 'It is your small escort against my entire tribe.'

'Then you should be prepared to lose several of your men. Are they ready to die, I wonder?'

Donal laughed, his hand resting upon a spear shaft. 'Are *you* ready to die, Patrick MacEgan?'

'What do you want?' Patrick asked. 'Isabel is of no use to you.'

Donal shrugged. 'Perhaps when you are dead, I'll wed her myself. If your alliance was good enough for the Baron of Thornwyck, so should mine be.'

Patrick did not reveal the rage boiling inside him. 'I want to see her. Is she alive and unharmed?'

'She is alive. As for unharmed…' He shrugged, a smirk crossing his face.

It took control Patrick didn't know he possessed to hold his position. The idea of men beating Isabel, or worse, forcing themselves upon her, made him grip the hilt so hard, his knuckles whitened.

'I challenge you for the right to her.'

Donal's smile never faded. 'I have no need to meet you in a challenge. As soon as you cross the gates, my men will kill you.'

Patrick nudged Bel forward in answer. 'Then it will be war between our people. We'll kill every last one of you, and the blood of your tribe will stain your hands.'

Donal pointed behind Patrick. 'I have my doubts of that.' A rumbling noise sounded, and Patrick turned to see a small group of men surrounding the forest entrance where his brothers waited.

He froze, not knowing if they were in danger or not.

'Order your men back to Laochre, MacEgan,' Donal commanded, 'and I'll let them live.'

Patrick drew his horse closer. 'I've another bargain in mind. It concerns your sons.'

* * *

Isabel tried to break free of the leather bindings, but could not. The men's attention was focused outside the ringfort, upon her husband.

She couldn't see Patrick from her vantage point. Why had he come? With the invasion, he could not leave their people. They needed his leadership.

Dust coated her cheeks, and her eyes stung. He shouldn't be here. They would kill him as soon as he entered the ringfort. She had overheard their plans of claiming Laochre for themselves.

'Get up,' one of the men commanded. He reached down and grabbed her arm, jerking her to her feet. Isabel stumbled, her arm burning with pain. The Irishman forced her inside one of the huts, down a narrow ladder leading to an underground storage chamber. He lifted the ladder away, imprisoning her in the small space. A moment later, she heard him draw the door closed, sealing off any light.

The stale air terrified her, along with the suffocating darkness. She could not see her fingers outstretched in front of her face, and her heart raced with trepidation.

Not knowing what they had done to Patrick was the most terrifying of all. Her cheeks grew wet, and oh, Blessed Saints, she blamed herself. He should never have left his tribe, not for her.

But he had. He had risked everything to bring her home, though it would be futile. Selfishly, she wanted to see him one last time. She wanted to rest in his embrace and feel his arms around her.

Her heart feared the worst, that they had already killed him.

Chapter Twenty-Two

Over the next few hours, Isabel explored the tiny space, feeling her way around the walls once she had worked her hands free. There was no other way out, save the ladder. And the distance to the top was well out of her reach.

She sank down against the wall, discouraged. Then a noise caught her attention. Men were shouting, and she heard the sounds of fighting. She pressed her hands to the cool earthen walls, wishing she knew what was happening. Seconds later, light shone down the chamber, momentarily blinding her. A figure dropped down into the pit, before all light was extinguished again. Isabel heard a groan, and she held herself against the wall, hardly daring to breathe.

'Bastards,' the man cursed, and she recognised his voice.

'Patrick?' she whispered, moving towards him. 'Is that you?'

'Isabel?'

She exhaled with relief when he crushed her to him. 'Are you hurt?' She touched his face and shoulders, thankful he was alive.

'Only a few nicks. Ó Phelan tried to do worse, but he failed.' His hand moved up her nape, stroking the hair. 'What about yourself?'

'I'm a little bruised, but it's nothing serious.' She closed her eyes, drinking in the luxury of his touch. Even in the darkness, she craved his nearness.

'Why did you come for me?' she asked. 'I saw the Earl of Pembroke's men.' Part of her wondered if her father had forced Patrick here.

'Why do you think I came, *a chroî*?' His deep voice washed over her like the answer to a prayer. Then his mouth descended, kissing her as though he would never stop. He took from her, stealing her very breath until her knees trembled. Isabel gripped him, moving her hands over his back, down to his hips. The rigid length of him pressed against her body.

She willed herself to ignore her own desires. This was not the time, nor the place, for a stolen moment. 'You shouldn't have risked it,' she managed, her voice catching. 'They're not going to let us go.'

His long silence unnerved her before at last he spoke. 'I swore I'd keep you safe.'

'Your tribe needs you as king,' she argued.

'I've done everything I can for them,' he said. 'If God wills it, they shall succeed against Strongbow's forces. When I left them, the men were standing together to defend the ringfort.'

A strange sense of hope encircled her heart. 'Together?'

'Both our tribe and the Norman soldiers,' he admitted.

There was no trace of resentment, only acceptance. She could hardly believe it. 'Can they withstand the enemy?'

'I hope so.'

She reluctantly moved out of his grasp. 'You have to go back.'

'I came to set you free. If your father learns you were taken, he'll destroy us.'

Was that the main reason he had come? She had wanted so badly to believe it was because he cared about her. *Careful, Isabel*, she warned herself.

'What bargain did you make with Donal Ó Phelan?' she asked.

'I offered him an exchange of prisoners. We hold his sons hostage. My brothers have gone to bring them from Laochre, and they will bring you back.'

'What about you?' she asked. When he gave no reply, her heart sank. He knew, as surely as she did, that Donal Ó Phelan wanted him dead. Only then could he claim Patrick's kingdom.

She didn't like the implications, that he was offering up his life for hers. 'I won't let you do this.'

His hands moved around her shoulders, pulling her to him. 'It's all right, *a chroí*.'

Tears burned her eyes as she gripped him around the waist. 'I won't leave you, do you understand? If I do, he'll kill you.'

'He may kill me anyway, Isabel. But it doesn't matter. Our tribe is safe, and so will you be.' He brushed away her tears, and Isabel was torn between wanting to strike out at him and wanting to sink into his embrace.

'When he comes for you, swear you'll go to Laochre. I've chosen my fate.'

'You've chosen death. I can't let that happen.' She let her tears fall freely, resting her head beneath his chin. His strong arms encircled her while he murmured soothing words in Irish.

'Our people may come for us,' he offered.

She didn't answer. With the Norman invasion happening all around them, never could their tribe leave Laochre. Even if they did, it might be too late. She didn't want to face being alone without him.

He tightened his embrace, pressing a kiss upon her forehead. 'We have tonight, *a stór*.' He sank down with his back to the wall, holding her close and Isabel prayed for both of them.

The hours slipped by, each one more precious than the last. She never knew if she slept, but she would not let go of Patrick, the man she loved.

At last, the noise of men broke through the stillness. Patrick raised her to a standing position. 'If something happens, if Donal does not keep his word, try to find the hut closest to the back of the ringfort. There is a storage chamber like this one with a passageway that leads to the outside.'

There was hardly time to argue when the piercing sunlight cut through the darkness. A ladder lowered into the chamber. Isabel didn't move.

'It's time for you to leave,' Patrick said softly.

'I don't want you to die because of me.' She touched his face in the darkness, as if to memorise every plane, every line of strength.

'I don't plan to die, if I can avoid it.' He gripped her tightly and, as her eyes adjusted, she saw the regret upon his face. 'Now go.'

She hesitated upon the ladder, her hand curling around the rung. The idea of leaving him behind struck her as selfish and unforgivable.

'Isabel, do this for me,' he urged. 'If you save yourself, there is hope for both of us.'

And though she hated herself for climbing each rung, she forced herself to leave him. He was right; they would not let him go, but she could bring back help. Somehow, she would find a way.

* * *

He'd lied to Isabel. He knew there was no hope for himself. Although Donal had agreed to let Isabel go free, in exchange for his sons, there would be no such bargain for himself. He suspected as soon as he was alone in the ringfort, they would take his life. Strangely, he did not fear death.

The ladder lowered again. 'Climb up,' came the order.

Patrick did, wary of the men. His eyes blinked to adjust to the light, and he saw one of the men holding a length of rope. The man tried to grab his arm, but Patrick anticipated the move. Crouching down, he swung his leg out and tripped his attacker. With a swift shove, he pushed the man down the storage chamber.

The second man was not as quick to strike. Patrick blocked a punch, ducking out of the way. Then the next blow caught him in the throat. He gasped, fighting to move away from his enemy, but more of them came, striking at every part of him with fists and wooden staffs. The last blow struck behind his knees, and he hit the ground.

Near the edge of the ringfort, he saw his wife. Isabel stood with two men gripping her arms, fury evident upon her face. At the sight of her, Patrick fought even harder to escape. He'd suspected Ó Phelan would not keep his word. But he'd be damned before he'd let anything happen to Isabel. If it meant keeping her safe, he'd willingly sacrifice himself.

He tasted the dirt, hardly caring about the blows that struck him. All he was aware of was her. The way she carried herself, the way she held her emotions in, though he could see the pain in her eyes.

No matter the cost, he wanted her to live.

'Isabel!' he called out. 'Do you remember what I told you?'

He used her Norman language, so that none of the Ó Phelans would understand.

'Be silent.' Donal Ó Phelan moved forward. 'Or I'll slit your throat.'

Patrick stared at Isabel, then looked towards the hut where he knew the *souterrain* passage led. It would bring her outside the ringfort and to safety.

'You promised to let her go,' he said grimly. What he wouldn't give for a weapon right now. Donal had stripped him of his sword and dagger. He'd like to skewer the chieftain for what he'd done. 'If she is not brought safely to Laochre, you will not see your sons again.'

Donal shrugged. 'She makes a good hostage. And once you are dead, she is free to marry again.'

'The Baron would sooner kill you where you stand.'

'Then she will also die.' Donal shrugged. 'Our men are strong enough to withstand the Normans.'

Patrick couldn't believe the man's arrogance. Donal had never witnessed the Norman forces, never seen their disciplined style of fighting.

The chieftain unsheathed a knife and moved towards him. Patrick glanced over at Isabel. She had precious seconds to run, and gods above, he prayed she would obey him. Time seemed to slow as he watched the blade lower.

At the opportunity he threw himself towards Donal. His motion caught the chieftain off balance, and he wrestled for control. He palmed the weapon, holding the edge to Donal's throat. 'Release my wife.'

The guards paused, but finally obeyed.

'Now go!' he ordered Isabel.

Instead of fleeing towards the hut, she moved to a completely different hut on the opposite side.

'Isabel!' he cried out, but three men were already going after her. Donal rolled over, and the blade nicked his own skin. He fought against the chieftain, who had unsheathed his knife. The blade slashed before him, but even as he avoided the weapon, he knew he couldn't reach Isabel in time to save her.

She'd gone inside the wrong hut. He felt sick, knowing she was trapped.

He wrenched himself free of Donal, slicing the knife at anything he could reach. When the chieftain retreated, Patrick started towards the hut where she'd gone. Moments later, one of the men stepped backwards, his hands raised in surrender. Isabel emerged from the hut, armed with a bow and quiver of arrows.

Patrick couldn't have been more stunned. She'd known where to find their store of weapons. And now she looked ready to kill the chieftain. Her arm held steady upon the bow as she stared at Donal.

'Open the gates. My husband and I are leaving.'

'The moment you turn your backs, our men will kill both of you,' Donal admitted. 'You've one choice, Lady Isabel. Stay as my hostage, or die with your husband.'

He had no doubt Donal would kill them. If Isabel refused to stay, her life had no use for the chieftain. She kept her arrow trained upon Donal. 'I've made my choice already. And I want the gates opened.'

Patrick joined her side, stepping inside the hut to retrieve his own sword and shield. The bodies of the first two men lay dead upon the ground.

With the weapon drawn, he stood beside Isabel. Any man who tried to harm her would have to go through him first. He raised the shield to protect both of them.

One of the Ó Phelans tried to rush forward, but Isabel loosed an arrow into his heart. 'Let us go.'

Slowly, they left the ringfort, Isabel's arms shaking with the effort of keeping the bow drawn. 'Give me the weapon, *a stór*,' Patrick murmured as he sheathed his sword. 'Take the shield.' His hand reached for the bow, and he kept the weapon drawn.

'I'm sorry, Patrick,' she whispered as she took the heavy shield from him. He kept the bow trained upon the tribe.

Isabel blamed herself for everything. If she hadn't been captured, none of this would have happened.

And now both of them would die. She knew it as surely as she knew that they were abandoned by everyone.

'It's not your fault.' They backed away slowly, Isabel casting quick glances over her shoulder. The meadow was silent, with no one to help them.

'We have to get out of their range,' she said.

'They aren't going to let us go. Our only chance of surviving this is if my brothers help us.'

'Will they arrive in time?'

He shook his head. 'I don't know. They were supposed to bring the hostages.'

Her heart ached. With her free hand, she touched his shoulder. 'I don't regret a moment of this. Being your wife, I mean.' Her voice broke as she continued, 'I only wish we had more time.'

He risked a look at her, and in his eyes, she saw a fierce determination. 'I'm not giving up on us yet, *a ghrá*.'

My love. The words slipped inside her heart, warming her. Though she wanted so badly to believe that everything would be all right, she clung to these last moments with him.

'When I give the signal, I want you to run to the forest. Don't stop, no matter what else happens.'

'What about you?'

'I'm going to hold them off and then follow you.'

She shivered, afraid of what would happen. She didn't want him to die, or worse, to know that she had caused it.

'My brothers would never abandon us,' he said. 'Have faith.'

'I love you,' she whispered, touching his shoulder. 'And I don't want you to die.'

His eyes darkened, and his voice turned gruff. 'There's no other woman I would willingly give up my life for. It's time for you to go.'

Her eyes filled with tears, as she prepared to run. Though she didn't want to leave, she understood there wasn't a choice. The wooden shield was heavy, but she held it to her back as she raced towards the forest. Behind her, she heard the swish of arrows as Patrick released them upon their enemy.

Then in front of her came a deafening battle roar, and she stumbled to her knees. From the hills, the silver of chain mail armour glinted in the sun. Isabel stared at the soldiers, her lungs gasping for air. The Norman army had come upon them.

She froze, glancing back at Patrick. He hadn't moved, but kept his bow aimed at the Ó Phelan ringfort. The Norman army advanced further, nearly a thousand soldiers surrounding them. Her pulse thrummed faster, and she got up, easing her way back to Patrick.

'Patrick?' she asked, afraid to run.

'Stand with me,' he ordered. He lowered his bow and Isabel returned to his side.

'What do they want?'

He shook his head. 'I suspect we'll soon find out.' He clasped her hand in his, and both of them waited while the men drew closer.

'Whatever happens, I'll protect you,' he said. 'And if I could give up my kingdom to let you live, I would do it.' His mouth brushed a kiss upon the top of her head. 'I love you.'

Isabel leaned against him, her heart filled with love for him. 'Give me the bow,' she said, and he exchanged the weapon for the heavy wooden shield. 'It's all right.' She nocked an arrow to her bowstring in readiness. 'I'd rather die at your side than alone.'

Unsheathing his sword, they stood back to back, awaiting the inevitable. There would be no escape for either of them.

Chapter Twenty-Three

The multitude of soldiers parted and behind them, wearing the MacEgan colours and carrying the tribe's banner, rode the rest of the tribe. Islanders and the men of Laochre all stood together, fully armed.

'Why are they here?' Isabel asked. Hope swelled inside her, and she relaxed the bowstring.

'My brothers brought reinforcements, it seems.'

She started to move towards them, but Patrick stopped her. 'Wait.' Seconds later, three arrows embedded in the wooden shield. 'The Ó Phelans haven't given up yet.'

Infuriated, Isabel released her own arrows, taking satisfaction when they struck their mark.

'Enough. Go towards our tribe.' He gave her a push forward, following her with the shield raised. Although arrows rained down upon them, miraculously none of them struck. When they were out of range, Isabel stopped in front of the MacEgan tribesmen.

Bevan and Connor were mounted, and they held the reins of Bel, Patrick's horse.

'Who is caring for Laochre?' she asked, afraid of the answer.

'Sir Anselm guards it, along with the Normans.' He shrugged. 'And all of the women, of course.' His scarred face held traces of anger, but he said nothing further.

'Thank you for coming to our aid,' she said quietly.

Bevan grunted. 'You are a MacEgan now. And we would never let anyone harm family.'

Isabel reached out and squeezed his hand. 'My thanks, brother.'

As she passed, she was startled to see the Irish raising their knee to her, bowing their heads in deference.

Ruarc came forward and knelt at her feet. 'My queen,' he said solemnly.

She offered her hand, raising him to stand. 'Do you accept my husband as your king now?'

'I do, yes. And I apologise for my wrongdoing.'

Isabel looked upon the faces of the MacEgan tribe, her eyes brimming with tears. She smiled, greeting each of them in their own language as she passed. When she spoke with the last man, she suddenly saw her father.

Edwin de Godred dismounted and strode forward. He wore full battle armour, and his gaze passed over her as if inspecting her for injuries. 'I understand this enemy tribe thought to take you hostage.' He glared at the ringfort. 'But at least your husband had enough sense to come after you. Even if he should have waited for our forces.'

'I thought your forces would attack Laochre,' she dared.

He shook his head. 'I gave you my word.' He reached out and touched her cheek. 'You are well, Daughter?'

'Thanks to my husband.' She heard Patrick come up behind her, and his arm moved around her shoulders in a protective gesture.

'Good.' Edwin glanced at the Normans. 'I think the Earl

of Pembroke will leave Laochre in peace. He has his sights on wedding King Dermot's daughter Aoife.' With a glance towards the ringfort belonging to the Ó Phelan tribe, he added, 'What of them?'

Patrick spoke up. 'Strongbow may do as he wishes. The Ó Phelan tribe seems overly confident that they can withstand the enemy.'

'Indeed.' Edwin cast a doubtful look. 'It's a small enough piece of land, but it may have its uses.' He paused a moment. 'I wish you good fortune, Isabel. And happiness.'

Without waiting for a reply, her father turned away and rejoined his army. Though he had not said as much, Isabel felt as though he'd given his blessing. And a part of her softened, inwardly forgiving him.

Patrick lifted Isabel into his arms, a possessive expression upon his face. He set her atop Bel, then swung up behind her. 'Send the hostages back to Donal Ó Phelan with an escort of Norman soldiers,' he ordered. 'And the rest of you return to Laochre.'

'Where are you taking me?' Isabel asked.

He spurred the horse into a gallop. Leaning forward, he whispered in her ear. 'I'm going to do what I should have done long ago.'

'What is that?'

His hand moved to caress her breast. 'I'm going to tie you to my bed and ravish you until you cannot walk.'

To Isabel's surprise, cheers erupted from the ringfort when Patrick rode inside. Though it was nearly the middle of the night, torches blazed inside the fortress. All the folk awaited them, down to the children sleeping in their mothers' arms.

Patrick lifted her down, and the Normans removed their

helms, kneeling in tribute. Isabel managed a smile, but inside she wanted to weep with gratitude. She was home, where she belonged. Patrick's hand rested upon the small of her back, a silent reminder of support.

Behind them rode the remainder of the tribe. They, too, joined in the thunderous noise of approval. Isabel walked among them, feeling overwhelmed by their acceptance. Her cheeks were wet with tears. She didn't know when she had begun to cry, but after so many weeks of being an outsider, it was hard not to release her feelings.

Patrick clasped her hand in his. 'We have brought our queen home safely.' He drew her in the centre of the *rath*, and Isabel dried her tears while the Irish and Normans offered their good wishes.

'Because of our lady and her efforts, Strongbow spared our fortress.' To the Normans he added, 'I thank you for defend ing Laochre in our absence.'

Isabel caught the look of understanding that passed between both sides. Although it would take time for the men to blend together and see each other as friends, at least they had built trust between them.

Then her husband addressed all of the people. 'It is late, but on the morrow we will host a feast in the Great Chamber. All are welcome.'

She translated Patrick's proclamation for the Norman forces, and then accepted the good wishes of both Irish and Norman alike.

Patrick stood by her side, his palm caressing her back until Isabel longed to retreat to the privacy of their chamber. At last, he dismissed the remainder of the folk and led her away.

They raced up the winding staircase, and when they reached the top, Patrick lifted her into his arms and carried her inside his bedchamber. He bolted the door behind them, staring at her like a barbarian warrior. Slowly, he let her slide down his body until Isabel couldn't wait any more.

She met his kiss with her own frenzied need. Their clothes fell away in a rushed tangle of hands until at last they stood skin to skin. Patrick lowered his mouth to her throat, and Isabel sighed as shivers erupted over her body. Her nipples tightened, and he kissed the tight buds until she moaned.

'I love you,' he murmured against her skin. He led her to the bed, laying her down upon the soft coverlet. 'I'm never letting you leave me, *a ghrá*. You're mine.'

She watched him with eyes filled with love. 'As you are mine.' Embracing him, she revelled in the feeling of his body against hers. 'I love you, Patrick.'

To her surprise, he leaned down and picked up her fallen veil. In a single motion, he rent it in half.

'What are you—?'

But the answer became clear when he gently tied each wrist to the bed posts. 'I told you what I would be doing to you, my lady wife.' He slid a finger beneath her bonds, testing to be sure they weren't too tight.

Isabel wanted to protest, but being unable to move offered a strange excitement. Her husband pinioned her body beneath his own, his mouth whispering what he planned to do to her.

And oh, sweet saints, he did exactly that. With his hungry mouth, he blazed a path across her naked body, teasing and tempting her. He spread her thighs apart, lifting her hips for a more intimate kiss. Heat shot through her, while her wicked warrior tormented her until she spasmed.

His hands moved over her breasts, lightly pinching the nipples until they rose up, heavily aroused. His mouth encircled each tip, sucking hard until wetness surged between her legs.

'I wanted you from the first moment I saw you,' he breathed, whispering across her skin. 'And I fell in love with you the day you swam the channel.'

He positioned his length between her legs, sliding deep within. Isabel wanted so badly to embrace him, but with her hands trapped, she could only accept the sweet torture.

With long strokes, he touched the very heart of her. 'I want to give you children and spend each day waking beside you.'

He reached out and untied her wrists, freeing her. Isabel embraced him, raising her knees to take him deeper. The fierce pleasure rocked her backwards, but she clung to him as the sensations built up higher.

He increased his pace, driving into her until at last Isabel screamed. He plunged deep inside, his face tightening as he poured himself within her.

She clung to him, shaking with the raw pleasure. Kissing him again, she revelled in the satisfaction of lying in his arms.

Patrick nuzzled her cheek, smiling wickedly as he withdrew from her body. 'It may take a while before you bear me a child.' His hands ran over the curve of her body to rest upon her womb. 'We'll have to make up for lost time.'

'Some day soon,' she whispered, praying his prediction would come true. 'But only if you let me stay here at Laochre.'

'Forever, *a ghrá*.' He kissed her deeply, and then rolled out of bed to cross the room. He returned, holding the silver diadem. 'This belongs to you, as is your right.' He placed the crown upon her head. The metal warmed against her skin, but her husband's touch distracted her more.

Isabel lay in his arms and offered up her own prayer of thanksgiving.

'What did you say?' her husband murmured against her lips sleepily.

'I thanked God for *not* saving me from this marriage,' she replied.

And then, as night cast its spell over them, her warrior king made love to her once again.

* * * * *

Love Inspired
HISTORICAL

Powerful, engaging stories of romance,
adventure and faith
set in the past—when life was simpler and
faith played a major role in everyday lives.

Turn the page for a sneak preview of
THE BRITON
by
Catherine Palmer

Love Inspired Historical—love and faith
throughout the ages
A brand-new line from Steeple Hill Books
Launching this February!

'Welcome to the family, Briton,' said one of Olaf's men in a mocking voice. 'We look forward to the presence of a woman at our hall.'

Bronwen grasped her tunic and yanked it from the Viking's thick fingers. As she stepped away from the table, she heard the drunken laughter of the barbarians behind her. How could her father have betrothed her to the old Viking?

Running down the stone steps towards the heavy oak door that led outside from the keep, Bronwen gathered her mantle about her. She ordered the doorman to open the door, and he did so reluctantly, pressing her to carry a torch. But Bronwen pushed past him and fled into the darkness.

Dashing down the steep, pebbled hill towards the beach, she felt the frozen ground give way to sand. She threw off her veil and circlet and kicked away her shoes.

Racing alongside the pounding surf, she felt hot tears of anger and shame well up and stream down her cheeks. With no concern for her safety, Bronwen ran and ran—her long braids streaming behind her, falling loose, drifting like a tattered black flag.

Blinded with weeping, she did not see the dark form that sprang up in her path and stopped dead her headlong sprint. Bronwen shrieked in surprise and fear as iron arms pinned her, and a heavy cloak threatened to suffocate her.

'Release me!' she cried. 'Guard! Guard, help me.'

'Hush, my lady.' A deep voice emanated from the darkness. 'I mean you no harm. What demon drives you to run through the night without fear for your safety?'

'Release me, villain! I am the daughter—'

'I shall hold you until you calm yourself. We had heard there were witches in Amounderness, but I had not thought to meet one so openly.'

Still held tight in the man's arms, Bronwen drew back and peered up at the hooded figure. 'You! You are the man who spied on our feast. Release me at once, or I shall call the guard upon you.'

The man chuckled at this and turned towards his companions, who stood in a group nearby. Bronwen caught hold of the back of his hood and jerked it down to reveal a head of glossy raven curls. But the man's face was shrouded in darkness yet, and as he looked at her, she could not read his expression.

'So you are the blessed bride-to-be.' He returned the hood to his head. 'Your father has paired you with an interesting choice.'

Relieved that her captor did not appear to be a highwayman, she pushed away from him and sagged onto the wet sand. 'Please leave me here alone. I need peace to think. Go on your way.'

The tall stranger shrugged off his outer mantle and wrapped it around her shoulders. 'Why did your father betroth you thus to the aged Viking?' he asked.

'For one purported to be a spy, you know precious little about Amounderness. But I shall tell you, as it is all common knowledge.'

She pulled the cloak tightly about her, reveling in its

warmth. 'This land, known as Amounderness, once was Briton territory. Olaf Lothbrok, my betrothed, came here as a youth when the Viking invasions had nearly subsided. He took the lands directly to the south of Rossall Hall from their Briton lord. Then, of course, the Normans came, and Amounderness was pillaged by William the Conqueror's army.'

The man squatted on the sand beside Bronwen. He listened with obvious interest as she continued. 'When William took an account of Amounderness in his Domesday Book, he recorded no remaining lords and few people at all. But he did not know the Britons. Slowly we crept out of hiding and returned to our halls. My father's family reoccupied Rossall Hall. And there we live, as we should, watching over our serfs as they fish and grow their meager crops. Indeed, there is not much here for the greedy Normans to want, if they are the ones for whom you spy.'

Unwilling to continue speaking when her heart was so heavy, Bronwen stood and turned towards the sea. The traveler rose beside her and touched her arm. 'Olaf Lothbrok's lands— together with your father's—will reunite most of Amounderness under the rule of the son you are beholden to bear. A clever plan. Your sister's future husband holds the rest of the adjoining lands, I understand.'

'You've done your work, sir. Your lord will be pleased. Who is he—some land-hungry Scottish baron? Or have you forgotten that King Stephen gave Amounderness to the Scots, as a trade for their support in his war with Matilda? I certainly hope your lord is not a Norman. He would be so disappointed to learn he has no legal rights here. Now, if you will excuse me?'

Bronwen turned and began walking back along the beach towards Rossall Hall. She felt better for her run, and somehow her father's plan did not seem so far-fetched anymore. Distant lights twinkled through the fog that was rolling in from the west, and she suddenly realized what a long way she had come.

'My lady,' the man's voice called out behind her.

Bronwen kept walking, unwilling to face again the one who had seen her in her humiliation. She didn't care what he reported to his master.

'My lady, you have quite a walk ahead of you.' The traveler strode forward to join her. 'I shall accompany you to your destination.'

'You leave me no choice, I see.'

'I am not one to compromise myself, dear lady. I follow the path God has set before me and none other.'

'And just who are you?'

'I am called Jacques.'

'French. A Norman, as I had suspected.'

The man chuckled. 'Not nearly as Norman as you are Briton.'

As they approached the fortress, Bronwen could see that the guests had not yet begun to disperse. Perhaps no one had missed her, and she could slip quietly into bed beside Gildan.

She turned to go, but he took her arm and studied her face in the moonlight. Then, gently, he drew her into the folds of his hooded cloak. 'Perhaps the bride would like the memory of a younger man's embrace to warm her,' he whispered.

Astonished, Bronwen attempted to remove his arms from around her waist. But she could not escape his lips as they found her own. The kiss was soft and warm, melting away her resistance like the sun upon the snow. Before she had time to react, he was striding back down the beach.

Bronwen stood stunned for a moment, clutching his woolen mantle about her. Suddenly she cried out, 'Wait, Jacques! Your mantle!'

The dark one turned to her. 'Keep it for now,' he shouted into the wind. 'I shall ask for it when we meet again.'

* * * * *

Don't miss this deeply moving story,
THE BRITON,
available February 2008
from the new Love Inspired Historical line.

And also look for
HOMESPUN BRIDE
by Jillian Hart,
where a Montana woman discovers that love
is the greatest blessing of all.